ROYALLY YOURS

New York Times Bestselling Author

EMMA CHASE

Royally Yours / Emma Chase – 1st ed.
Library of Congress Cataloging-in-Publication Data
ISBN-13: 978-1726473781 | ISBN-10: 1726473783

PROLOGUE

NO WOMAN IS BORN A QUEEN, no matter the title attached to her name at birth.

Kings are crowned. But queens . . . queens rise.

They lift themselves from the depths of tragedy and heartbreak that always seem to follow them. They break the chains of society, and they soar through their triumphs and joys. They are forged by the burn of betrayal and they are shaped by the constant, cold clash of wills.

Still they rise, and then . . . they reign.

For good or bad, in sickness and in health, until death do they part.

The vestiges of that reign are the true inheritance of the descendants. For most, that birthright is duty, tradition and loyalty.

But the two of us were different. Right from the start, and in every way.

Passion that could tear the whole world down around us. Love that would not be ignored or denied. Devotion that would last beyond a lifetime.

These would be our legacy—our gifts to the ones who would follow in our footsteps. It would be scored on their bones and branded on their souls.

We just didn't know it then.

Every dynasty has a beginning. Every legend starts with a story.

This is ours.

CHAPTER
1

Lenora

Averdeen, 1945

"YOU SHOULD HAVE SEEN HER, Alfie. She was so damn *impressive*. More dignified than any of those bawbags in Parliament could dream of being."

My father, Reginald William Constantine Pembrook, the King of Wessco, often talks about me like I'm not in the room. My mother calls it a sorry habit. But I don't mind, especially when he's proud of me.

"And my *advisors*," he says, spitting out the word like a curse. "They don't understand the people at'all. Damn fools, the lot of them."

Father's advisors talk about me like I'm not in the room too.

"Eight years old is too young," they'd said. *"She will humiliate herself,"* they'd warned. *"The Crown Princess is*

just a girl after all."

When the war finally ended last month, we had a parade through the city. There was music and sweets, banners and balloons, and golden confetti floating everywhere you looked. The crowds waved and cheered and welcomed the men home as they marched down the street in their handsome uniforms.

This morning, the rest of the lads came home, but no one was cheering.

The bagpipes played and a sea of sad faces—crying mums and dads and little brothers and sisters—watched as the flag-draped caskets were loaded off planes in a parade that seemed to go on and on and on.

I wanted to cry too. My heart felt like a lead ball, and my stomach pinched from the awfulness of it all.

But I didn't let it show. I kept my eyes dry and my face solemn. I nodded my head and told them we would never, ever, forget their brave boys. And I think my being there, my words, made it better . . . a little less awful for them.

Just like Father had told me it would.

"I'm glad it worked out how you wanted, Reggie," Alfie Barrister replies from the leather chair by the fireplace.

Alfie is Father's best friend. I like him very much. He's large and round and happy—like a redheaded Father Christmas.

"There's a call for you, Your Majesty," a servant says from behind me.

"I'll take it in the study."

I hear the library door close behind Father as he

leaves the room, but I continue to look out the window. Across the carpet of green grass to the rear of the sun-streaked yard, where a rope swing hangs from a thick black branch of a tree that's as big as a monster.

The cheery kind of monster.

It's my favorite part of visits to Alfie's. Because while our palace has hundreds of rooms and endless hall-ways, and fountains and gardens with flowers of every color you can imagine . . . there's not a single swing hang-ing from one branch of any tree in the whole damn place.

I'm not supposed to say *damn* out loud, but it feels good to say it in my head sometimes.

Alfie steps up next to me and looks out the window too.

"Would you like to go swing, Chicken?"

I grin all the way up at him, and nod.

A hop, skip and a jump later, Alfie's pushing me on the swing and it feels like I'm flying—like I'm a bird who can go anywhere—with the sun on my face and the wind in my hair. My navy-blue dress is tucked under my legs to keep it from flailing.

"Did you hang this swing for yourself, Alfie?" I ask. The wooden plank that makes the seat would fit him.

He chuckles. "No. It's for my children."

I twist around in the seat to gape at him. "You have children?"

"That's right. Two boys and a little girl."

I turn back in the swing and contemplate this unex-pected development.

"I don't think I like children. They seem confusing and badly behaved."

I don't actually know any children—not officially. Miriam goes to school while I'm tutored at the palace.

"But I'm sure I would like yours, Alfie." I look up, scanning the yard. "Are they here? Why haven't I met them when we visit?"

"They live in Scotland with their mother," Alfie explains.

"Why does their mother live in Scotland and not here with you?"

Alfie thinks a moment and then he sighs. "Well . . . I wasn't a very good husband. Married to the store and all that."

Alfie's store, Barrister's, is the biggest in Wessco—it has toys and clothes and all sorts of amazing things. I heard him tell Father he's opening another one in London soon, and after he's finished taking over the world, he'll be nice and let Father keep Wessco.

"Do you miss them?" I ask.

"Yes." Alfie nods. "But my wife is happier in Scotland with her family. And children belong with their mums."

My mother is beautiful, with a soft voice and long dark brown hair like mine, and eyes that are the exact color of the sky on a sunny day.

"I'm hardly ever with Mum," I say quietly.

When I'm not with my tutors, I'm with Father. Sometimes, when they think I can't hear them, the staff call me HRS—His Royal Shadow.

"Yes, I know," Alfie says, sounding a bit sad for me. "But you're special, Chicken."

I'm special because one day I'm going be queen. Father said so.

There were two babies before me—and one was a boy. But they came too soon, were born too small, and didn't survive. After my younger sister, Miriam, was born, Mother was very sick and the doctors told Father there would be no more babies.

And that means I'll be the first Queen Regnant Wessco has ever had.

It's important that I'm good at it.

"Why do you call me Chicken, Alfie?" I wonder on the upswing.

"Because I saw you the night you were born at Ludlow Castle. I was there the first time your father held you —and that's just what you looked like. A pale, squawking chicken with no feathers."

The description is disturbing. I frown.

"I hope I don't look like a chicken anymore."

Alfie steps to the front of the swing, watching me. Then he rocks his head from side to side, his blue eyes sparkling. "Eh . . . depends on the day."

My mouth drops open. "Alll-fie!"

And his belly shakes in time with his deep chuckle. "It's a pet name, Lenora. An endearment. Every child should have one." He gives me another push from the side of the swing. "And believe it or not, Your Highness, you are, in fact, a child."

Alfie turns toward the main house, shaking his head. I hear him say softly, "God knows someone has to treat you like one."

Guthrie House, Palace of Wessco, 1953

The color of clothing is important. It's the first thing people notice about you. Black is gloomy, white is sanctimonious, fuchsia too garish, pastels too girlish. Patterns are important too. Polka dots are too frivolous, florals too shallow, stripes and plaids can do nicely—but you mustn't overdo them.

And for everyday-wear . . . gray.

According to my personal secretary, Miss Crabblesnitch, dove gray is the perfect color. Not too drab, not too bold, it's soft but not weak, attractive but not superficial.

I'm probably going to die in a gray dress. And that will be my ghost outfit.

Forever.

"That one today, Megan." Miss Crabblesnitch points to the ensemble in the maid's left hand—a tweed short-sleeved circle-dress with attached bouffant petticoats and matching jacket.

In gray. *Of course.*

After I'm dressed, I sit at the vanity table and Megan begins to arrange my long hair in its typical bun, leaving my bangs swept to the side and a few strands loose to soften the look.

"Good afternoon, ladies." Mother sweeps into the room, elegant and smiling, wearing a willowy dark blue silk dress with a dainty white floral pattern. Miriam trails in behind her in pale green with a matching band in her curly, light brown hair.

"Thank you, Megan. I'll finish up here," Mother says, taking the maid's place behind me. Miss Crabblesnitch and Megan curtsy and leave the room.

"Never cut you hair, Lenora," Mother says as she pins it. "It's so beautiful."

Mother is the only one who calls me beautiful and sweet and a hundred other words that make me feel delightful inside. That make me feel . . . normal. Or what I imagine "normal" must be.

She finishes my hair and catches my eyes in the mirror, wrinkling her nose. "Miss Crabblesnitch chose gray again?"

I sigh dramatically. "Gray like the dreary Wessco sky . . . and my soul."

"Cheeky girl." Mother laughs. Then she turns and gazes at the sparkly, poofy gown hanging just outside my dressing room. "At least you'll be able to mix it up tonight at your birthday ball."

I stand up beside her. "Yes, because silver is so very different from gray."

Mother presses her soft hand to my cheek. "It complements your eyes. You will be a vision."

"I want to have a black-and-white ball for my birthday," Miriam says. "And everyone will wear black and white—except I'll be in electric blue. And I'll meet the love of my life and we'll dance and dance and dance. And no one will look at Lenora."

My fourteen-year-old sister sticks her tongue out at me.

Charming.

"You can have all the looks," I tell her. "If no one ever turned my way again, I'd be perfectly happy."

Mother checks her watch. "Come along, darlings. Your father is downstairs and you know he hates to be kept waiting."

Father stands at the bottom of the steps, spine straight, hands folded behind his back. He's many years older than Mother, with lines on his face and more white in his hair than brown. But together they're an attractive couple, and as he gazes up at her, his gray-blue eyes are bright, like those of a much younger man.

We don't wait for compliments from the King, and he gives us none. It's never been his way. But he offers Mother his arm, and the four of us walk across the grand marble foyer toward the car that will take us to the Parliament luncheon to celebrate my birthday.

"Remember, Lenora—no dancing tonight," my father says without turning around.

"Oh, Reggie. It's her sixteenth birthday," Mother complains.

"Precisely. I won't have rumors spreading about her with this or that randy son of a lord because she was seen dancing too closely."

Rumors are like a dent from a sledgehammer—you can repair it, but it will never be as it was before. The Archbishop of Dingleberry . . . don't even get me started on his name . . . told Father that once. He has a puckered, bitter face like a piece of fruit that's gone bad, and you can just tell his mother never let him have sweets as a child.

Mother tries again. "For goodness sakes, it's not the eighteen hundreds."

And my father says one of the truest things I'll ever hear:

"Within these walls, it still is."

The Parliament luncheon progresses just as I would expect from a room full of old men whose favorite sound in the world is their own droning voices. I look up to the ornate, mural-painted ceiling and pray for an act of God to save me from my boredom. Nothing flashy like an earthquake or a volcano, but perhaps a little plague? Frogs would be good. I'd settle for locusts at this point.

But God has forsaken me—because the afternoon drags on uninterrupted.

"Warts."

It's funny how just when you think things can't get any worse, they always do.

"Pardon?"

The Marquis of Munster's beard is so overgrown, I can barely make out his mouth. But I can see the leftovers from his lunch—bits of ham and cheese dangle from the gray, wiry hair like horrific Christmas tree ornaments.

I don't gag. Or grimace. My self-control is outstanding. I should give myself a medal.

"I used to be the best rider in Parliament," he grumbles, "but I've had to cut back because of the warts on my feet. Springing up like weeds. There's one on my large toe that's as big as a juicy grape."

And my gag reflex is put to the test.

"Would you like to see, Your Highness?"

"See?" I repeat, because . . . he didn't really just say that, did he?

"It's quite magnificent actually—medically speaking."

And he reaches for his left boot.

"Uh, I—"

"Good afternoon, Lord Munster!"

Miriam, my favorite sister in the whole wide world, skips up beside me, threading her arm through mine. "I'm afraid I have to steal my sister. Woman talk. You understand."

"Oh, yes, of course." Munster bows. "A very happy birthday to you, Princess Lenora."

"Thank you."

Arms linked, Miriam and I slide away.

"You owe me," she whispers. "I want to wear your sapphire necklace at the ball tonight."

"You can have the necklace and the earrings too. You've earned them."

"Was he trying to show you his *magnificent* wart?"

"How did you know?"

"He tried the same thing with Elizabeth Montgomery at her uncle's knighting ceremony last month! I think it's a bizarre mating-ritual kind of thing."

"What does that even mean?" I snort.

"Well, first he shows you his toe, but that's just the start. The next thing you know it's 'Come along now, dearie, and let me show you *all my other parts* that have warts!'" She wiggles her eyebrows and I cover my mouth, and we dissolve into a fizzy giggle fit.

Sometimes, when I let myself think about it, I almost can't believe how incredibly strange this life is. And I look out at the city from the palace window and I wonder if it's strange for everyone—maybe not in the same way it is for me, but odd, just the same.

A young man walks into the room then, and I'm sure I haven't seen him before. He's pale, with thick, dark, neatly trimmed hair and boyish features behind square, black-rimmed glasses. He moves through the room like an enthusiastic puppy in a new yard—all wide-eyed eagerness.

"Miriam, who is that boy?"

Gossip is petty, but in the world of politics it's also essential. I try to keep up, but Miriam's knowledge puts mine to shame. Hell, she'd put an MI6 spy's to shame.

"He's the new Duke of Anthorp," she whispers back.

The Duke of Anthorp is the title of the Rourke family—a name that's as old and prestigious in Wessco as Pembrook.

"He's so young."

"Just a year older than you." She nods. "Father had to give him a special dispensation so he could take his family's seat in the House of Lords. Didn't he tell you?"

I shake my head.

And Miriam tells all. "Oh, it's the juiciest bit! The new Duke is actually the second Rourke son. His brother—older by eight years—had a falling-out with the old Duke when he joined up for the war against his father's wishes. When the war ended, the older son came back home and the Duke offered to reinstate him. But he wanted nothing to do with it! He left!"

"Left?" I can't imagine it—walking away from your home, your family . . . your duty. It's as inconceivable to me as walking down the middle of the street without your clothes on.

"Where did he go?"

"Anywhere he wanted." Miriam sighs. "They say he's traveled all over the world climbing mountains, exploring jungles, and holds a record for deep-sea diving. He finds treasure."

"Treasure? The Rourkes have as much money as we do."

"But that's why it's so dreamy! He doesn't find the treasure because he needs to—he does it just because he can. He gives it to charities—they say he once gave a rare diamond to an orphan boy begging on the street. Changed his life."

Oh . . . that is rather dreamy.

"The old Duke kicked it a few months ago." Miriam snaps her fingers. "They say the older one didn't come home for the service, but the two brothers are supposedly very close. And now the younger brother is the Duke of Anthorp."

I watch the boy for a moment as he smiles and chats with the old men crowding around him—like they're trying to siphon off his youth through proximity. There's an openness in his expression, an unguardedness in his stance that's rare around here. He seems . . . kind. And genuine.

Parliament is going to eat him alive.

"What's his name?" I ask.

"Thomas."

My birthday ball is turning out to be a huge improvement from the luncheon. I feel luminous in my silver gown with my hair piled in shiny curls on my head, encircled by a flawless diamond tiara. And I haven't heard the word *warts* once.

It's an extravagant affair—long tables laden with caviar and sparkling Champagne in crystal flutes. The gilded mirrors on the ballroom walls reflect the rainbow blur of dancing gowns, glittery jewels, top hats and tails, and the lilting music of a twenty-piece orchestra is in fine form. The guests include a former American president, royals from every country in Europe and all the noble families of Wessco.

I stand to the side, along the wall, beside a marble column—my feet tapping in time to the music I won't be dancing to.

Occasionally a well-wisher stops to chat—like Mr. Elvin Busey, a middle-aged, well-connected entrepreneur who wanted to tell me all about his new upholstery business, in case I wanted to invest. Once in a while, an upper-class boy passes by—the son of a Duke or an Earl or one of the several foreign Princes—each with expressions of greedy lust or squirrelly unease on their faces when they glance my way.

"That dress is the tops, Lenora!" My cousin Calliope gives me two thumbs up as she whisks past with her entourage.

Calliope's hobby is writing detailed horror stories about the grisly death of every member of the royal family who stands between her and the throne. Including me.

These interactions aren't genuine. They're not real or sincere.

The rest of the guests tend to watch me from across the room, while trying to look like they're not. But attention is tangible and weighted—something you can feel. As if by reflex, I stand stiffer, straighter, and my features slip into that unreadable mask of indifference.

"Are you having a good time, darling?" my mother asks.

She looks like a jewel tonight. Her gown is red velvet and there are winking rubies pinned all through her dark hair.

"Yes, I'm enjoying myself."

The same way a Fabergé egg must enjoy itself while it's admired, in its guarded museum glass case.

Laughter and chatter come from the group of young nobles behind us. Mother hears it too.

She wraps her arm around my lower back, squeezing with a gentle strength. "Your time will come, Lenora."

"I know." I shrug.

"I don't mean when you become queen. I mean your time for laughter . . . for love. Joy and excitement—that will come for you too. I'm sure of it."

"How can you be sure?"

There are old, shushed stories about my mother's

great-aunt Portia. They say she was a strange bird who sometimes had dreams that had a funny way of coming true.

She cups my jaw in her hands. "Because you, dear girl, are extraordinary in every way. It only makes sense that every part of your life will be extraordinary too." She kisses my forehead. "I'm so proud of you . . . so proud to be your mother."

I don't spend a lot of time with Mother, not as much as I'd like. But when I do, she's always able to do this—chase away the melancholy as easily as a fairy waving her wand.

"Thanks, Mum."

She looks over my shoulder and her smile drops like a bomb. "Oh hell . . . the Marquis of Munster has the Queen Mother of Spain cornered. If he flashes that damn warty foot, we'll end up in a bloody war."

As my mother scurries away to prevent an international incident, I spot the young Duke of Anthorp again. He's two columns down, leaning against the wall, his position almost a mirror image of my own. And because he can most likely feel me looking, his head turns my way—and he squints, like he still can't see me well, despite the thick glasses on his face.

And then he's strolling this way, hands folded behind his back. When he reaches me, he leans on the wall beside me, bowing his head, giving a start of a smile.

"Happy birthday, Princess Lenora."

"Thank you, Duke Anthorp."

He flinches. "Please, call me Thomas. Or Rourke. Every time I hear the title I look around for my father. He was a miserable old bastard when he was alive and I don't expect two months of being dead would've improved his disposition, so the thought of him being close by is . . . disturbing."

A chuckle swirls up my throat. What an oddly honest thing to say!

I nod. "How are you finding Parliament, Thomas?"

"Challenging. I've heard there are no friends in politics—only enemies and men you don't yet know are your enemies. I'm beginning to see how accurate that is." He shakes his head. "I just have to figure it out. I'm the youngest member of Parliament—it's important that I be good at it."

"Yes, I know the feeling."

A swell of sympathy rises inside me for him. Like spotting a doe in the woods, when you know the wolves are near.

"The trick is to guard your opinions," I tell him. "To not let anyone know what you're thinking. You should work on your poker face." And because he seems so young and alone, I offer, "I could help you with that. Show you the ropes, so to speak. Give you some pointers."

And it's as if I've offered him the world.

"You would do that for me? That's very kind." He looks off toward the dance floor and his voice drops lower. "I don't have many friends—especially not here in the city. I'm more of a lone wolf, you know? A rebel." He shrugs then and gives me a self-deprecating smile. "Well . . . an oddball may be more accurate. A strange duck."

I smile. "I know that feeling too."

Thomas adjusts his glasses. "May I ask you something?"

"Of course."

"It's your party—why aren't you dancing?"

My eavesdropping sister pokes her head out from behind the column like a nosy squirrel popping out of a tree.

"She's not allowed."

"Why isn't she allowed?" Thomas asks.

"Chewing gum," Miriam explains—too happily.

"Yes, of course." Thomas nods. "I see."

And then his nodding head turns to a shaking one.

"No, wait, I *don't* see. What's chewing gum have to do with it?"

Yes, it's as ridiculous as it sounds.

"A lady is like a lovely stick of chewing gum," Miriam parrots. "Sweet and unblemished, but if you're not careful, every lad around will take a taste."

"But no decent man," I continue, mimicking a crotchety old sod, "will want to put a used stick of gum in his mouth."

Thomas seems to consider the idea seriously.

"That's a load of bollocks, if I ever heard it. Who said that?"

"The Archbishop of Dingleberry," I reply. "My father took it straight to heart."

"Dingleberry, eh? The name sort of says it all, then, doesn't it?" Thomas winks.

And I laugh out loud.

Miriam does too, then she grabs Thomas's wrist. "Now, Lenora may not be allowed to dance, but I am. And this song is one of my favorites. Let's dance, Duke."

Thomas seems surprised. "Well, all right."

And Miriam drags him off to the dance floor.

Two dances later, they come back.

"We've concocted a plan!" my sister whisper-yells.

Oh no.

I'm already shaking my head. "The last time you had a plan, I ended up sitting next to Stinky Winky at dinner. No thank you, very much."

Thomas looks back and forth between us.

"Stinky Winky?"

"The Viscount of Winkerton," Miriam explains.

"The man smells like a pig's arsehole," I add.

Thomas chuckles.

"But this is totally different!" Miriam bounces on her toes. "This plan will actually *work*! I'll create a distraction —I'm good at those. And you'll get a chance to dance, Lenora."

Thomas's soft green eyes meet mine. "Everyone should get to dance on their birthday—chewing gum be damned."

Excitement fizzes in my stomach and an unfamiliar wicked smile tugs at my lips.

"I shouldn't."

"Which is why it's fun," Thomas insists.

"I don't know . . ."

"Oh, come on!" my tempting serpent of a sister whines. "For God's sake, live a little."

I glance around the room, searching for the prying eyes that always follow me, then I take a quick breath and nod. "All right."

"Brilliant!" Miriam claps her hands, then looks at

Thomas. "Wait for the signal."

She rushes off to my father, pulling the King out to the dance floor. The bulbs of the palace photographer's cameras flash, and you can practically hear the whole room sigh with the preciousness of watching the King of Wessco dance with his youngest daughter.

Thomas stands beside me, staring straight ahead, his hand just inches from mine. "Wait for it . . . wait . . ."

"Oh no!" Miriam screeches, and if all eyes weren't on her and my father before, they are now.

"Now!" Thomas whispers, grabbing my hand and rushing us through the door behind us, as Miriam carries on about losing her beloved sapphire earring that was a gift from the King of Bermuda.

The room Thomas and I dive into is the mauve and gold drawing room, which was used in the corset days for all the fainting ladies who dropped like flies. But tonight it's empty.

Thomas peeks through the crack in the door, listening—and after a moment he smiles. "The coast is clear."

For most people, this would be a small, silly thing. But I'm not most people.

I've never disobeyed my father—I've never disobeyed *anyone*.

And I feel . . . alive. Maybe the most alive I've ever felt.

The beautiful music comes clearly through the walls—a fun, fast jig of a tune.

Thomas straightens his tuxedo jacket and his glasses. Then he bows, holding out his hand. "May I have the honor of this dance, Princess Lenora?"

And for the first time, to someone who is not my father or a direct relation, I reply, "I would be delighted."

Thomas clasps our right hands together, squaring our arms, and rests his other hand on my waist. And beneath the dim, golden chandelier, we dance. We skip and spin, twirl and shuffle. We almost fall once, and Thomas steps on my toes . . . more than once.

"Ouch!"

"Sorry."

"Ow!"

"My fault—won't happen again."

By the time the song ends, my head feels light and my heart races. Not in a swoony, romantic kind of way, but sillier—sweeter—how it would feel to dance with a dear brother. "You're not very good at dancing, Thomas."

He grins, wheezing. "Yes, I probably should've warned you. But I figured bad dancing was better than no dancing."

He reaches into his pocket and removes a small metal device that he puts in his mouth and breathes on deeply. I've read about them—a new way of administering inhalant medicine.

He lets out his breath slowly, then shrugs, explaining, "Asthma."

I nod as he slides the device back in his pocket. And when a new song begins, Thomas lifts his eyebrows. "Want to go again?"

I nod and put my hand back in his.

But we've only taken a few steps when a sharp scream comes from the outer room. And the music cuts off. And a still, eerie silence covers us like a blanket.

Thomas and I look at each other, and then we run for the door.

The guests are clustered on the dance floor. I push my way to the center and there, on the floor, my father cradles Mother in his arms.

"Anna, Anna!"

She doesn't answer.

Her eyes are closed and her face is still and a trickle of red-black blood seeps from her nose.

"Anna . . ."

Miriam is curling into me, hiding her face against my arm. There's a rush in my ears, a whole ocean crashing against my brain. And it's as though I'm leaning over the edge of a cliff, about to plunge into the jaws of the dark, bottomless sea.

But then, from the other side, there's a hand on my shoulder—warm and strong.

I tear my eyes from my parents and Thomas's soft green gaze catches me. He holds on tighter—tethering me, anchoring me, letting me know I'm not alone, that he's there.

And he won't let me fall.

CHAPTER
2

Lenora

"**Y**OUR MOTHER HAS DIED."
Such sad words. Terrible words—the most awful words I ever heard.
"Your mother has died."

The King seemed to age ten years as he spoke them. And I watched as all the joy was leached from Miriam's dancing eyes.

"Your mother has died."

Nothing would ever be the same. Nothing would ever be as fun-loving and wonderful as it could've been. No one would ever call me sweet or beautiful again.

A cranial aneurism, the doctor said. A freak occurrence, he explained. No warning signs, no treatment that could have prevented it.

My father is a good king, a gentleman.

But he is not a *gentle* man.

So the day after my mother died, he lectured us in

firm, harsh tones on what was expected. We would walk every street in Wessco behind Mother's casket, as was tradition. Mother was beloved and the people would be devastated, and it was up to us to lead them through their grief.

Our own mourning would be done privately—not in view of the maids or the secretaries or security—we must only show composure. Strength. Dignity.

"Your mother has died."

And so, the morning of my mother's funeral, the maid drew my bath. And alone in that porcelain tub, I slipped beneath the water and cried until there were no tears left inside me.

"Can I ask you something?"

A week after Mother's funeral, we've come to Alfie's for the weekend, fishing for carp in the large pond on his estate.

According to Father, it's important for me to be skilled in all sorts of manly leisure activities—because that's where deals really get done. At card tables and hunting grounds and fishing ponds. He'd have me on a rugby field if he thought he could get away with it.

"You can ask me anything, Lenora."

My eyes dart beside me to Alfie, then back to my father. "It's personal."

"Go ahead."

I look up at this man—my father, my king, my mentor—who most times I feel like I don't know at all.

"Did you love her? Mother?"

He casts his line into the water and his steel-colored eyes—the same shade as mine—cloud over.

"I know you cared for her, but did you love her? Truly?"

My father has this way of imparting a lesson without making it feel like a lecture. His voice is a wise, resonant, baritone—like the voice of God—that makes you want to follow and obey.

"Your mother was a good woman. Gracious . . . jubilant. When you sit on the throne, everyone wants a piece of you—a piece for the people, a piece for the press, a piece for Parliament, a piece for your spouse, a piece for your children. Eventually, you have to cut yourself up into pieces so small, you feel as if you've shortchanged everyone. But your mother never begrudged me."

He turns his head and puts his hand on my shoulder. "It will not be that way for you, Lenora. Some part of your husband will always resent you."

"Why?"

"You're a smart girl—you tell me why."

I think about all I know and all I've seen, and the answer isn't difficult.

"Men don't like to bow. To anyone. But especially not to a woman—to their wife."

My father taps my shoulder and nods, then his gaze goes back to the pond.

"When the time comes for you to marry, we'll find you a good, greedy man."

"Greedy?"

"A greedy man will appreciate you for the wealth and power you give him. And because he'll want to stay in your good graces, I'll know he'll treat you well."

When you can't think of anything clever to say, sarcasm will never let you down.

"Greed, wealth and power? Oh my—it's like a fairy tale. I may swoon."

My father reels in his line. "Don't fill your head with fairy tales, child. Or thoughts of love. They are not for us. They will only bring you sorrow."

With that, he walks away, to the footman to change his bait. I stare at his back.

"He didn't answer my question," I say to Alfie.

"'Course he did," Alfie says kindly. "He loved your mother, very much."

I tilt my head. "How can you tell?'

"Your father will never lie to you . . . and he didn't tell you no."

"Then why didn't he just say yes?"

"Because love is bloody awful, Chicken. And fantastic. A beautiful, horrible, messy thing. It will make you feel like you can fly one day and rip your guts out the next. It's complicated." Alfie shrugs. "And your father wants you to have simple, as much as you can. Because he knows there's already a whole crown of complications just waiting to be put on your pretty head."

The next morning, I'm back at the palace at my vanity table, as Megan holds up two outfits for Miss Crabblesnitch to choose from.

And it feels like a lifetime has gone by. Like so much has changed.

Like *I* have changed.

I look at the ensembles in the mirror—a dove-gray skirt and blouse and a yellow, short-sleeved dress with buttons down the front. I already know which one Miss Crabblesnitch will choose.

There's an old story about Vincent van Gogh eating yellow paint. Some say he did it because he wanted to die; others say that he was trying to raise his spirits by ingesting the cheery color. Maybe it was neither. Maybe he just said what the hell—and did it because he wanted to.

Because he could.

Because the choice was his to make.

I stand and turn toward the clothing in Megan's arms. And I point to the yellow dress. "I'll wear that one today."

My secretary blinks at me. Then she lifts her pointy nose and sniffs. "Princess Lenora, that is not—"

"*That* one."

I barely recognize my own voice. It comes from somewhere deep inside me, cold and clipped. And final.

Today, I will be yellow. Tomorrow I will be some other color.

But I will not be gray.

In-between, indecisive.

I will not float like a feather caught in a current, while others pull me in the direction they want and make my choices for me.

If I want to dance, I will dance. And if I choose to wear yellow, then yellow it will be.

Because what I know now, which I didn't before, is that life is too short, too unpredictable and too cruel for anything less.

CHAPTER
3

Lenora

Palace of Wessco, 1955

I T'S BEEN SAID THAT ONE PERSON can change the world—and because of who my family is, I know for a fact that this is true. What I didn't know was that one person can change your life. Fill in the empty, hollow spaces inside that you didn't even know were there.

That's what Thomas Rourke has done for me over the last two years. He's become my rock and my fun skipping stone. The someone I'd been missing my whole life.

My friend.

The first and only and very, very best.

"There you are," Thomas says from the stoop of Guthrie House. "I was just coming to see you."

It's dark out and late, and even the crickets in the garden have settled down for the night.

"You missed brandy and cigars."

Brandy and cigars in the library after dinner is the manly powwow session of the powers that be—and Father always insists I attend. Because . . . politics. Keep your friends close and your enemies right up your arse. That's how it works.

Thomas puts his hand over his heart. "And I'm all torn up about it, really. I had to finish reading the trade legislation for the vote tomorrow. Did you review it yet?"

I groan, like a student cramming for exams.

"No—I was planning on forgetting."

"Sorry." Thomas reaches into his jacket pocket and slips out a green glass bottle. "Maybe this will make up for it?"

Thomas Rourke isn't just the young Duke of Anthorp —he's a naughty boy. A terrible influence. And he's taken me firmly under his wing.

"What is it?" I ask.

"Irish whiskey. *Old* Irish whiskey from my father's personal collection. The bastard used to guard it like gold. I thought we'd crack it open together." He wiggles his eyebrows. "A few nips will make that legislation go down a lot easier."

I look over my shoulder—there's not a guard or maid or a spying judgey secretary in sight.

"Come on, then." I smile.

There's a shadowy spot behind a big evergreen, hidden from the view of the guards at the palace wall. Thomas and I sit on the grass and I reach under the tree like it's Christmas morning, for my secret white box. A moment later, I light my cigarette and tilt my head back to blow out a long, languid stream of smoke.

"If a photographer ever snaps a shot of you with a fag in your fingers, your father's going to lock you in your room for a month." He pulls the cork out with his teeth and takes a deep swig from the bottle—because we're classy like that.

Then he chokes and sputters.

I give the bottle a sniff, then before I change my mind, I bring it to my lips and gulp quickly.

And I immediately regret the decision. It's like drinking fire. I drop my cigarette and cough my esophagus up into my hands.

Like a lady.

"It burns," I rasp, eyes watering.

Thomas winks. "That means it's good."

There's more drinking—and coughing—and by my second cigarette I feel light and wonderfully floaty. Thomas pulls an arched, intricately hand-carved wooden pipe from his pocket.

"Oh, no, Thomas—not the pipe."

"I like the pipe," he mutters around it. "It makes me look distinguished."

"It makes you look like Sherlock Holmes."

"Exactly. Holmes is distinguished."

I shake my head. "You keep saying that word—I don't think you know what it means."

He points at me with the hideous pipe. "Shut it, you. Or I'll keep *this* all to myself."

He holds up an envelope—with sharp, masculine handwriting on it.

Thomas gets a letter from his brother about every two weeks—it's the most exciting thing in both our lives. And if I let myself think about that too much, I'll drown myself in this terrible-tasting whiskey.

I pluck the letter from his fingers, turning it over in my hands.

"Did you read it yet?"

Thomas snatches it back. "No. But if I were a gentleman I would have. Especially after the last one that was all about the luscious tits and arse of the Egyptian girl who liked him so much."

Naughtiness is strong in the Rourke family. But Edward's is different from his brother's.

Dirtier. Manlier.

I suppress an embarrassed giggle. "There were *two* Egyptian girls. And he liked them right back, from what I recall. At the same time."

Edward's letters are the perfect mix of eloquence, wit and vulgarity—sometimes he draws pictures, and he's one hell of an artist. They're more interesting than any film and more fun than that Elvis Presley hip swing all the American parents are losing their minds about.

They're my peek into the outside world. The real world. A world of sweat and sex and fighting and dancing —where people walk on the grass barefoot and eat with their hands. A world where life doesn't revolve around titles or etiquette and double-damned political mind games.

Thomas opens the envelope and reverently unfolds the letter. He gives his pipe a puff—coughs twice because he shouldn't be smoking it—then begins to read.

"Dearest Thomas,

"I've stopped in Sweden for a few days, to stock up

on gear on my way to a climbing expedition in Greenland. I arrived by train—hopped a boxcar—not the most elegant way to travel, but it's quick and interesting. And there's something freeing about having everything you own in the world strapped to your back in a pack. If you get the chance, I recommend it.

"I met a family of indigents in the car—a pretty mum, dad, little boy and cute girl. They shared their supper with me and despite their circumstances, they seemed happy. Content. Grateful for the food in their stomachs and the temporary roof over their heads. The lad was about seven or eight—with dark hair and glasses that were too big, but close enough for him to use. He reminded me of you. I left the few hundred kroner I had beside him while the family slept, then I jumped off at my spot, while the train rumbled on."

I've never seen a picture of Edward, but in my mind he's taken on a life of his own. Roguishly handsome, strong and charming, he lives the life of a hero-pirate-Viking-god. The kind of man who works in the sun, shares a pint with a friend, flirts with the prettiest lass, and manages to rescue an orphan or two from a burning building before he calls it a day.

Edward Rourke is the most exciting man I've never met.

"I'm writing to you now from a quiet hillside, with a campfire and tent beside me and the Northern Lights over my head. I'd heard aurora borealis is a stunning sight, something you have to see to believe—and Christ, they were right. It's like a river in the sky of the most magnificent colors. Swirls of greens and reds and deep purple—

all dancing together, a living symphony of color. It's magic made real, like I can reach out and touch it. I don't have the words to do it justice. I wish you were here, Thomas. I wish you could see this.

"I'll be in Sweden until the end of the week; send your reply to the post address in Greenland below. I hope all is well with you, little brother, and I look forward to hearing from you more than I can say. Stay out of trouble —or, more to the point—don't get caught making trouble. And don't do anything I wouldn't do (which of course isn't much).

"Yours,

"Edward."

Sometimes he stays in one place for a few weeks or a few months, but never for good. I watch Thomas's eyes light on the bottom of the page, before his lips curl up into a grin.

"PS—give my regards to Lenny."

Warm, rushing sparks of electricity spread under my skin like some incurable rash.

Lenny. That's me. What Edward calls me in his letters, because Thomas has told him we're friends. It's the most ridiculous name. Only slightly less ridiculous than the effect it has on me.

"Are you blushing, Lenora?" Thomas asks.

I turn up my nose. "I don't blush. It's your stupid Irish whiskey going to my head."

I grab the letter and lie back on the cool grass, scanning it to make sure Thomas didn't leave anything out. Then, subtly, I bring the paper to my nose and inhale. There's a hint of pine and freshly cut wood.

"Did you just smell my brother's letter?"

Perhaps not so subtle after all.

I lie like the stellar politician I'm being raised to be.

"I have no idea what you're talking about."

"You did! You sneaky, sniffing, lying princess—you smelled the letter!"

"You're batty."

Thomas's tone turns singsongy teasing.

"I think you have a crush on my brother."

"I think that pipe is making you soft in the head."

"You think he's top-notch."

I refuse to answer; my lips are closed. My cold shoulder has been known to freeze people to death.

"I'm going to tell him." He pokes. "I'm going to say, 'James Dean has nothing on you, Edward, because Princess Lenora is totally gone for you.'"

Like a cobra striking, I reach up and yank a few strands of his hair out, at the nape of his neck where it'll really hurt.

"Ow! Fucking hell!"

"I'll have you killed. I know people. I'm a princess on the edge—don't push me."

"You can't have me killed—I'm the only friend you've got."

I flop back on the grass, shrugging. "That's a sacrifice I'm willing to make."

Chuckling, Thomas tucks the letter in his pocket, then lies back on the grass beside me, our heads just a few inches apart.

"I think Winston fancies you," he says softly.

Maddox Winston is the newest addition to my personal security team. He's mysterious in a cold, brusque sort of way. Rumor has it he was a notorious assassin during the war.

I roll my eyes. "Oh, bollocks."

Thomas glances at me. "No, truly. The way he watches you . . ."

"He's on my security team—he's supposed to watch me."

Thomas shakes his head. "Not the way he does it."

I ignore that comment and gaze up at the sky. There are no clouds tonight, just a thousand silver-white dots of light glowing brilliantly. And I think about Edward's letter.

"Do you ever wish you could trade places with Edward? That you had left and he had stayed here?"

In the dim light, Thomas's face is as pale as the stars —it makes him look like a bespeckled marble statue. A rascal angel.

"No. I couldn't serve in the military because of the asthma, but I've always wanted to do my part. Something more than just inheriting the Rourke money. Parliament is my chance to do that. To make a difference, leave my mark. And maybe if I do it well, someone somewhere will remember me. I think I'd like that . . . to be remembered."

I turn my head toward him.

"*I'll* remember you."

He smiles softly. "Well, that's one person, at least."

"I'm heir to the throne, silly. My remembrance is worth a thousand commoners'."

Thomas snorts. "What about you? Do you ever wish you were Miriam?"

Miriam went a little mad after Mother died. If I'm a rule-breaker now, she's a full-out revolutionary. Sometimes she goes out wearing trousers . . . and no bra. Yesterday she was caught for the second time this month with a boy in her room—an earl's son we're actually distantly related to—a fourth something-or-other twice removed. Father's ready to box her up and ship her to a convent on the next train out.

"No, I wouldn't trade places with Miriam. This life can be suffocating and stupid, but one day I'm going to be able to do amazing things, Thomas. I feel it in my bones. Being first anything is always hard, but I'm going to do it. And when I do, I'm going to change the world."

I tilt my head back to the sky, but in my mind's eye, instead of black, I see vibrant swirls of green and deep purple and fiery orange-red.

"Still . . . aurora borealis . . . it must be incredible." I can hear the longing in my own voice. The yearning for a piece of something outside the palace walls. Something new and wild and real.

"I would love to see it."

"So, fuck it all and go see it." Thomas sits up and plucks the blades of grass out of the ground. "Like Edward, he gets an idea in his head, something he wants to do—and he does it. Simple as that. No hesitation. No doubt."

I shake my head. "I'm needed here; Father would never let me. And even if he did, it wouldn't be like Edward—on a hillside with a tent and a campfire. There'd be press and security and servants. It would all be a . . . shitshow."

Thomas laughs, but in a subdued, sympathetic sort of way.

I wave my hand—I have no patience for self-pity, even when it's my own.

"Oh, listen to me going on—the poor princess. Irish whiskey makes me go all pitiful."

Thomas stands, brushes off his trousers and offers me his hand, pulling me up. "Then it's time for you to sleep it off, Pitiful Princess."

"I will. *After* I do my required reading."

The dark-haired joker lifts his hand to the sky, like he's reciting Shakespeare. "Mirror, mirror on the wall, what is the boringest of them all?"

"Trade legislation!" we say in unison.

I heard a new term the other day on an American television show—*nerds*. I'm fairly certain that's what Thomas and I are.

He walks me to the door.

"Good night, Thomas."

"Pleasant dreams, Lenora."

Thomas bows, then he slips his hands in his pockets and heads down the path, whistling a quick, cheery tune.

CHAPTER 4

Lenora

Palace of Wessco, 1956

I T BEGAN SLOWLY, subtly, the way terrible things
often do. A flinch, a pause, a grimace of pain—my
father hid it well, but I noticed. And I wasn't the only
one—rumors and whispers filled the palace like a moldy
stench. Within months it graduated to the occasional post-
poned meeting, then missed functions that I attended in his
place, delayed starts to his schedule and finally, whole
bedridden days.

And here is where it ends.

In the royal apartments, the antechamber of the
King's bedroom. My uncle is here—my father's youngest
brother, the Duke of Warwitch. They've never been especially close, but he's on the Advising Council, so he's
here. A few of the men in this room have genuine affection
for my father, and they chat easily with the ones who

don't. The ones waiting like vultures, ready to swoop in and claim their chunk of the carcass.

Because that's how this works.

"The King is dying."

Those words were delivered to me two days ago by Alexander Bumblewood, the Prime Minister, who was the only man the King's doctors informed. Like a morbid version of the telephone game.

That's the way it goes. Secrecy is paramount. Because governments don't do change well, and monarchies . . . despite all our rules and laws and traditions . . . we're bloody awful at it. Historically, change brought power struggles—it used to be all false imprisonments, murders, full-out wars and royal heads rolling.

We're better now.

More . . . outwardly civilized. But the hidden, hushed motivations—ambition, fear, greed—those will remain for as long as humans are humaning.

Miriam and Alfie step out from my father's bedroom. Alfie's nose is red and he wipes at his watery eyes with a handkerchief. He tries to give me a smile, but he can't quite manage it.

And that cracks something inside me—a small fissure in the veneer I've lacquered to perfection.

Miriam shudders with great, gasping sobs—openly and unashamed. My sister's always been emotional, wearing her heart on her sleeve for all to see. A young blond footman guides her from the room with his arm around her. If I had it in me, I'd make it clear he's being too familiar—but I'm too drained.

"The King is asking for you, Your Highness," The

Prime Minister says.

I look to Thomas beside me and his kind green eyes offer me comfort. *I've got you*, they say. *I'm with you.*

And none of it feels real. It's like a foggy dream. A day I knew would come but didn't really believe ever would.

The inner room is as well-equipped as any hospital's. Beeping monitor wires and pain-relieving tubes stick out from beneath Father's papery skin. His doctor, the King's Physician, is here; he bows to me before stepping back to a respectful distance.

If a praying mantis and a human had a baby, the result would be Oscar Pennygrove. He's a tall, emaciated man with strangely long fingers that give the impression of two spiders attached to the ends of his arms. He's the Home Secretary—an official witness to assure the country and Crown that there is no trickery or foul play at the births and deaths of any royal in the line of succession. He was in the room when I was born, and he was at Miriam's birth too. He was present at the births and deaths of the siblings before me, and he stands silent in the corner now, like one of those portraits whose eerie eyes move when you do.

I put my hand on top of Father's.

"It's Lenora, Father. I'm here."

Slowly, his eyes open and a moist rattling sound comes from his chest. His lips are blue-tinged and chapped, but they smile at me.

"Lenora." His voice is reedy, so thin I lean forward to hear him. "I love you, my dear girl."

You do?

It's the first thought that springs into my head, and

though I don't say the words out loud, he reads them on my face and his fragile smile falters.

"You didn't know. I should have done better by you. There was so much to teach you . . . but I should have done better."

I take his hand in both of mine, holding it gently and close. Because I see it now—I understand. This man may have not given me everything I wanted—tickles and cuddles, laughter and pushes on the swing—but he spent his life giving me everything I will *need*.

And I won't let him die thinking he failed me.

"No, Father. No . . ." My throat constricts. "You did wonderfully by me, I promise. I'll make you proud. I'll serve Wessco with dignity and honor, and I'll make you so proud of me."

He squeezes my hand back.

And though his breathing is ragged, he tells me, "I have always been proud of you. Do not serve . . . Lenora. *Reign.* With an iron grip . . . and a velvet touch. Trust . . . only . . . yourself. And reign."

I nod, and though my eyes are full, I don't let any tears fall. I hold them back, for him. To prove that even now, especially now . . . I can be strong.

His eyes close, and for many minutes the only sounds in the room are the beeping machine and Father's frail breaths.

Alexander Bumblewood steps up beside me. "Would you like to return to the antechamber to wait, Princess Lenora? They're having tea."

Of course they are. Because tea fixes everything.

"No. I'll stay with him."

Kings are men . . . they die like any other man.

And this one will not die alone.

I get to my feet, lean over and kiss Father's rough, leathery cheek. For the very first time, and the last. Then I sit back down, hold his hand, and in my head . . . I talk to him—telling him all the things I can't say in front of the doctor and Prime Minister and Pennygrove.

I tell him about Thomas and the trouble we've gotten up to through the years. I tell him about my hopes and dreams for Wessco—ideas I didn't share before, because I wasn't sure if he'd approve. I tell him about me—a side he's never seen that can be silly and wild. I tell him how desperately hard it is sometimes to be me—how awfully lonely—and then how stupid I feel for feeling that way, because I know I'm the most fortunate girl in the whole world. I say how grateful I am for all he's given me—his support and attention and guidance.

I say . . . goodbye.

And still, none of it feels real. It doesn't seem like he's gone.

Not when the monitor stops beeping, or when the doctor checks for breathing and a pulse, and finds neither. Not when the time is announced or the sheet is drawn up or when the Home Secretary tells the Prime Minister to formally certify that His Most Royal King Reginald William Constantine II has passed from this life.

"Your Majesty . . ."

I don't look up; I don't move.

"Your Majesty . . ." Oscar Pennygrove says again.

And it's only then that I realize he's speaking to me. There can be several royal highnesses in a bloodline, but there is only ever one ruling majesty at a time.

Pennygrove offers me his bony hand. I take it as I stand and the bedroom door is opened, and I step into the room full of waiting, watching aristocrats—their eyes fixed on me.

Pennygrove's proclamation is crisp and definitive.

"The King is dead. Long live the Queen."

Like their ancestors before them, the lords reply in one resounding voice.

"Long live Queen Lenora!"

And that's the moment. The moment the fog clears and the circumstances of who I am—*what* I am—becomes as real as real can be.

Queen Lenora.

Ready or not . . . here comes the crown.

Two months later
St. George's Cathedral

The day of my coronation is bitterly cold—long, shining icicles hang from every corner of the palace and breaths come in exhales of puffy white bursts. My gown is a masterpiece of ivory satin, long in the back, cinched at the waist, with the Rose of Wessco intricately embroidered in silver filigree across the skirt. My lips are ruby red, my lashes sooty black. Glistening diamonds—my mother's—dangle from my earlobes and the coronation robe rests on my shoulders, stretching out behind me in yards of pristine white fur.

It makes me feel like a mythical arctic huntress . . . a Winter Queen. A ruler of snow and ice.

When I emerge from the carriage—the same one my father rode in, and his father before him—in the shadow of St. George's Cathedral, the camera flashes go off like fireworks and the endless crowd gathered along the streets roars. I hear them, but I don't look their way. With my head held high, I ascend the stone steps, focused on the sacred ceremony before me. There will be massive celebrations—a coronation is a joyous event—but they will come later.

I stand in the atrium, alone, surrounded by only the vivid prisms of color shining from the stained-glass windows. The double doors open, and the members of the packed congregation rise to their feet, as the drums begin to pound out a deep imperial rhythm.

It's the same beat that was played when royals were marched to the chopping block.

My ancestors enjoyed irony.

While I stand in the doorway, I experience a moment of terror, when it feels like my knees have disappeared. The faces of the lords and ladies all bedazzled in their best formal-wear seem to morph into some dark goblin nightmare—their eyes demon-black and their teeth-baring grins sharp and menacing.

I close my eyes.

And my mother's lilting voice whispers in my head.

Breathe, my darling. Just breathe.

My father's voice joins hers—an echo of his final command.

Reign.

And my knees return, solid and sure. Because I was raised for this.

Born for this.

I take my first step down the aisle, shoulders back, spine straight. In my periphery, I spot Thomas and Alfie and Miriam—and I know they are there for me, that they have my back. But it's only now that I realize no one will ever be there to guard my front again. To shield me, to step before me.

I will always be first and on my own—for the rest of my life.

I reach the altar, where the Archbishop waits. I step up to the throne, turn to face the congregation, and the ceremony begins. The Archbishop anoints me with oil and says all the magic Latin words. I recite my oath, my solemn vow. The Lord Chamberlain invests me with the golden scepter and jeweled orb, and the Lord Chancellor slides the ring on my right hand.

And then I take my place upon the throne.

Saint Michael's Crown—the jeweled and velvet glory of the Crown Jewels of Wessco—is brought forward by the Dean of Ansaline. The Archbishop prays, then slowly, reverently, he places the crown on my head.

And I wait for the transformation from Princess to Queen. The surging inner shifting that I'm sure must occur as one rises to the level of most royal sovereign.

I wait and wait some more.

Then, after a few moments, I blink.

Because it doesn't happen. *Nothing* happens.

I don't feel different. I still feel like me, only . . . me with a big crown on my head.

How anticlimactic.

Stealthily, I glance at the bishops and the crowd filling the cathedral pews. No one else seems to notice.

So, I carry on.

Regally, I walk back down the aisle, and every head bows before me. Outside the cathedral there are more flashes and cheers as I wave, then descend the steps and return to the carriage that carries me back through the palace gates. For the next hour, I'm greeted and congratulated by all government officiants and visiting dignitaries. I smile and nod and say the right things—but still it feels all so disappointingly make-believe.

Like pageantry. Like I'm a little girl, wearing her daddy's crown, which is too big for her head.

And then it's time to step out onto the balcony—the press loves this bit.

As I proceed alone, a frigid breeze wafts over me, tickling my skin with icy fingers. I rest my hands on the stone balustrade . . . and look down.

There's an ocean of faces, men and woman and children—and they're all smiling, cheering, waving and clapping. Tens of thousands of them—maybe millions. Some have tears running down their faces, but all have a look of complete adoration.

For me.

They're here for me.

I've seen crowds before, my whole life. I've met the public—but not like this, never like this.

These are my people. And for the first time, I understand what that means.

Because I don't just see them—I feel them. Their energy envelops me in its warm embrace. Their joy, their
trust, their love . . . their acceptance. I feel it from the top
of my head to the tips of my toes. My soul sings with it.

This is what it must be like to fall in love for the first
time—this flying, breathless sensation. Or, how it must be
to hold your own child and know instantly you will love
him or her forever. You'll do anything to keep your children safe, to do right by them, to give them the best life
they can possibly have.

Slowly, glittering fluffy snowflakes drift down from
the sky. Everywhere and all around.

It's magical. Like a blessing.

I wave to the people. "Thank you! Yes, hello! Thank
you!"

They can't hear me, but I want them to know that I
hear *them*. I *see* them. I care for them as they care for me
. . . and I will never, ever let them down.

It's only when my vision goes blurry that I realize I'm
crying. Crying with joy and relief, overwhelmed by so
much feeling. And still I wave. I wave until my arm aches
—but it's not enough.

With my heart galloping, I walk back inside.

"I want to go down. I want to speak to them, shake
their hands, be among them."

A dozen ancient disapproving faces look back at me.

The Lord Chamberlain steps forward, clearing his
throat.

"Your Majesty . . . it's not done."

A government is a machine with many moving parts. The Crown is the key—but Parliament, the Advising Council, the Lords and Secretaries of State, they're the gears. It's a balancing act, a constant grinding tug-of-war —because the one who controls the key controls every-thing.

"You mean, it hasn't been done before, not that it can't be."

"It's not safe," he insists.

I scan the room, and I spot my very own dark-haired guardian angel.

"Winston," I call, using my commanding voice. "I wish to go down to see the people. Can you help me do that?"

He dips his chin and gives the Lord Chamberlain a piss-off sort of look.

"If that is what Your Majesty wishes, then that is what will be done. My men and I will keep you safe."

I turn to the Lord Chamberlain and smile sweetly.

"See now, it's no problem at'all."

I walk through them, and Winston and his men close in around me, as I go down the stairs and out of the palace gates to let the people meet their new Queen.

And this crown feels like it fits just right after all.

CHAPTER
5

Lenora

THE AVERAGE PERSON WASTES a third of her life sleeping. My great-aunt Matilda told me that— she was a bouncy, wiry woman who drank too much black tea and rushed about like she was perpetually late for some important event that didn't exist. I've never been much of a sleeper—three or four hours a night is more than enough.

Insomnia is a mark of genius. And insanity.

I tend to ignore that latter part.

On the third day after my coronation, I rise especially early—before sunrise. I dress in a kelly-green sweater and matching pencil skirt—with white gloves, my grandmama's pearl broach and my hair twisted high into its usual bun. It's a stylish look, but professional, and today, I'm all business.

A bit later, after a light breakfast and reading all three of the major newspapers, I pull up in the Rolls-Royce to the curb of Barrister's department store. Nearly half of my face is covered by big, round sunglasses despite the drizzling rain, and I tip my head back and gaze at the mammoth stone building. Over the years, Alfie Barrister has built quite an empire. He has five stores now in cities across the world—with a sixth opening soon in Hong Kong.

My security team precedes me through the gleaming glass doors, across the shiny black-and-white-tiled floor, to the elevator up to the top, where I'll find a jolly, redheaded man—who's just the bloke I need to see.

"Hello, Chicken." Alfie stands and bows from behind his giant mahogany desk. It's a desk fit for a queen, and I make a mental note to commission a new one for myself straight away.

"Alfie."

"Tea, Your Majesty?" Jones, Alfie's secretary, asks.

"No, I'm fine." I wave my hand. "You may leave us."

"This is a pleasant surprise." After I take one of the cushioned chairs across his desk, Alfie sits in the large leather one behind it. "Have you come by before we open to shop?" He winks. "I can get you a discount."

"No shopping today. But I do have a request—a big one."

"Request away. You know I could never tell you no." He brings his china teacup to his lips.

And I drop the proverbial bomb. "I want you on the Advising Council."

Alfie chokes on his tea.

"The Advising Council?" He dabs his mouth with a napkin. "That's . . . unexpected."

It's unheard of, actually, but that's just semantics.

"It's a full-time commitment, Lenora. I don't have room in my schedule."

"Make the room. I need you, Alfie."

Father said to trust only myself, and I do. I trust myself enough to know that I need men around me I can depend on.

"You once told Father the whole world is an advertisement and we're all customers. Do you remember?"

That looks comes over his face, the same one he always gets when we talk about my father—warm and affectionate and still a little sad.

"I remember."

"I need your business sense and marketing skill, Alfie. Father used to say if you have the people on your side, you have everything. I need you to make sure my message, my vision for the country, makes its way to the people."

Alfie folds his hands across his belly, tapping his thumbs.

"You think Parliament will work against your vision?"

"I don't know what Parliament will do. I must be prepared for anything."

"Only nobility can serve on the Advising Council," he points out.

Alfie had the ear, the confidence and the friendship of a king. But he wasn't an aristocrat. Until now.

I hand him a large, sealed envelope—with a thick, folded sheet of paper inside that's inscribed with black elegant writing, my signature, and stamped with the golden seal of the Crown.

"You are now the esteemed Earl of Ellington. Congratulations."

Alfie takes the envelope like it may bite him.

"Can you do that without Parliament's approval?"

I shrug. "The land is mine, the titles are mine—I can hand them out any damn way I please. If you'd like an official ceremony, I can organize one for you."

"That won't be necessary."

I watch his face and can practically see the wheels turning in his big, brilliant red head. Being a wealthy international businessman is all fine and good, but being a titled aristocrat is a whole other level of success.

Of stature.

So, I make my other request.

"I also need Cora to come work for me, as my private secretary."

Alfie's eyebrows lift high and mighty. "You're commandeering my schedule *and* my only daughter?"

When Alfie's children finished their schooling in Scotland, all three came to live in Wessco and work with him in the family business.

"You only have yourself to blame," I tell him. "You're always going on about her organizational skills, her energy and initiative. I could use some of that at the palace."

Traditionally, the king's private secretary has been a man's position, but I think it's time a lady filled the role. And Cora Barrister, with her father's business sense and jovial personality, is just the woman for the job.

When Alfie continues to hesitate, I tease him.

"Don't make such a fuss, old man. You still have Albert and Louis—they'll continue the expansion of your great retail empire."

"When did you start calling me Old Man?" He frowns.

"When you were still calling me Chicken after I was old enough to begin wearing a bra."

That gets a chuckle out of him.

"So what do you say? Are you with me?"

And he smiles—the same warm, reassuring smile he's given me my whole life.

"Of course I'm with you. Did you have any doubt?"

No, but it's still nice to hear him say it.

I stand. "Welcome to the peerage, Alfie. Brace yourself—it's not as much fun as it looks."

His forehead crinkles. "It doesn't look fun at'all."

"Exactly."

My next destination is a good four hours' drive away—not quite the middle of nowhere, but far from anywhere that's considered somewhere. In the car, I review the latest tax report. Since the war ended, revenue has been in steady decline and Parliament wants to hike up taxes. But the issue isn't that taxes are too low; it's that jobs are too scarce.

And you can't get blood from a stone, no matter how many times you bash it with a meaner, heavier rock.

I set the report aside as we pass through the wrought-iron gates and head up the winding drive. The rain has stopped, a thick foggy mist rises from the ground and a fragile glimmer of sun peeks out from the clouds as the massive gray structure comes into view.

Anthorp Castle.

It's the stuff of fairy tales. All smooth, shiny stone, arched windows, floating footbridges and soaring turrets—with the angry green sea crashing against the rocks below the cliff on one side, and miles of wild forest on the other. I was raised amongst castles; they are as common to me as bed linens . . . but this one still manages to take my breath away.

Two flags fly from the highest tower—the Wessco standard and just slightly lower, the banner of the Rourke family, proclaiming that the master of the house, the dear Duke of Anthorp, is in residence.

I find Thomas in the morning room with his feet up on a leather ottoman, his hands tucked behind his head, his white shirt open and his chest on display in all its pale gleaming glory.

And he's not alone.

"Good afternoon, Your Majesty."

Michael Fitzgibbons bows his dark auburn head as he greets me. Michael's the third son of a viscount and an artist, a painter. He's a beautiful young man—how the statue of David would look if it came to life and walked out of the museum. He's Thomas's *special* friend. They spend time together as often as they can when Thomas is away from his parliamentary duties.

Michael sits down in his chair and refocuses on the chessboard on the table between them.

"We were just about to have lunch, Lenora," Thomas

says in a raspy voice. His glasses are off and his eyes are closed, his head tilted back. "Would you like to join us?"

"That would be lovely."

And then my nose begins to burn with an odor—as if something had crawled from the sulfur pits of hell and died under Thomas's chair.

"Holy God, what is that stench?"

"Eucalyptus ointment," Thomas says. "For this bloody chest cold that won't go away. You get used to it after a bit."

Michael slides his rook across the board. "Yes, after the nerve endings in your nostrils shrivel and die."

Thomas makes the "tossing off" motion with his fist. A gesture I didn't even know existed until he taught it to me when I was seventeen. That and "the finger."

Very cathartic.

Thomas opens his arms and wiggles his fingers toward me. "Come, let me hug you. Then we can all be offensive together."

"No thank you. You're offensive enough for all of us."

Michael raises his glass of wine. "Here, here."

Despite the smell, I shift Thomas's feet and sit on the ottoman, taking over his chess game with Michael, moving his bishop into a more aggressive position against the king.

"I have a proposition for you, Thomas."

That gets his eyes open. "Is it a naughty proposition? You know those are my favorite."

"Depends on your definition of *naughty*. What do you think of taking a place on the Advising Council?"

He'll have to give up his family's seat in Parliament

—those are the rules—and we are nothing if not sticklers for rules. But the Council is a loftier position, more coveted, and more powerful. If Thomas wants to leave his mark on Wessco, the Advising Council's the place to do it.

"I think the sods on the Council will say it's borderline degenerate," Thomas replies.

"Probably."

Michael moves his knight and I take it with my queen.

"They'll fight you on it," Thomas says. "They'll say I'm too young, too reckless, not nearly wise enough."

"Highly likely," I reply.

He sips from his brandy glass. "Though what I lack in age, I make up for in experience and a bombastic personality."

Michael raises his glass. "Agreed."

I pick up one of the chess pieces, gazing at it for a moment.

"The queen is the most powerful piece on the board—did you realize that? But without her bishops and knights around her, she never lasts long." I place the piece back down. "I plan on lasting, Thomas. So I didn't come here to ask you what *the Council* would think. I want to know what *you* think."

A grin spreads across Thomas's lips.

"I think their heads may actually explode. Won't that be fun?" He lifts his glass. "Count me in."

"Excellent." I smile. And then I make my final move. "Checkmate."

The King's Advising Council is an institution as old as the monarchy. There's a room in the east corner of the palace where they meet. Where they've always met since the royal palace was completed in 1388, fifty years after Wessco was founded by its very first king, a former British general and husband to the daughter of Robert the Bruce, my ancestor John William Pembrook.

That's over five hundred years' worth of meetings . . . in the same room.

Despite my belief that the Council could use a little shaking up, I'd be lying if I said I wasn't a bit awed by the institution itself. I want to make a good impression. These are the men who'll be working side-by-side with me, who will guide me through the political and legislative land mines to turn my dreams for my people into reality.

They're here to help me do my job—and do it well.

At least, that's the idea.

For the last few weeks, I've conferred with Alfie about tax revenue and researched the legalities of the jobs program with Thomas. I have reports that I dictated to Cora. I have colored charts, and they're magnificent.

I have the cure for all of Wessco's ills. I'm ready.

There are no windows in the Council Meeting Room —better to prevent assassination attempts—but the room is accented in calm, deep purple with pleasant landscapes in oil framed on the walls. There's a sideboard for meals, tea and wine, and while the long, rectangular table and chairs in the center don't exactly look comfy, they are majestic.

There are six lords on the Council—eight now, if you count Alfie and Thomas.

There's my uncle, the Duke of Warwitch—a younger, lesser version of my father.

The Tweedle twins—Bartholomew and Bertram—the Marquis of Kooksbury and Fernshire, respectively. However, behind their backs they're known as Tweedledum and Tweedledee because of their name . . . and because of the odd egg-like shape of their bodies.

Next there's Christopher Alcott, the Duke of Sheffield, a distinguished former ambassador and highly respected scholar.

There's also dear Montague Spencer, the oldest man in the government and the Earl of Radcliffe. He's so old, no one can recall a single memory of him as a boy—not even himself.

Finally, there's Elliot Blackburn, the pious and powerful Marquis of Norfolk, who is rumored to have never smiled a day in his life.

I walk in the door promptly for my first meeting with my Advising Council, my reports and trusty charts tucked beneath my arm.

And it all starts off so well.

They stand and bow and I greet them with a "Good morning, my Lords." Then they sit and I sit and I begin with, "Let's get started."

And that's it. That's the good part.

It all goes straight to hell from there.

Because next I say, "There are several issues facing our country that the Crown and Parliament must work together to resolve. But I believe it's very clear to all of us here which issue must take precedence before any other can be addressed."

They all nod and I nod and we're all nodding along . . .

Until we give voice to what each of us believes is the top priority.

Alfie, Thomas and I say, "Jobs."

The rest of the tossers blurt out, "Marriage."

That's when the nodding comes to an end.

And the chaos descends.

"Pardon?"

"What?"

"Who?"

"How, now?"

"Eh?" Lord Radcliffe cups his ear. "Did she say *jobs*? *Jobs* doesn't sound like *marriage*."

"Whose marriage?" I ask.

"Your marriage," the Duke of Sheffield responds.

"I'm not getting married," I choke out.

This gets Tweedledee in a tizzy. The first of many.

"But, but . . . of course you are!"

"You must!" Tweedledum concurs.

"The people are looking forward to a grand wedding," my uncle says. "It's all they're talking about in the pubs and cafés and knitting circles—what handsome prince is going to ride off into the sunset with our lovely new Queen."

"I have no desire to get married," I try.

My uncle fancies himself a comedian. "I don't blame you. I've been married twice and I'm still not keen on it. But you really must."

"It's imperative!" Old Man Radcliffe shakes his fist and shouts so he can hear himself.

"Why is it imperative?" Thomas asks.

Tweedledee's tizzy worsens.

"Wh . . . wh . . . why? We've never had a queen, let alone an *unmarried* queen! What about tradition and propriety?"

Tweedledum makes the sign of the cross.

"Parliament must have assurances," Sheffield explains. "With all due respect, Your Majesty, they are concerned that you are a woman. They worry your ideas may be somewhat radical or . . . hysterical. They believe a husband would curb you of such tendencies."

"Curb me!" I gasp. "If marriage was such a priority, why didn't my father arrange it years ago?"

Norfolk speaks for the first time.

"Because he wanted you to have a say in the final decision."

I look to Alfie to confirm that statement, and with a nod, he does.

"Well, my say is, 'No.' Now, then—"

"But who will be your escort on state visits?" Tweedledee exclaims.

"Or when visitors come here to the palace!" Tweedledum adds. "The American president is set to visit next spring. You can't stay in the palace with him. Alone!"

Thomas rolls his eyes all the way up to heaven.

"Yes, they'll be right on top of each other in the fucking palace. And that Eisenhower looks like a wily one, all right."

"Precisely!" Tweedledum has no concept of sarcasm.

"You are only nineteen, Your Majesty," Sheffield explains calmly. "And you look even younger. You must mature your profile on the international stage if you hope to be taken seriously."

"Elizabeth the Second of England was only a few years older than I am when—"

"Elizabeth was a married woman with two children when she became queen," Uncle Warwitch interrupts. "To the world you are a young girl—a virgin princess."

Norfolk leans forward. "You are a virgin, aren't you?"

Oh for the love of Christ.

"I don't see how that's—"

"And she's pretty!" Radcliffe shakes his head like it's a catastrophe. And all my fault. "Terribly pretty!"

Norfolk narrows his eyes. "Yes, pity, that."

"If you were ugly or more masculine in countenance, then maybe . . ." Tweedledum says.

"But no, you must be married," my uncle agrees.

"It's the only solution," someone—I don't know which one—says.

"As soon as possible."

"Absolutely."

"No other option."

"Married."

"Married.

"Married!"

The word echoes in my mind like a death knell. And all my amazing plans waft away in a puff of smoke. Before I can stop myself, I'm standing up and crying out.

"But . . . but I have charts!"

And the room goes silent.

I was ready for the Council to disagree with me on some points, to have to fight for Alfie and Thomas's seats. I was prepared for them to be stodgy, stubborn—they're old men and I've been dealing with their old-men attitudes my entire life. But I wasn't expecting this. The utter disregard. The dismissal.

That they would reduce me to nothing more than pretty mortar, to be used to shore up the bricks of alliances. Only this time it's the alliance with our own Parliament.

The disappointment is fucking crushing.

Alfie looks at me with pity, and I can tell Thomas is raring to cut them all down on my behalf. And somehow that makes it even more humiliating.

"Excuse me, I . . . need a moment."

I walk out the door and down the hall to the washroom. I rinse my hands with ice-cold water and press a wet cloth to my face. And then I stare at my own eyes in the mirror.

And I will myself to become steel. Coated inside and out. Even if just for a little while. Cold, hard, undentable—nothing can hurt steel; you can pound your fist against it a thousand times and all you'll have to show is a wounded hand.

There's a knock on the door. When I open it, Thomas is in the hall. He adjusts his glasses worriedly. "Are you all right?"

My knees tremble beneath my skirt, but it's not from upset.

"They think I'm weak. All of them."

He nods somberly. "Yes."

"They think I'm just a girl."

Thomas looks ashamed of the entire male species.

"They do."

I look up into his eyes.

"Then it's time to show them that they are very, very wrong," I say.

He stares at me, and slowly a gleam rises in his eyes and a smile slides onto his face.

"All right. Let's do that."

He gestures for me to lead the way and follows behind me as I walk back through the door.

They all stand when I enter. But now I know it's just for show. The pageantry of respect.

"Please, my Lords . . . sit."

Once they're seated, I walk around the room with my hands folded behind my back. Slowly, like a shark that doesn't want to worry its prey.

Or that American Al Capone chap—with his baseball bat.

"I have taken your advisement under consideration. I believe we should speak plainly in this room—all of us. There is much to be done and I have no patience for polite words for protocol's sake."

Everyone agrees—there's more nodding of heads and tapping of canes and the rapping of knuckles on the table.

"In the spirit of frankness, I need you to understand . . . times are changing. Those who refuse to roll with change get run over by it. Buried beneath the weight of their own outdated views."

I pause at one end of the table, turning toward them.

"I may be a new queen, a young queen, even a *pretty* queen—but the fact remains, I am *the* queen. *Your* queen. I'm all you've got, gents. I'm all Parliament's got. There is no prince coming to *curb* me. The next man on this council who brings up the topic of my marriage to anyone . . . will no long *be* on this council. Is that perfectly clear?"

No one has ever been kicked off the Advising Council—but there's nothing in the law that prevents it. It would be an embarrassment, a public shaming, career ending . . . and absolutely, perfectly legal.

They look at me—some in surprise, maybe shock or fear, others with barely concealed anger and resentment simmering on their faces.

And I look right back at them. Daring them to contradict me. Feeling the power of my name, my position, the history of my nation and the generations of kings that came before me, who sat and ruled and made decisions in this very room.

I will not be cowed by small men with oversized opinions of themselves. I will not be cowed by anyone.

When the final member of the Council, my Uncle Warwitch, lowers his eyes, I move back to the head of the table.

"Good."

I sit down gracefully and fold my hands.

"Then let's begin."

And I thought it was done. I thought that settled it.

It turns out I was also very, very wrong.

CHAPTER
6

Lenora

FOR THE NEXT TWO MONTHS, the gears of government in Wessco grind to a halt.

"Parliament will not bring this legislation to the floor. They refuse to consider it."

"But they must."

"No, they don't. And they won't."

Worse than a halt. If we were a racehorse, we wouldn't just not be out of the gate, we'd be trotting arse-backwards around the track.

"Do you have any idea what you're asking, Your Majesty?"

And it's all my fault.

"Mandatory military service will be a drastic change to our system. Change requires time and will . . ."

For having ideas that will actually bloody work.

"It's a jobs program! An education program. The people will have money in their pockets and come out of the service with skills for employment in the private sector. The national defense will be strengthened and tax revenue will go up. This is not difficult to understand."

"It's a never-ending draft. You are asking the people to send their sons to war for you, without any choice in the matter. Yet you have no son or brother . . . or husband to sacrifice."

"I wanted to include the women too," I shoot back. "To give the ladies of Wessco more occupational opportunities."

Tweedledee makes the sign of the cross again.

I believe he thinks I'm a demon. Sent from hell to distress him. I won't be surprised if one day he pours holy water in my tea, just to see if I'll melt.

"You didn't even carve out an exemption for your noblemen. No wonder the House of Lords refuses to consider it."

I rub at the throbbing between my eyes.

"We rise together or we don't rise at'all. I will not put the burden of defense on the lower class alone. That is how revolutions are seeded."

I tap the table with my fingernails, all frustration and nervous energy.

"Get Bumblewood on the phone—I want to speak with him. No—I want a meeting, face to face."

"You can meet with him all you like—it won't do any good. Only one thing will change Parliament's mind." Sheffield raises a meaningful eyebrow. "And that is the act that dare not speak its name in the Council Room."

And then two weeks later, as it always seems to work, things go from bad . . .

"Princess Miriam has eloped."

. . . to fucking disastrous.

"With a footman."

I'm going to kill her.

Not literally—but I'd be lying if I said I didn't have a whole new understanding of my ancestor's penchant for fratricide.

That damned footman—the one from Father's death-bed room. I should have sicced Winston on him.

Since my coronation . . . no, since Father's death, actually, I haven't seen much of Miriam. I should've kept a closer eye on her, made her more of a priority. But she has her own duties and I've been so very busy.

I fold my hands, resting my lips against them.

"Where are they?"

"Italy."

"Have them brought back immediately. I can declare the marriage invalid. She's seventeen and did not have my permission."

"The people are overjoyed for Miriam." Alfie gestures to the newspapers on the table and the celebratory headlines across every front page. "They think it's all very romantic."

"Invalidating the marriage will not be a good look for you politically," Thomas advises.

"Why not?"

He opens his mouth to reply . . . and hesitates.

Norfolk jumps in to fill the silence.

"You're gaining a reputation as cold . . . bitter. An ice queen, Your Majesty."

"I'm not bitter!" I argue. "I'm bloody delightful, considering all I have to deal with around here."

Norfolk continues. "If you dissolve the Princess's marriage, you'll become a destroyer of true love as well."

Wonderful.

"There is another, more grave matter we must discuss," Christopher Alcott, the Duke of Sheffield, says.

"Of course there is." I sigh. "What is it?"

"According to my sources, there are murmurings in Parliament and other dark corners of the government about replacing you on the throne, Queen Lenora."

"Replacing me with whom?" I bite out.

"Your sister."

And I laugh. Out loud.

"Miriam? On the throne? Miriam is . . ."

"Malleable," Norfolk supplies, his face grim and hard like a rock. "She would be easy to control. Those are not characteristics you are known for, Queen Lenora."

"The fact that she is married will strengthen the case for her," Uncle Warwitch adds.

"The fact that she is married to a commoner disqualifies her from the line of succession," I counter.

"Actually," Sheffield lifts his finger, "that's not accurate. The laws regarding the requirements of virginity and royal lineage or a natural-born citizenship refer only to the future *wife* of the king. There is no such language in the law regarding the *husband* of the queen."

This cinches it. The men who wrote those requirements were the absolute *worst*.

Norfolk picks up the thread. "Theoretically, a case could be made that Princess Miriam is perfectly within her rights to sit on the throne with a footman for a husband."

I rub my temples. "You have got to be joking."

Norfolk stares me dead in the face.

"I never joke, Your Majesty. About anything."

Frustration pounds through my veins like lava. I stand up and pace, wanting to explode. "This is treason."

"Yes, Your Majesty." Old Radcliffe nods.

I thought things like this only happened in books.

Or . . . England.

Even Tweedledee and Tweedledum look grim.

"Is my life in danger?" I ask.

"You are a monarch," Radcliffe answers in his shaky, ancient voice. "Your life is always in danger. At the moment, your position is solid but not secure."

"If Princess Miriam has a child before you are married, it could lead to a full-blown constitutional crisis," Norfolk says.

And that just caps it all off.

I turn on them, smacking my hand on the table. "This is absurd! There must be something we can do to quash this immediately."

"There is something." My uncle stands, looking as agitated as I feel. "But you've forbidden us from discussing it."

"Not that! You don't get to use this situation to back me into the corner you wanted me in all along. I will not be a pawn in these ridiculous games men play."

I stamp my foot—like a child refusing her bedtime.

"I am the Queen of Wessco!"

A lion doesn't need to tell anyone it's a lion . . . so if it does, you can bet it's really in trouble.

"Then act like it!" my uncle shouts.

For a moment we stare each other down, eyes sparking like the clash of swords.

"What did you say to me?"

He shakes his head and adjusts his tone. "You are my Queen, you are my brother's daughter . . . but this is not how he raised you."

"I do not want—"

"Your *wants* are immaterial! The only thing that matters is your *duty*—your responsibility to Crown and country."

The room is silent, frozen with icy tension . . . and the cold truth of his words.

"Your people want a wedding. Parliament demands a marriage. You are not the first monarch who has been nudged down the aisle and I swear you will not be the last. If getting the government functioning again means you must be the royal sacrificial lamb, then *that is what it means*. You don't wear the crown to do what you *want*— you wear it to do what must be done. Because you are the only one who can."

He's right. Totally and completely. God damn him straight to hell. I have nothing to say, no clever retort that would make it any less true. I've avoided doing what needs to be done for as long as I could.

And there is no avoiding it anymore.

"Fine! Bloody fucking fine!"

In a huff of swinging skirts, I turn and walk down to my chair at the head of the table. There, I take a deep, long breath and sit.

As they all just stare at me. Like idiots. Like I'm speaking another language.

"Well?" my voice whips. "I said *fine*. If marriage is the ransom, then I'll pay up." I straighten my back and fold my hands. "So, who've you got for me? Let's hear it."

It turns out my father had anticipated this day after all. He made a list of potential suitable husbands. *An actual list.* Who would ever do such a thing?

"Figglescunt. The Viscount of Redmere."

I stare at Sheffield with dead eyes.

"I'm not marrying anyone named Figglescunt."

"He's well respected. Reputed to be highly intelligent."

"Then he should've been smart enough to change his name. Next."

Tweedledee brings up the royals of Greece. But I strike them from the list with a wave of my hand.

"If one of the goals of this exercise is to raise my status on the national stage, then the future Prince of Wessco and Royal Consort to the Queen must be a man *of* Wessco. We must be . . . what's the term?" I snap my fingers. "A power couple. Next."

And so it goes. For three days. Names are batted around like a tennis balls over a net and then ultimately . . .

discarded.

"Lord Lancaster."

Too stupid.

"The Duke of Portchester."

Too ugly.

"Rupert Haddock, The Duke of Cavanaugh."

Too stuffy.

"Sir Dunspotty."

Too low in rank.

"Baron Ivan Von Titebottum."

Alfie frowns. "I've heard stories about the man. He's violent. A sadist."

"Would that be an issue for you, Your Majesty?" Tweedledum asks.

"Yes," I reply, my tone dry as tinder ready to light. "Actually, it would."

"Seymour Gilfoy, the Duke of Barburry."

"He's old enough to be her father," Thomas objects, then flips through the papers in front of him. "Possibly her grandfather."

"As long as he's still able to give her children. That's all that matters," my uncle explains.

And it's the damnedest thing.

It doesn't feel like we're discussing me. My future. My husband. The father of my children. It's as if my heart has been encased in thick, impenetrable ice. I feel no disgust or resentment or fear.

I feel nothing at all.

Marriage is just mechanics now. Calculated choices and transactional obligations.

"No." I shake my head. "The people want a fairy tale

—that is what we must give them."

Sheffield agrees. "We need a young lord with an old name."

"Good luck with that." Thomas snorts. "The aristocrats in Wessco live forever. Like they all made deals with the devil."

Alfie stares at Thomas for a beat longer than normal.

"*You* are a young lord with an old name."

"Yes." I chuckle. "Pity I can't marry Thomas."

And the whole room goes still.

And quiet.

Someone whispers, "Of course."

And another. "Why didn't we think of it before?"

Bertram Tweedle holds up his hands, framing Thomas and me with his fingers. "I can already see them on the tea napkins."

And the ice around my heart cracks. Blood rushes through my ears and I can feel my pulse convulsing in my neck. I don't look at Thomas—I don't look at any of them.

"Well . . ." I stand quickly. My words are chipper and rambling, because denial isn't just a river in Egypt. Denial is now my best friend.

"I believe that's enough for today. We'll resume tomorrow. Meeting adjourned, my Lords."

And I almost trip over my own feet, running from the room.

An hour later, he finds me in the south garden, on the white marble bench near the cherub fountain that I always thought was bit evil looking.

Thomas sits down beside me, resting his elbows on his knees.

"The cherry blossoms are my favorite," I say quietly. "They're never here long, though. Only a few days until the petals start to fall. I try to enjoy them as much as I can while I can."

I know he's looking at me, but I don't turn his way.

"There have been several times in the last few months when I've had to separate myself as your advisor and your friend. The two opinions haven't always agreed."

"And who are you now?"

"Both."

Thomas turns his gaze toward the cherry blossoms too. And he sighs.

"I think we should get married, Lenora."

I nod slowly. Because it's a bang-up idea. Makes perfect sense.

Except not at all.

"I need to have a child, Thomas. Preferably more than one. We'll have to . . . sleep together, and I don't mean sharing a bunk."

He snorts. "That's occurred to me, yes."

"And you don't find it repulsive?"

He squints. "Remind me, why am I your friend again?"

We both laugh. But Thomas's chuckle descends into a succession of coughs. When he catches his breath, he's still smiling.

"You know what I mean," I tell him.

"Yes. I see massive amounts of awkwardness in our future."

And then his voice drops lower—a gentle whisper of sincerity.

"But . . . I would work very hard every day to make you happy. It would matter to me, Lenora. I worry that it won't matter at all to any of the others."

The beauty of that statement slashes through me, making my throat tighten. Because my whole life I've been surrounded by people concerned with my decisions, my plans, my train of thought, my opinion *of them*.

But my true feelings? They don't really occur to them.

I rest my hand on Thomas's forearm. Because his feelings matter to me too.

"What about Michael?"

His chin dips and he shakes his head. "I have no illusions about the world we live in. His father is already on him to get married. Michael will understand."

His hand covers mine on his arm, squeezing.

"My mother is gone; Edward is out there somewhere. You're already my family. This would just make it official."

And it's all there in those gentle green eyes. Warmth, laughter, comfort, trust . . . yes . . . Thomas is already my family too.

"So." He takes a breath. "What do you say? Wanna tie the knot?"

Slowly, my lips slide into a smile.

"Oh, what the hell . . . I guess so."

His grin is so bright, it lights up his eyes. Thomas holds out his palm—and I smack it a high-five.

Definitely, "nerds."

We laugh at ourselves until Thomas starts coughing again. A string of choking coughs like machine gun fire that leave him gasping. He takes his inhaler out of his pocket, puffing on it twice.

I check his forehead, but his skin is cool, clammy, not feverish. "You need to see the doctor. That cough is terrible."

"I *have* seen the doctor," he wheezes. "Nothing he's given me has helped. I feel like utter shit."

"Well, see him again. We'll tell the Council, but we'll hold off on any public announcement until you're feeling better."

CHAPTER 7

Lenora

WHEN I WAS A GIRL, I didn't read fairy tales. I know the stories, everyone knows the stories, but the actual reading—I could never finish them. They were too cruel, too sad; no matter how happy the ending might be, it wouldn't undo the pain the hero and heroine had to go through to reach it. It wouldn't balance it out.

I've always been a practical person, a realist—even when I was a child. I see things as they are, not as I want them to be. Which is why I should have known. I should've seen it—it was there in front of me the whole time.

But I didn't. I didn't have an inkling.

And that made it so much worse.

Thomas doesn't get better.

Not the day after our conversation in the garden, or the day after that. In a week, he's too ill to attend council meetings. In two, he's admitted to the hospital for treatment and tests.

But I don't worry, not really. I go through my busy business days, sure that he'll be well again soon. That he'll be better than fine.

Because he's Thomas.

It's as simple as that.

After a month, when he tells me he's going home to Anthorp Castle, to properly rest—because it must be the old-man aura wafting over from Parliament that's making him ill—I laugh and agree with him. When he promises to knock this sickness on its arse and come back as soon as he can, I believe him.

Because I'm a double-damned idiot.

My idiocy continues right up until the head physician of Royal Hastings Hospital comes to my office to brief me on the results of Thomas's tests. There is no right to medical privacy here—and as the sovereign, it's my prerogative to know the health of the men who serve in my government. Normally, this information would be conveyed to a secretary, a staff member—but again, this is Thomas.

So the esteemed Dr. Nevil sits across my shiny, new desk and explains the situation.

"Large-cell undifferentiated carcinoma. There is a mass in each of his lungs. Inoperable."

And still, it doesn't sink in.

"I see." I nod, folding my hands on the desk. "And what is the treatment?"

Silly, stupid, foolish, fucking girl.

Dr. Nevil snaps his eyes to mine.

"There is no treatment, Your Majesty."

"I don't . . . I don't understand. How will the Duke recover without treatment?"

The doctor's face blanches with sympathy. And something else—an emotion that's not often aimed in my direction, but I recognize it straight away.

Pity.

My stomach roils, and I think I may vomit on the spot. Because finally, I understand that something is terribly wrong.

"The Duke of Anthorp's condition is terminal."

Terminal.

The word ricochets around my skull, before embedding in my brain like shrapnel.

"He's twenty years old. Twenty-year-old titled, upper-class boys do not get *terminal* conditions."

Dr. Nevil's voice is gentle, but certain.

"Sometimes they do."

I breathe slowly through my nose, in and out. Contemplating this information. Processing and planning. Strategizing how to control this, fix it. How to bend the situation to my will.

Because I am the Queen now and that's what queens do.

"You are dismissed as the Duke's physician. Another doctor will be appointed to take charge of his care. You can go."

This seems to shock him. "May I ask why?"

I stand. "One does not charge into battle waving the

white flag and expect to win, Doctor. Good day."

He stands and bows, then leaves the room.

And I pace behind my desk, twisting my fingers to-gether, brimming with unspent energy and urgency. I buzz for Cora on the intercom and she enters the room while the sound still lingers in the air.

"Yes, Queen Lenora?"

"I need specialists—oncologists—the best in the world. Make a list. We have to keep it out of the press, but I need them here straight away."

"Yes, ma'am." She writes it down.

"Clear my schedule as much as you can, cancel any upcoming engagements and have my bags packed. I'll be conducting all government business from Anthorp Castle and I wish to leave as soon as possible."

She doesn't ask why; she only nods. "How long do you expect to stay at the castle?"

I glance out the window. There's a doomsday sky above us, with gathering clouds the color of ash and not a glimpse of sunlight to be found.

"As long as it takes."

Late that night, when I arrive, I find Thomas in the library, in light blue pajamas and a black robe, staring into the mouth of the stone fireplace from a leather chair that seems too large for him. He glances at me in the doorway, then his eyes return to the golden glow of the flames.

"Have you spoken with Dr. Nevil?"

"I have."

He bobs his head in a nod, bringing a glass of amber liquid to his lips.

"Promise me you'll look after Michael. This is going to be hard on him."

"Thomas—"

"And for fuck's sake don't bury me beside my father. I don't care where you plant me, as long as it's not there."

I rush forward, still in my coat, and kneel down beside his chair. I don't think about the impropriety of it—that I'm not supposed to kneel to anyone. Because he's my sweetest, dearest, truest friend, so I'll kneel for him.

"I'm going to save you."

It's not a promise—it's a solemn vow. I swear it because I believe it.

The fire casts dancing shadows on Thomas's glasses.

"Lenora . . ."

"I couldn't save Mother, I couldn't do anything for Father . . . but I can save you. I'll use every resource I have. I won't let you die, Thomas." I hold his hand in both of mine. "I'll fight this with everything I am. Please fight it with me. Please."

He gazes down at me for several still moments, and I can feel his affection and caring and love. They wrap around me like a soft, safe blanket, warming me inside and out. Then the corners of his mouth inch up, and for the first time since I walked in the room, he looks like the Thomas I know.

"I'd fight next to you any day of the week and twice on Sunday. You're small but you're plucky. And that pissed-off, determined look that you get on your face," he points at me, "that's the one, there—absolutely terrifying."

I laugh softly, even as my eyes go wet. I kiss the back of Thomas's hand and he presses his palm to my cheek.

And then he's making vows too.

"We'll sort it out, Lenora. And whatever happens, I promise it's all going to be all right."

For a time, things don't get significantly better or worse; it's just steady as we go. Doctors come to see Thomas and appointments are scheduled. I have breakfast with him every morning, pushing him to keep up his strength and eat his porridge. Sometimes I plead sweetly for him to take just one more bite, and if that doesn't work I tell him I'll have Winston hold him while I shove it down his bloody throat.

That's what friends are for.

The rest of the days are filled with calls and briefings, reports and legislation, and meetings here at the castle because the business of government stops for no man . . . or queen.

Late one afternoon, I'm on a call with Prime Minister Bumblewood, who has the temerity to ask about the rumored upcoming betrothal announcement. *Inquiring minds want to know,* he teases in a tone I'm sure he believes is charming.

Wankmaggot.

I end the call and push back from the desk, rubbing my eyes and stretching out the knot in my neck. I walk through the grand hall to the stairs and up to Thomas's room, where I intercept Michael in the outer sitting room.

"How is he?" I ask.

"Sleeping." Michael forces a tight smile, cracking open the door behind him. Thomas lies on his back, pale and still, in the center of the big canopy bed. His breathing is labored, in spite of the oxygen tubes in his nose, and despite my best efforts to get him to eat, he's lost weight—his lively face now gaunt, with cheekbones too prominent.

"Good. He needs his rest." I swallow past the lump in my throat. "I think I'll go for a ride—get some air."

Michael nods kindly. "That's a fine idea."

After changing into my riding clothes—snug black jodhpurs, a white shirt, a black riding jacket and high leather boots—I walk out the back toward the stables. The air is cold enough to see my breath and my lungs expand with icy invigoration every time I breathe it in.

Winston, as always, is just a few steps behind me.

"I want to ride alone," I tell him.

I can feel his frown boring into the back of my head.

"That's not—"

I stop on the path and spin around.

"Is the perimeter secured?"

"Of course."

"Then I'll be fine. I'll stay on the property. Don't worry so much, Winston—it'll give you wrinkles and I'll have to fire you because you'll be too ugly to look at."

He doesn't smile exactly, but his scowl softens—like he's smiling on the inside.

"I'll try my best, Queen Lenora. I do aim to please."

At the stables, the groom brings me a gigantic, angry

brown beast of a horse named Hector. I like him immediately. As I swing up into the saddle, he dances with frantic
energy that needs to be burned off. I know exactly how he
feels.

In the grassy field beyond the castle, I open him up—
letting him gallop toward the forest as hard and fast as
those brawny legs will go. My cheeks and the tip of my
nose go numb with cold and I tuck my chin and enjoy the
speed, the blur. The crashing sound of the ocean mixes
with the whistle of the wind and it feels like I'm flying . . .
like I'm a bird that can go anywhere.

Someplace where there are no duties or schedules or
terminal conditions. There is only the sun on my face and
wind in my hair.

An hour and miles later, Hector is calmer. I duck my
head under a branch as we trot through the canopy of trees,
until we come to another clearing. When I glance up at the
sky, I see a storm coming in—a great swelling wall of in-
digo clouds that have already enveloped the sun.

Leaning forward, I stroke Hector's velvet neck.
"What do you say, my boy? Think we can get in one more
run before the rain catches us?"

He snorts, pulling at the reins.

"I think so too."

I tap his hindquarters, and we're off again. I close my
eyes, to better soak up the sensations, and squeeze Hector's rippling flanks with my thighs and knees.

And then I let go of the reins and hold my arms out,
palms forward. Trying to catch the wind in my hands.

It's the stupidest bloody thing I've ever done—but it
feels amazing.

It feels like freedom.

For about three seconds.

That's when Hector lets out a sharp, indignant shriek. He rears up on his back legs and before I can grab the reins, I'm flying—falling—like Alice down her endless rabbit hole. Before landing on my arse in the cold, hard dirt.

"Ooof!"

The vibration of Hector's thundering hooves on the ground beneath me gets fainter and fainter. *Traitor.*

I don't move at first. I lie on my back breathing, making sure all four limbs are still attached. Then I open my eyes and blink up at the darkening sky. Until something obscures my view.

Some*one.*

It's a man—standing over me, gazing down at me.

His hair is wavy and blond and slightly too long. It falls forward over his forehead, giving him a reckless, rebellious look—like an archangel who came down to earth against orders.

I sit up slowly, my head spinning a bit. He drops his bag on the ground and crouches down, assessing me. His eyes are an unusual green—a very dark shade of emerald —and his jaw is strong, taut, and scattered with more than a day's worth of rugged, golden stubble. Tingling goose bumps that have nothing to do with the icy air race up my arms.

When he speaks, his voice is deep but refined, like rough silk.

"Are you injured?"

I've been educated by the finest minds in the world.

I speak seven languages fluently.

And yet the only response I can muster is, "Huh?"

Brilliant.

His brows draw together and his full, wicked mouth quirks—like he can't decide if he should be worried or entertained.

"Did you hit your head?"

And now he thinks I'm concussed—how lovely.

"Uh . . . no, no, I think I'm all right."

He nods, standing up, all tall and broad and muscly beneath a white shirt with the sleeves rolled up and casual trousers. He holds out his hand and when I take it, his swallows mine whole. But when I get to my feet, a hot pain slices up my ankle.

"Oh!"

I take my weight off it, hopping, and the man guides me to sit on a large boulder. Without asking permission, he grasps behind my knee with one hand and slowly slides my boot off with the other. Then he cradles my ankle in his hands, pressing here and there with his thumb, his touch surprisingly gentle.

"Can you wiggle your toes, lass?"

Lass? I look at his face to see if he's being impertinent, but he just gazes back at me, waiting. Because he has no idea who I am. None. To him I'm just a lost babe in the woods—like in one of those fairy tales I never finished reading.

I've never met someone who didn't already know who I was—how utterly bizarre.

I flinch when I wiggle my toes.

"It's not broken, but you've twisted it good." He

glances up and down the field, then he turns those pene-trating green eyes back on me. "Looks like I'll be carrying you."

I am not a blusher. Or a giggler. I don't get flustered.

I fluster everyone else.

Yet the thought of him carrying me with those im-pressive arms makes my insides go all gooey and my cheeks flush like they're on fire.

"That won't be necessary." My voice is breathless, because I can't seem to get enough air. "I'll wait here and you can have them come fetch me with the maintenance buggy."

On cue, a blast of thunder booms overhead—the kind that shakes the ground and sounds like the sky is cracking.

Thanks, God. Thanks a lot.

"No, this storm's going to be a nasty one. I won't leave you out here all alone."

"That's very kind, but I'm perfectly—"

It's a very strange thing to not being listened to. To be overruled. Is this what everyday life is like for everyone else?

I don't like it at'all.

He lifts me effortlessly in his arms, cradling me against his chest. His shirt is clean, soft cotton and smells like earth and fresh grass. I don't know what I'm supposed to do with my hands, so they stay folded in my lap as he walks us into the forest.

"That was a hell of a horse you were riding." His rich voice has a hint of teasing to it. "You may want to stick to something smaller until you get better at it."

"I happen to be an excellent rider."

The fact that he thinks I'm not prickles me more than it should.

"Excellent riders usually know to keep their hands on the reins." He winks.

"I'll try to remember that," I reply dryly.

Another blast of thunder comes and lightning bursts in the sky. He dips his head, leaning in closer.

"Are you staying at Anthorp Castle, then?"

"Yes. The Duke and I are good friends."

There's a glint in his eyes as he nods, as though I've said something amusing.

"And you?" I ask. "You seem to know the property well."

"Aye. It's been some time since I've been back, but I was raised here."

"Oh?" I take in his clothes, his hair, his gruff demeanor. "Were you . . . one of the groundskeeper's children?"

His lips slide into a devilish grin and he's definitely laughing at me now.

"No."

There isn't a chance to elaborate—or to tell him he's being rude. Because the skies open and a torrent of pounding rain begins to drench us both.

CHAPTER 8

Edward

FTER YEARS OF RESEARCH I've come to the uncontestable conclusion that no good news ever comes in a telegram. They are bringers of bad. Harbingers of depressing. The equivalent of a call at two in the morning—whoever's ringing on the other end, you can bet your balls they're not going to have anything happy to say.

When my mother died, it was a telegram that told me and Thomas. When the six-member team of a river expedition I was set to join was unexpectedly wiped out by a mudslide, the telegram struck again. When my father died, a telegram informed me—though that wasn't exactly *bad* news, but . . . that's a story for another day.

The story for today is, I've come back home.

And Christ, it hasn't changed a bit.

Every tree, each stone is exactly like I remember it. The churning ocean is the same shade of blue-green and the waves crashing against the rocks beat in the exact same rhythm.

Like it's been sitting, waiting for me to return all this time.

When I was young, it chafed at me. The sameness. The monotony. It seemed so pointless. The rigid expectations and traditions of an heir to an old dukedom wrapped themselves around me like an iron chain—weighing me down, making it impossible to breathe.

But that was then.

Today, standing back on Wessco's shores, it doesn't feel like that anymore. It feels like . . . coming home. The land may not have changed, but I have. A decade away will do that to you. There's a comfort in the steadfastness of the landscape now—in knowing every path and trail the same way I know the look of my own hands. There's a wistful nostalgia in the air that I couldn't appreciate when I was wild and young and hungry for recklessness.

Speaking of recklessness . . .

It's not every day you find a beautiful girl in the woods, riding free, arms stretched out, head tilted up to the sky like a submissive angel awaiting her master's command.

It would only have been better if she were naked.

I think it's a good omen—a welcome-home present from God.

I didn't get her name before the torrential downpour began . . . but I plan to. I can tell from her demeanor that she's a lady—some Parliament member's daughter perhaps, or maybe a cousin of Thomas's friend, Michael Fitzgibbons.

Even with water pouring down her face and her hair stuck like a drowned rat on her head, she's lovely. With full, pouty, petal-pink lips that inspire all sorts of dirty thoughts and skin that smells like lilacs and rainwater. She's almost nothing to carry—but pressed against me, she's soft and full in all the right places.

The castle comes into view through the rain. The girl gives a little shiver from the cold and I hold her tighter and walk a bit faster. A few minutes later, my wet steps echo across the stone floor and gently, I place my pretty bundle in the foyer chair. I tug down a God-awful tapestry that's hung ugly on the wall for a hundred years, wrapping it around her shoulders and rubbing heat into her arms. Then I stand up and push my dripping hair back off my face.

And the fun really starts.

When a maid I don't know comes in from the great room, looks at the woman in the chair and gasps, "Oh, Your Majesty, are you all right?"

At the exact same time as Horatio, the butler, comes in from the other side and says, "Welcome home, Master Edward."

And I stare down at her and she stares at me.

"Edward?"

"Your Majesty?"

"*You're* Thomas's brother?"

"*You're* the Queen?"

When Thomas first wrote me about his little friend, Princess Lenora—or Lenny as I'd christened her, because Lenora is an old woman's name—it was stories of a laughing, lively girl who was game to tag along on his misadventures. And that's the image that's been frozen in my mind—a young girl with a taste for the wild.

But this creature—with enticing gray eyes, a pert nose and a lush, plump mouth, wearing saturated riding clothes that cling to every gorgeous curve like a second skin—she's no girl.

"Why didn't you tell me who you were?" she demands, her eyes glinting like two sharp blades.

"Why didn't you tell me who *you* were?" I demand right back.

She scoffs at the question as if it's the most ridiculous thing she's ever heard.

"The Queen does not *tell* people she's the Queen."

"Why not?"

"Because they're just supposed to know."

"How?"

She throws up her arms. "They just do!"

Fuck, but she's an entertaining little thing. So much indignation and fire in such a tight, shapely package. It makes me want to grin—if only to infuriate her more.

"That's ridiculous."

"*You're* ridiculous." She pushes herself up from the chair, standing. "And rude."

"*I'm* rude?" I hook my thumb over my shoulder. "I left my bag in the bloody woods for you. I carried you five miles through a monsoon. Does the Queen also not say 'thank you' when a man helps her?"

She crosses her arms and lifts her nose, somehow making it feel like she's looking down at me even though I'm a foot taller.

"No, she doesn't. It's an honor to serve me, so . . . you're welcome."

Well, would you look at that—the Queen's got balls. Good for her. It's more than I can say for most of the aristocrats I know.

"Brilliant, you're getting along already."

The voice comes from behind me—a voice I know as well as my own. I turn around . . . and all thoughts of sparring with the haughty Queen rush from my head.

Because when Thomas's telegram first reached me, I told myself it was a prank. A bit of fun. Just the kind of thing he would do—use dark humor to lure me home. But now, as I look at him, I know every word of it was true.

And it's like the floor falls away beneath my feet.

Because my baby brother is here in front of me, but at the same time . . . it's not him. Not the him I remember, not the him he's supposed to be. He looks like an old man—a pale, young old man—in a wheelchair, with a blanket over his lap, being pushed by Michael.

Only his eyes are the same, behind the lenses of the thick, dark frames that he's worn since he was six. They dance with green mischief. With life.

"Hello, Edward."

It's been three years since I've seen him, when he and Michael joined me on holiday sailing near Jamaica. Three years too long. Too late.

"Thomas." I go down to my knees and hug him—embracing him tightly—wanting so much to pass him my strength, my health. To make this better, now that I'm here, now that I'm home.

He smacks my back and looks me in the eyes as I straighten up. Then he turns his attention over my shoulder.

"What happened, Lenora?"

There's a staff member at each arm as she takes tender steps up the stairs.

"Just a little mishap with the horse. I'll be fine." She says, all dignity and controlled composure. "You two get reacquainted. Don't wait for me for supper—I'll dine in my room tonight."

"Stay off your feet," I say, the words naturally coming out like an order. "And get some ice on that ankle."

She nods stiffly. Her eyes dart to me quickly, then away—like she's trying not to look, but just can't help herself.

I watch her go until she turns the corner at the top of the stairs and Thomas touches my arm. "Lenora has commandeered the library, so let's go to the study. We have a lot to talk about."

Horatio brings me towels and a change of clothes. In the study, Michael pours us three brandies, then takes the seat beside my brother's wheelchair, close to the fire.

Thomas raises his glass. "It's good to have you home, Edward."

"It's good to be home, little brother."

"Liar. You hate this place with the heat of a thousand suns."

I shrug. "Maybe only a few suns now. I've mellowed in my old age."

My brother takes a sip of his drink. "Did you find what you were looking for? Your purpose?"

He's talking about a conversation we'd had when he and Michael had visited.

I left Wessco in search of adventure and excitement—

ROYALLY YOURS | **97**

and to stick it to my old bastard of a father. But that's not why I stayed away. I stayed away because I wanted more out of life than a title and vaults full of money I didn't earn. I wanted a purpose. A reason for being. I was searching for it.

I still am.

"No," I tell him.

"I didn't think so," my brother says. Then he glances at Michael and some secret communication passes between them.

I look him over again—his frail frame and sunken cheeks. And my voice turns as gutted as I feel.

"Why didn't you write me sooner?"

He lifts his shoulder, taking a mouthful of brandy.

"It's not really something you put in a telegram. 'I'm dying. Stop. Come home. Stop. Hope you make it in time. Cheers.'"

I take the folded telegram from my back pocket.

"But that's exactly what you wrote. Literally that."

He laughs. "Well . . . I guess it took some time for me to work up the courage. To accept it."

"I don't want you to accept it," I growl through clenched teeth.

I want him to live. And I'm ready to do anything, to make that happen.

"I want—"

He reads my thoughts or my expression. Or both.

"Don't start. It's lung cancer, Edward. Aggressive. I've spoken to the doctors, specialists. There's nothing to be done."

"Doctors don't know everything. There are alternative treatments. When I was in India—"

"No." He shakes his head. "I'm not going to spend my final days being dragged around strapped to your back." His tone goes somber. Determined. "I want to go on my own terms, while I'm still myself, while I still have a say. It matters to me."

"For fuck's sake, Thomas. There must be something I can do."

He gazes at me with that mischievous twinkle in his eyes.

"Well, now that you mention it. There is one thing . . ."

The next morning, after I shower and shave, I sit with Thomas in his room. He's dressed, but still in bed. We talked for several hours last night—about many things, but about one thing in particular.

Lenora—the Queen—walks into the room, her expression smooth and composed, wearing gray slacks with a red sweater and a chiffon scarf tied around her neck.

"Good morning." I stand and bow, watching her carefully.

When you travel the world and live amongst cultures different from your own, you become observant. You note body language and facial expressions; you learn how to read people.

"How's your ankle?"

She gives the barest shrug. "It's fine."

I saw her ankle yesterday—it's nowhere near fine. It was already swelling out in the woods. It must be hurting her, but she doesn't limp or grimace even as she walks in black baby-doll pumps.

Little Lenny either has a sky-high pain threshold or self-control made of iron.

She pulls up a chair beside Thomas's bed and reaches for the porridge on the tray. "You need to eat your breakfast."

"There's things we need to talk about, Lenora."

"Thomas—"

He holds up his hand, swearing, "I'll eat the whole bowl after we talk."

She sighs. "All right. What did you want to talk about?"

And my brother, ever diplomatic, just puts it all out there.

"I think you should marry Edward."

She pauses, but her expression doesn't change. She doesn't laugh or gasp or frown. Her tone is cool and reserved.

"Your brother? How biblical."

Her gray eyes slice my way. "You've agreed to this?"

"Yes."

"Why?"

"He's my brother. He asked. I won't deny him, not now."

And it's the truth. But it's not the only truth. Something about her intrigues me—this beautiful, guarded woman, who rides wild in the woods when she thinks no one is looking.

She turns back to Thomas.

"We've discussed this. We've agreed. I'm marrying *you*."

"You will put me in the ground before the month is out."

That gets a flinch out of her.

"Don't talk like that."

"Why not? It's true."

"I said stop it." Lenora gets to her feet. "I won't listen."

Thomas gives in, closing his mouth and nodding his head. But only for a moment.

"No, you know what?" He swipes his teacup with the back of his hand and it explodes against the wall. "To hell with that. If I can do the dying, you can damn well listen to me talk about it."

"Thomas—"

"There are unpleasant truths we have to deal with. That *you* have to deal with—you can't stubborn them away, Lenora." His jaw is clenched and he's as angry as I've ever seen him. "You have to get married—that's a fact. You need to be married before your sister gets pregnant—another fact. When I am gone, you'll be back in the same precarious position you were in two months ago. So who's it going to be, hmm? Who's left to choose from? The sadist, who'll want to smack you around a bit before he fucks you?"

"Stop it—"

"Or the old man, who I don't even want to know what he'll have to do to get it up before he crawls between your legs."

She doesn't back down; she doesn't retreat a single inch.

"Don't be obscene."

My brother's words are harsh and furious. "If any situation on earth called for obscenity, it's this one."

He barely gets the sentence out, when the coughing starts. So hard it wracks through his body and bends his back, hunching him forward. I pour him a glass of water and give him a handkerchief from my pocket. Thomas presses it to his lips and it comes away with blood on it. After a few moments, he settles.

"I thought you'd be pleased with the idea," he rasps. "There was a time when we read Edward's letters that you—"

"Don't." Her cheeks flush pink. Whether it's from embarrassment or anger, I can't tell. "That girl is gone."

I wonder about that girl—where she's run off to and what happened to make her go. I would've liked to have met her; I think we could've gotten on well.

Thomas's expression turns searching and sad. He shakes his head.

"Wouldn't you do it for me?"

"What?"

"If you were leaving forever, and you knew there was something you could do to make it easier on me, wouldn't you do it?"

"Of course," Lenora swears, and the sincerity in her voice rings clear.

"Then for God's sake, consider it. If not for yourself then for me. So I can have the peace of knowing that I'm not completely abandoning you."

Another round of coughing starts up, this one worse than before. And it's so damn hard to watch him struggle. I just want her to fucking agree—agree to anything, as long as he can rest easy.

It's as if she reads my mind.

"All right. All right." Lenora nods, her face pinched. "I'll consider it."

Thomas rests back on the pillows, breathing hard, but short of breath.

"Thank you."

She nods, giving me the barest glance, then looking back to my brother. "I have to . . . I'll be gone for the day. I'll be back later."

Then she's gone, the click of the door echoing in her wake.

My eyebrows lift. "That went well."

"She'll come around. She's stubborn but logical; she'll see the reason in it. She always does."

I watch my brother, trying to see the answer on his face.

"Do you love her, Thomas?"

He doesn't even hesitate. "Yes, but not in the way you're thinking. The first time I saw her, I knew she would get me. That she was just like me."

"Just like you, how?"

"Lonely."

And I hate myself more than I ever thought possible. The guilt is suffocating and irrevocable, and deserved.

"But it's worse for her, Edward. She's the most alone person in the whole world."

"She's the bloody Queen! She's surrounded by people every moment of every day."

"And yet she has no one. No one who cares about her. Not really. No one but me . . . and I hope, soon . . . you."

Lenora

I GO TO ALFIE'S ESTATE in Averdeen. To the back of the house, to that old monster of a tree and the rickety swing. Eventually, when Alfie comes out he finds me there, my forehead resting on the rope. And the words pour out, hushed and awful.

"Thomas is dying, Alfie."

"I know, Chicken. I'm so sorry."

"He wants me to marry Edward."

"Edward who?"

"Edward Rourke."

"No one's seen Edward Rourke for years. He's practically a legend these days—like William Wallace, the rogue adventurer."

"He's at Anthorp Castle right now. Thomas sent him a telegram and—poof—he came home, just like that."

Alfie looks up at the cloudy sky. "Thomas always was a sharp one. Edward has the right name, and when his brother passes, he'll have the title once again. He'll be a suitable match for you."

"I don't know him," I argue harshly.

"You won't know any of them."

My head snaps up. "But I would know *of* them. Their motivations, their goals . . . I would have information. Edward is a blank slate to me. I won't be able to anticipate him."

"You mean you won't be able to control him."

"That too." I nod.

He chuckles then, shaking his head, and his voice goes soft.

"You are your father's daughter."

And suddenly I'm just so tired. From the weight of it all—the choices and changes. It's exhausting.

"What do I do, Alfie? What would Father tell me to do?"

He rubs his chin, considering the question. "He would tell you to make a decision, don't dawdle. He could never abide dawdlers. Your father would want you to look at your options and make the best choice."

"What if there is no best choice?"

"Then choose the least worst." He looks down at me with kind affection. A fatherly look. "If you want my opinion, from what I know of the man he is, you could do worse than Edward. It says a lot about a woman, a queen, the man she chooses to tie herself to."

I stare at the ground and there's a bitterness on my tongue, flavoring my words.

"And what would Edward Rourke say about me?"

"That you are fearless, bold, unpredictable . . . perhaps a bit wicked. In your position, those are not bad things to be, Lenora."

"No . . ."

I cannot disagree.

"Not bad at'all."

It's dark by the time I return to Anthorp Castle. I step soft-ly into Thomas's dimly lit room and walk to the bed where he's sleeping, propped up on pillows. Edward sits beside the bed, following my every move. I don't look at him, but I can feel the intensity of his gaze. The questioning.

I put my hand over Thomas's and slowly he opens his eyes.

"I accept," I tell him.

And it feels like a failure. Like accepting defeat. Because this fight for his life is one we can't win.

Thomas's voice is barely a whisper. "Smart girl. Thank you."

Only then do I turn to Edward and meet his gaze straight on.

"I accept," I tell him too, but it feels very different.

It's like accepting a challenge.

For a moment, his intense green eyes hold me posses-sively as I wait for his response.

It comes in the form of a sharp, deliberate nod.

And quick as that, the course of my life is set.

CHAPTER
9

Lenora

THINGS GO QUICKLY AFTER THAT, as if Thomas was just holding on, to set things straight. A doctor comes and stays at the castle, monitoring his condition, setting up an intravenous drip to treat him for pain. I'm there as much as I can be—putting aside everything but the most urgent, unavoidable business. Michael is there, doing anything he can for him, whispering to him, holding his hand. Most of the time Thomas sleeps. Occasionally, he'll open his eyes and give me a smile when he can manage it.

Give *us* a smile.

Edward is always there as well, always in the room. He takes his meals there; he rests in the chair beside the bed—when he rests at all. He's showered and wears fresh clothes, but otherwise, he doesn't leave Thomas's side.

One evening, Thomas opens his eyes and turns toward his brother. And in a reedy voice, he tells him,

"Don't be sad, Edward. This time I'll be the one traveling. I'll try to write and tell you all about it."

Edward gives him a smile—and it's a beautiful smile. Then he presses his hand against Thomas's cheek, patting him gently.

I don't think about the country, the Advising Council or Parliament. I don't think about the "after" or the promises I've made. And Edward must feel the same. Because we only speak to each other about Thomas.

The rest will be for another time, another life . . . another us.

Early on Saturday morning, the heavy drapes are shut, and Michael has finally given in to his exhaustion and is napping on the sofa in the sitting room. Thomas's eyes are closed, his lips moving soundlessly, his skin pale with a bluish hue, despite the oxygen mask that rests over his face.

The maid moves to turn the light down. And Edward practically bites her head off.

"Leave it!"

She startles, but then recovers, and lifts the tray from the night table before silently leaving the room. And we go back to waiting, watching the slow rise and fall of Thomas's chest.

"He didn't like the dark," Edward says quietly. "When we were young, before I left, he would come into my room at night because he was afraid. He'd always ask me to leave the lights on. And I did."

"He's not afraid of the dark anymore," I tell him, just as quietly.

He turns his eyes to me. "How do you know?"

"There are catacombs below the Palace of Wessco. I've lived there my whole life but never stepped foot in them. Until last year, when he talked me into going exploring. He had a flashlight, but otherwise it was pitch black. And he told me a ghost story—about a man wanting his golden arm—the whole time. Thomas thought it was hilarious . . . I didn't sleep for a week."

A hoarse bark of a chuckle comes from Edward's throat. And I almost laugh with him, even while the memory makes me want to cry.

"Good," he whispers.

And we resume our vigil.

Edward

I DO THE MATH IN my head . . . mostly to keep from losing my mind. I was gone for ten years, eleven if you count the war. I wrote Thomas about a letter a week, sometimes more, sometimes less—an average of four per month. Four, times twelve months a year, times eleven.

Five hundred and twenty-eight letters, tens of thousands of words, countless moments between my baby brother and me.

I don't have any of his letters; they were burned in

campfires all around the globe. When you live on the move, you must travel light, and sentimentality is too heavy to carry. But I don't need them—I already know every word and every curve of every letter he wrote, by heart.

It'd be a mistake to think we weren't close just because we didn't live in the same place. I know brothers who shared the same bloody bed who couldn't stand the sight of each other.

But Thomas was with me all the time. Every new place, new experience, new memory . . . he was there, in my thoughts—I couldn't wait to share them with him. And I know it was the same for him. Thomas confessed his deepest secrets to me in those letters, like he thought it would matter to me. As if there was anything in the world that he could write about himself that would make me think less of him. That would make me not love him fully and completely—the same way he loved in return.

There wasn't and I told him so.

I know how to live in a place where my brother's not. But I don't know how to live in a world where he doesn't.

And as I sit here at the side of his bed and watch his life slowly slip away, it's like a part of my soul is slipping away with it. Leaving it hard and barren. Like the parched, cracked earth without water. Like the arctic without the sun.

I watch him and think of when he was a little lad—all head and glasses and short, skinny limbs.

"Show me, Edward! Show me how to kick the ball like you."

"Can I sleep in here with you? You'll keep the shadows away."

"When you go away to school, Edward, can you take me with you?"

His breathing gets slower and slower, and I know Lenora and Michael see it too.

And I look at his face and he's not wearing his glasses. They're folded on the bedside table because he doesn't need them. Because he'll never need them again.

And it's so fucking wrong.

And there's absolutely *nothing* I can *do*.

Except sit and watch him go, and feel the fury at the injustice of all of it.

Thomas lets out a deep, slow breath—peaceful—longer than any that came before. And I lean forward, waiting, praying for him to inhale just once more. To stay just a little longer.

But it doesn't come.

The only sound in the room is the click of the clock in the corner—it's deafening against the still, perfect silence. The doctor steps forward and checks for a pulse, a heartbeat, with his stethoscope. He lifts each of Thomas's eyelids gently and even before he utters the words, Michael's face collapses into his hands and the silence is overwhelmed with his sobs.

"He's gone," the doctor tells us.

And it's over, just like that. But I don't feel empty or drained. My muscles tighten with a rage I've never known. I want to destroy something. I want to tear this damned castle down, stone by stone, for no other reason than because it's still here and my brother is not.

I pat Michael's back, trying to channel the seething energy into comfort because I know that's what Thomas would've wanted.

The doctor lifts the sheet and covers him. And still—stupidly—I wait for it to billow with his breath. When it doesn't come, when the white cotton lies quiet over his features, a wave of crushing disappointment presses down on me. Slowly I get to my feet and move over to the bed-side table. With reverence, I pick up those thick-framed glasses, and my vision blurs as I hold them in the palms of my hands. I choke back the burn of wetness that's drowning my throat and slip the glasses into my shirt pocket, above my heart—where I swear they will stay every day for the rest of my life.

"There, there . . ." I hear from behind me, in a lovely feminine voice. Nothing should be so lovely on such a terrible day.

"It's better this way," Lenora tells Michael.

I spin around, ready to attack.

"Better for whom?"

She looks up at me with wide, dry eyes and perfectly composed features.

"It's better that he didn't suffer," she says.

And even that rationale infuriates me.

Lenora stands. "I will go to the chapel and pray for his eternal soul." She looks to the maid. "I'm not to be disturbed."

The maid nods.

I have an altogether different reaction.

"Prayers? That's all you've got? My brother's final days on this earth were filled with concern for you. Your welfare, your future—and all you have for him are fucking prayers? Not even one tear? Or does the Queen not grieve either? Not feel *anything* for *anyone* except herself?"

She regards me with as much emotion as stone.

"I don't have to explain myself to you."

"I think your relationship with my brother was lop-sided. I think he cared for you a fuck of a lot more than you ever cared for him."

Her gaze remains infuriatingly steady. As calm and flat as the surface of a breezeless gray lake.

"I don't care what you think."

She turns her back, dismissing me.

"Winston?"

The dark-headed guard who barely takes his eyes off her steps forward.

"I'm here, Your Majesty."

"Stay with the Duke," she says. "He shouldn't . . . I don't want him to be left alone."

The guard dips his head. "I won't leave his side."

With her shoulders back and head high, like she's wearing some invisible crown, the Queen walks from the room.

Later, I don't know how long it's been, Michael and I sit together in the great room. Drinking whiskey. Lots of it. And staring at the enormous wall of ancient, nasty-looking weaponry hanging from it. The wall of death.

We don't speak, not yet. That will come later, when

we're strong enough—or drunk enough—to actually form words. But when I hear the door open, and see men walking through the foyer and up the stairs rolling a gurney, I rise to my feet.

"Who the hell are they?"

"They're from the palace," Michael explains. "Thomas is to be buried there."

"What? Why? And you're all right with that?"

He swipes the back of his hand across his nose. "The Queen says I'm welcome to visit at the palace whenever I like."

Then he shrugs, and pours himself another glass.

"No—no, they can fuck right off. We have a family plot on our land where generations of Rourkes are buried. He belongs here."

I don't know why I care, it's idiotic—Thomas wouldn't give a single shit. Maybe it's because I'm feeling possessive and protective of him. Or maybe I'm just itching for a fight.

I march through the foyer, toward the door. The maid —the one from upstairs; I think she came with Lenora from the palace—intercepts me, as if she's reading my mind.

"The Queen doesn't want to be disturbed, sir."

"Well, we don't always get everything we want in life. If the Queen hasn't learned that by now, I'm happy to instruct her."

I stalk around the maid, out the door and across the courtyard to the family chapel on the northern-most side of the estate near the cliff. There's no security guarding the door, so I don't pause before tearing it open and letting it slide closed behind me. The small rear vestibule is cloaked in darkness, except for the dim, red-tinged light that comes from the glow of the late-afternoon sun through the high stained-glass windows.

Houses of worship each have a distinct scent, depending on the faith and country. Sometimes spice or incense, sometimes clay or earth. Here, I'm enveloped in the scent of my childhood—the perfume of burning candles and the heavy flora of lily of the valley. I close my eyes and breathe it in, and the memories that come with it are not exclusively unpleasant.

My eyes spring open when I hear a muffled sound. I move to the double doors that lead into the chapel and open one slightly. And the sound is louder. Clearer.

It's pain. Heartbreak. Devastation. Raw and inconsolable.

Lenora is prone before the altar, on her knees, her spine curved, her face in her hands, crying so hard she trembles. And the sounds that come from her—sharp, stabbing, wrenching sobs over and over again. I can feel her anguish, even from across the room—her sadness and sorrow and terrible loss.

It's the same for me. Those same feelings rip through my chest and echo in my heart.

I close the door, gently so she won't hear. And I lean my back against it and sink to the floor. Though she'll never know, I stay there with her. And the Queen cries her heart out, for both of us.

CHAPTER
10

Edward

One month later
Palace of Wessco

"NOW TELL US, Your Majesty, what do you and the Duke do in your leisure time?"

I forgot about this part. The fakery and arse-kissery, the etiquette and protocol. I forgot about the boredom. The hours of mundane pageantry and useless tradition.

"We discuss literature, art, politics," the Queen says pleasantly. "We go to the museum and take long horse-back rides on the estates."

This is exactly how I imagine hell. Hot artificial lights and glaring cameras and sniveling wankers who call themselves journalists asking stupid questions.

"And picnics?"

"Of course. I love picnics."

Hell is a thick, itchy suit and a necktie so tight it might strangle me.

"Now, on to the topic viewers really want to know: the wedding dress."

And at this point, I hope it fucking does.

"I'm afraid that's top secret." Lenora smiles like a professional charmer.

She has a dozen different smiles—the tight frustrated smile, the sarcastic I think-you're-a-goddamn-idiot smile, the patient persuasive smile. All of the them are beautiful, but none of them are real.

None of them light up her eyes.

Well . . . except for maybe her pretty, vicious, victorious smile—the kind a cat wears after swallowing a mouse. That's one of my favorites. When it slides onto her lips, I can't help but imagine how pretty that rosebud mouth would look when she gasps.

Or moans my name.

"And will you be taking a honeymoon?" the reporter asks. "Any hints you can give us as to the location?"

"There's too much work to be done to go for long, but we'll be taking a brief honeymoon after the wedding," the Queen replies. "Somewhere tropical."

"Ah, an island holiday," the tool croons. "How romantic."

I reach over and take Lenora's hand, threading our fingers together, even though I know it may irk her. Have to do my part, after all.

"*Romantic* is practically one of our middle names."

She digs her nails into my hand, where the camera can't see, and I have to swallow a laugh. Because this is

the dance we've fallen into, two fencers circling each other
—*lunge, parry, lunge, parry*. Prodding and poking and
feeling each other out.

"And how are you finding palace life, Your Grace?"
the reporter asks. "Politics must be very different from the
mountain climbs and deep-sea dives you're known for."

"Not so different. In each case it's important to watch
your step, and keep a mind out for sharks just waiting to
strike."

He nods. "It seems almost kismet that you were
brought together by the untimely illness of Lord Thomas,
your dear friend and your younger brother."

Immediately, the bite of Lenora's nails disappears.
And I slowly stroke the pad of my thumb back and forth
across her knuckle, the way I'd calm a skittish horse.

"Our falling in love was a comfort to Thomas, knowing we would have each other after he was gone," she
says. "We are grateful that something so wonderful could
come from something so tragic."

On that note, the interview ends. The journalist gives
us his farewells, and we're barely able to take a sip of water before a new one sits down and it begins all over again.

Repeating the same thing over and over and hoping
for a different result isn't insanity. That's hell too.

"You're very good at that."

The final, eighty-seventh interview on the royal betrothal tour has concluded, and it's just the two of us now,

out on the balcony waving and smiling like idiot manne-quins to the crowd below.

"Good at what?" Lenora asks.

"Lying."

She gives a little shrug that doesn't disrupt the rhythm of her wave.

"I prefer to think of it more as . . . performing. And it wasn't all a lie. I do enjoy picnics."

I glance down at the crowd—at the cheering, elated expression for the slip of a woman beside me.

"They adore you."

Her face softens, like a mother gazing at her newborn.

"Yes. I'm quite fond of them as well."

Then Lenora glances toward my waving, waving palm—because this is what I do now.

"You shouldn't have held my hand during that inter-view. The Palace frowns on physical contact between members of the royal family. I've told you this."

"I won't be dictated to. If I want to hold my fiancée's hand I'll fucking hold it."

My fiancée. Still not used to that.

I've seen firsthand how life can turn on a dime, but this has got to be the damnedest turn of all.

"What does that mean, anyway?" I ask. "*The Palace frowns?* Who is The Palace and why do we give a shit that they're frowning at us?"

Lenora's gentle brow furrows, like she hasn't consid-ered it before. "The Palace is the advisors, the ministers and secretaries, sometimes Parliament and the Prime Min-ister." She shakes her head, throwing off the thought. "In any case, you should also stop swearing. We're being photographed, filmed, and there are lip readers."

"So many rules. Your whole life is a list of shoulds and shouldn'ts." I lower my arm and drift closer to her, close enough to smell the lilac in her hair. "Don't you ever have the urge to chuck them all out the window and just do what you want, Lenny?"

"No, I don't." Her lips part, and she seems a bit flustered. Breathless. "And I've told you—you should address me as Queen Lenora or Your Majesty."

Another *should*.

I hover over her.

"But you're not, are you?"

She lifts her chin to look up at me.

"Not what?"

"*My* Majesty," I say softly. I drop my eyes, dragging them over every inch of her, all her delectable swells and valleys. And she is glorious to look at.

"At least . . . not yet."

After the balcony, we have tea on the back terrace with the Palace's head press secretary—a middle-aged man with milk-white skin, orange hair, a nasally voice and a habit of sniffing after each sentence he speaks.

I take my tea with a heaping helping of whiskey.

"Now, as I was saying, I'd like to schedule a photo shoot for you, Your Grace." *Sniff sniff.* "At your family estate." *Sniff.*

"No." I shake my head. "I'm not going to have another photograph taken of me gazing off into the horizon, like an utter arse."

The secretary glances down at his notes. "But we need to give the establishment press something to counter the stories circulating in the tabloids." *Sniff.*

"What stories?"

He passes me a folder. "Several are reporting that the Rourke fortune has been squandered and you're only marrying the Queen for money and title." *Sniff, sniff, sniff.*

"That's ridiculous. Lying bastards."

"You can't let it bother you, Edward," Lenora says.

"It doesn't bother me; it pisses me off. There's a difference."

The butler, Jonathan, announces that the press secretary has a call—the man sniffs his apologizes for the interruption—and heads inside.

When it's just the two of us, Lenny runs her finger along the handle of her teacup thoughtfully. "My very first front-page headline was the announcement that I'd begun menstruating."

I freeze and my eyes dart to hers.

"You're joking."

Lenora holds up her hands like a banner. "'Palace staff confirms: Crown Princess Is Fertile.'"

"Christ, you're not joking."

And I'm furious. For her. For the innocent, trusting girl she must've been, once upon a time.

"Your father should've burned the paper's offices to the ground."

She looks up, surprised by my answer. But after a moment, she shrugs. "You have to learn which headlines to pay attention to—which ones can do you damage and which ones you should pretend aren't even there. If you take them all to heart you'll go mad. Believe me, I know— I had an uncle who went out that way. My mother's brother—batty as a loon."

I laugh because Lenny can be very funny . . . when she's not trying so hard to be a pill.

"I've been meaning to ask, where did you get that?" I gesture to the egg-sized diamond surrounded by a dozen blood-red rubies sparkling on Lenora's right ring finger.

"The Palace requested it from the conservator of the Rourke family jewels. It was your mother's."

"I'm aware. You should toss it in the river or bury it on consecrated ground. My parents couldn't stand each other."

Especially not after my father caught my mother boffing the chauffeur and tossed her out. He was never a pleasant fellow, but after that he worked very hard at making everyone around him every bit as miserable as he was.

Lenora stretches out her hand, tilting her head and examining the jewel.

"It's tradition for the bride to wear the groom's mother's jewelry."

"It's bad luck, is what it is. I'll get you a new ring."

Whether she's going to argue or agree, I don't know —because suddenly, the double doors to the terrace open like a whirlwind is coming through.

A whirlwind named Princess Miriam.

"The Prodigal Princess has returned!" she announces. Then throws herself at the mercy of the Queen—literally. She falls to her knees and hugs Lenora around the middle, almost climbing on top of her. "Don't hate me!"

I watch Lenora's face. She lets her sister accost her for a moment, then she sighs and hugs her back, before finally rolling her eyes.

"Oh, get up. I don't hate you. Stop being dramatic."

I don't think Miriam knows how to be anything else.

They stand and Lenora holds out Miriam's hands, examining her little sister's wild, curly light brown hair, her bright beaded pink dress, her sparkling wrists and ears and neck that are laden with jewels, her hopeful, robin's-egg-blue eyes.

"Where have you been, Miri?"

The young Princess shrugs and plucks a tart from the plate, popping it in her mouth and answering around it.

"Rome, Venice, you know . . . around."

"And your husband?" Lenora says it lethally, with a smile to match. "The footman. Is he with you? I've so been looking forward to meeting him."

That meeting will not go well for Miriam's husband.

"Dmitri? Oh, I left him."

Lenny is confused.

"Left him where?"

Miriam reaches for another tart. "I was sure Dmitri was the one—that I would love him to bits forever and ever. It was so fun at first. But once we got to Italy he became so *boring*! All he wanted to talk about was 'the future' and 'children.' I don't know what I was thinking marrying him. But, it's all right now—I've had the whole thing annulled. Well . . . almost annulled. I was hoping you could speed things up a bit and put in a good word with the Pope?" Miriam wags her finger. "He always liked you."

Lenora sits back in her chair. "Annulled? Just like that? Is it really that easy for you?"

A servant hands Miriam a glass of Champagne—she sips it, nodding.

"Do you have any idea what you've done, Miriam? The chaos you've wrought?"

Her sister hugs her again—like an apologetic chimpanzee.

"I am sorry about that." She straightens and gestures to me and then her sister with her glass. "But look how it's all turned out! You've found your gorgeous prince . . . and you've found your queen of hearts, and it's just like a storybook ending!"

She offers me her hand then. "It's a pleasure to meet you, by the way, Edward. Lenora and I heard stories all about you when we were girls. She thought you were dreamy!"

I like this Princess.

"Dreamy?" I give my fiancée a self-satisfied smirk. "Really, Lenny?"

Lenora scowls. "No. She's exaggerating. It's what she does. And don't call me that."

"Lenny!" Miriam throws her head back, cackling and clapping her hands. "Oh, that's fabulous!"

Lenora glares at me with deadly, dagger eyes. And I grin arrogantly back.

When Miriam notices our expressions, she sobers. "Hmm . . . yes, I see we're not quite there just yet. But don't worry. I have faith in you two—you'll find your happily ever after, I know you will."

Lenora shakes her head with embarrassment.

"You've read too many fairy tales, Miriam."

Miriam pops a kiss on the top of her head.

"And you, dear sister, haven't read nearly enough."

CHAPTER
11

Lenora

R ULE BREAKING RUNS IN the Rourke family—
if I didn't know that already, it becomes abun-
dantly clear the next day when Edward walks
right through the Council Room door without knocking.

As if he owns the place.

"Sorry to interrupt." He stands beside my chair with a
sack slung over his shoulder, all tall and broad-shouldered
and arrogant—and not the least bit sorry. "I'll be kidnap-
ping the Queen for the day."

This is new. I've never been kidnapped before. I
don't know whether I should stand my ground and insist
that he let us get back to work or grab his hand and run out
the door. That happens a lot around Edward. He's a very
confusing man.

"But—" Sheffield begins.

Edward cuts him off.

"Tomorrow."

Norfolk tries. "Duke Anthorp, we need the Q—"

"She'll do it tomorrow," Edward replies in a way that dares them to argue.

Or more to the point, he confuses *me*. I feel a mixture of frustration and fascination, because he hardly ever does what he should. He's not my friend like Thomas was . . . but sometimes it feels like he could be, like he wants to be.

Like he wants to be so much more. And in the most locked-away parts of myself, that I've never shown to anyone . . . I want that too.

So many thoughts, so many new and swirly, upside-down sorts of feelings.

And I thought being Queen was difficult.

Edward takes the decision out of my hands—he does that a lot too. He grabs my hand and before I know it, we're walking through the door. On the way out, I hear the Tweedle brothers chattering like two meddling aunties.

"They do make a stunning couple, Bertram."

"Indeed, Bartholomew. The tea napkins will be lovely."

Oh for God's sake.

Edward and I descend the large, curved staircase that Miriam used to tempt death sliding down when she was small and her nanny wasn't paying attention. And each step feels like I'm walking on one of those giant billowy clouds, like my feet aren't really even touching the ground.

So this is what "playing hooky" feels like. Thomas

said he used to do it often when he was in school—and he was right.

It's brilliant.

"Where are we going?" I ask Edward.

He opens the sack and shows me what's inside—a blanket, food and a bottle of wine. "We're going riding and then on a picnic." Edward winks. "You love picnics."

I laugh as I recall my answer to one of the many interview questions.

"Ah, but that's nice," Edward says.

"What's nice?" I glance around to see what he's talking about. What's made his eyes go dark and his voice rough.

But he's only looking at me.

He strokes his thumb across the apple of my cheek.

"That smile. I'll call it . . . your giddy, girlish smile. Very, very nice."

And just like that, my knees go squishy, and my stomach contracts, and I feel like I may just pass right out. Swooning is real . . . and it's rather brilliant too.

It's noon when we arrive at the royal estate in East Leopold, a large brick mansion with stunning grounds—oak trees and apple orchards and acres and acres of forested land. After I change into riding clothes, we go out to the stables. Edward chooses a mammoth black stallion, while I opt for a camel-colored mare who looks like she has a penchant for speed.

Security rides ahead and behind us, far enough away to give us privacy.

Once we're both mounted our horses dance around each other, and the sunlight glints off Edward's hair, giving him a golden glow.

"Do you want to race?" he asks in a taunting tone.

"All right. To the tree line?"

Edward nods. "But fair warning, Lenny. I'm not going to let you win."

I tsk, shaking my head.

"Fair warning, silly man . . ." I grip the reins and set my feet. "You won't have to."

I tap my horse's flanks with my heels and I'm off. Flying. With the sun on my face and the wind in my hair.

In a gallop of hooves that sound like approaching thunder, Edward gains ground, coming up alongside me. He's very good. I want to look over at him—to watch the way those large hands grip the reins and the wind tousles his hair—but I don't take my eyes off what's right in front of me.

We approach the tree line fast, our horses barreling down, neck-in-neck for several strides. Drops of dirt kick up behind us and then, nearly at the same time, we rumble past the trees.

But . . . I cross it first.

I slow my horse and turn to face Edward, with laughter in my lungs and smiling so wide my cheeks ache. I pat my horse and whisper praise for her.

Edward dips his chin, his gaze shining. "Well done, lass."

I shrug, lifting my nose. "I told you I was an excellent rider."

We ride slowly side by side, down a rocky path that leads to a noisy stream. The bright sun peeks between the branches of the trees, making odd shadows on the forest floor.

"What does a Consort to the Queen do exactly?" Edward asks. "Am I just the stud of the kingdom? The cock for the Queen to ride?"

I thought I wasn't a blusher, but Edward just might be turning me into one. My cheeks blaze like there's a fire beneath my skin. When I glance up at him, the bastard is smirking.

I defend myself—and my blush.

"I don't remember you sounding so crass in your letters."

"Maybe Thomas kept a few from you."

"Anyway." I shrug, straightening my spine. "Historically, the wife of the king spends her time on philanthropic work. What the kingdom needs and what's close to her heart. Social programs, charities, that sort of thing."

I gauge his reaction, because Edward Rourke is a man's man—rugged and capable. "Would you think that's beneath you?"

He snorts. "Only a genuine article of an arse would find altruism beneath him. Many of the places I've traveled would've been wiped off the earth without charities.

Philanthropy makes the world go 'round."

We emerge from the canopy of the forest at the top of a hill. Without speaking, we stop at the same time, gazing at nature's beauty—the way the long grass sways with the wind, making waves in a great green sea.

"Thomas was lonely," Edward says quietly. "Before he met you."

"Yes, I think he was. I think that part of him found a kindred spirit in that part of me . . . and then neither of us was alone anymore."

Edward squints against the sunlight, shaking his head slightly. "I didn't know. I hate that I didn't know that." He clears his throat roughly. "I've been thinking—I'd like to do something in his honor. Create something permanent. A boys' club. An organization that would pair up lads who don't have anyone. And they won't have to be alone anymore either. What do you think of that?"

My eyes go warm and wet, even while I smile.

"I think that would be lovely. Thomas would be just chuffed to bits."

Later, we sit beside each other under a tree on the blanket, eating grapes and cheese and drinking blackberry wine. Edward seems to get a strange enjoyment out of watching me eat—I feel his gaze on me the whole time.

"Did it bother you when I held your hand during the interview?" Edward asks. "I'm not talking about the frowns of the Palace or the should and should nots . . . I'm asking you. Did you not like it?"

I think for a moment, and tell him the truth.

"I didn't dislike it, no. But . . . I'm not an affectionate person. It's not how I was raised. I don't know how it's done."

"Can I hold your hand now?"

My eyes snap to him. "Do you want to hold my hand?"

"I wouldn't have asked if I didn't, Lenora."

His grin is seductive and secret, like there's an undercurrent of dirty thoughts constantly running through his head.

Or perhaps that's just me projecting—because he's the most alluring man I've ever met.

I hold out my hand and he cradles it gently in both of his—with reverence—like it's something precious. Fragile. Then, with the tip of his finger he traces the delicate bones that run along the back, stroking up each finger. He turns my hand over and skims each line of my palm, slow and deliberate, like he's memorizing it.

And warm liquid heat spreads up my legs, filling my stomach, trailing up my spine, until my limbs feel languid and my breasts feel heavy, tingling.

"You have very pretty hands." His voice is deep and melodic. "I bet you're pretty everywhere."

Edward aligns our palms, like two hands in prayer, and then he folds them together and rests them on top of his thigh. And for a time we sit, side by side, hand in hand, enjoying the calm and the company.

"Tell me something?" I ask.

"What kind of something do you want me to tell?"

"Something about your life out there. Where is the first place you went when you left?"

He nods as he recalls it.

"The Philippines. There's a village of fishermen—the Bajau—their children learn to swim and dive before they learn to walk. They're the best divers in the world, they can hold their breath longer than any other man—they've taught themselves, trained their bodies over years and years. The livelihood of their families and their village depends on it."

I watch him, listening to the steady pull of his voice, like the best kind of bedtime-storyteller.

"I stayed with them for . . . five months."

"That's longer than you stayed anywhere."

"That's right, it was. They taught me how to dive. Turned out . . . I had a talent for it. And I have this to remember it by."

Edward reaches into his front shirt pocket and pulls something out. Then he turns my hand over and drops a pearl into my palm. A perfect, pretty, translucent little pearl.

"It's beautiful." I hold it up to the sunlight, admiringly. "And you carry this around with you all the time? Aren't you worried you'll lose it?"

"I don't have many belongings that are important to me—this is one of them. I don't lose things that are precious to me," he says meaningfully.

And I shiver a bit—because I think it would feel amazing, to be precious to Edward.

Edward

AFTER THE FOOD IS DEPLETED and the wine bottle is empty, I stand, brushing off my trousers, and hold out my hand to Lenora.

"Come on, then. Let's go."

I glimpsed her today—the girl my brother wrote me about. During our race, Lenora's eyes sparkled like two shooting stars and her cheeks were flushed and her laughter rang out in the air—so wild and free and beautiful she made my chest ache.

And I'm hell-bent on seeing that girl again.

Lenora stands and mounts her horse, and after I stuff the blanket back in its sack, I walk over and swing up behind her.

"What are you doing?" she asks, surprised.

I reach around, taking the reins from her hands, and turn the horse.

"I want you to do it again," I say close to her ear.

"Do what again?"

"Close your eyes, stretch out your arms and try to catch the wind. Like that day in the woods. Be that girl again."

For a moment her eyes are unguarded. Innocent and wanting. Yearning to trust someone . . . to trust me.

"I think I learned my lesson the last time," she says.

A fierce, savage protectiveness rises up inside me.

"But I'm here now." I wrap my arm around her waist, tight enough so she'll feel it. "I won't let you fall."

CHAPTER 12

Lenora

"I'M LEAVING," he says.

I look up to Edward, standing beautiful and straight in front of my desk, his face serious and somber. And my heart plummets. Because Edward is hardly ever serious or somber.

"Pardon?"

He pushes a hand through his thick hair, tugging a bit.

"I have a prior commitment I have to see to. From before."

Before he came home. Before Thomas died . . . before me. From the life he loved, when he could go wherever he wanted, do whatever he wanted, and there were no cameras or interviews or public or press.

"A man I've worked with—Ian Kincaid—he's the best bloke. I thought he could replace me, but he can't. He can't do it without me, Lenora. And . . . I gave my word."

Edward's word is very important to him. He plays at

being a carefree wanderer and in many ways he is—but the core of him, his character, the part of a man that says what he means and does what he says—that runs deep. And is unshakable.

I swallow. "Where . . . are you going?"

"Indonesia."

"Indonesia?" I repeat like a silly parrot.

"There's a gold mine . . ."

"A gold mine in Indonesia?"

The corner of his mouth quirks.

"Not all treasure comes in a chest, Lenny."

I nod. "No, no, of course not."

I could put my foot down. Demand he not go—command him to honor his commitments to the Crown before any other. But I won't do that to him. I won't trap or chain him—he'll be chained enough after the wedding.

Some part of your husband will always resent you.

I won't do that to myself either.

I straighten the papers on my desk and the high steel walls go up and up all around me. Closing me in, sealing me off. I feel the mask come down over my features. Indifference and disinterest. The nonreaction. The appearance of feeling nothing at all. It's my weapon, my costume . . . if only it were true.

"Well . . ." I stand. "Have a nice trip, then."

Sometimes I think Edward can see behind the mask.

"Come with me, Lenora."

"Come—what?"

He leans his hands on my desk, his eyes and voice intense and determined. And perfectly serious.

"I'll show you everything. How to explore the jungle,

how to mine gold—it's dirty work, but I bet you'd have a knack for it. It'll be an adventure. Our adventure."

The idea of it calls to me with an almost painful sweetness. To imagine going with Edward, leaving everything behind and exploring the world while holding his hand.

It's a lovely fantasy. An exciting thought.

And completely infeasible.

"Edward . . . that's not possible for me. At all."

His jaw tightens, and he looks out toward the window and nods. Because he knows I'm right. And it's as if a hand is wrapped around my heart, squeezing and squeezing.

"There aren't phones at the site," he says. "I won't be able to call."

I just nod.

"My secretary has adjusted my schedule. I'll be gone a few weeks . . . but I'll be back in plenty of time for the wedding. And for the events that lead up to it."

My voice is soft, ashen. "That's good. The people would be very disappointed if you weren't here for all that."

He strides around my desk until he's standing so close, I have to tilt my head to look in his eyes.

"I'm coming back, Lenora." He says it in a voice that's strong and clear, like a vow. "You know that, don't you?"

I take a breath and exhale with a small smile. "Of course I do."

But I wonder if it will be all of him that returns. Or if some part of his soul will always be searching, gazing out the window and dreaming of all the adventures he missed out on because he married me.

I put my hand over his and give it a quick squeeze, before stepping back away from him.

"I have to go. I have a meeting. Safe travels, Edward."

And I walk away.

It's been three weeks since Edward left, and I try very hard not to think of him. Of course, the *not* thinking of him requires some effort. Which makes me think of him more. Since he's been away, it's as if the world has lost its luster. The walls and rooms, the sky and sun seem dimmer, duller, a bit tarnished.

We're moving forward with legislation to present to Parliament immediately after the wedding and I'm staying very involved. So I've been spending long hours and many days working in my office. For the country and Crown.

I'm not doing it to keep busy. At least that's what I'm telling myself.

I'm not very convincing.

I close the folder on my desk and glance out the window at the moonless black sky. My stomach growls at me for missing lunch. I step out into the hall and Cora isn't at her desk, but someone else is there looking for her.

"Good evening, Alfie."

He dips his head.

"How are you tonight, Chicken?"

"Mmm . . . I'm famished, actually." I glance down at the diamond-and-sapphire broach gleaming on the bodice of my pale blue dress. "So hungry I could eat the crown jewels."

"Sounds like they'd be hard to swallow." He winks.

"Would you like to dine with me tonight? The new cook in the private quarters is fantastic."

Before he can answer, Cora comes scurrying down the hall, her red hair styled beautifully and her purse in hand.

"All right, Dad. I'm ready to go now."

Alfie kisses Cora's cheek tenderly. And watching them, my smile slowly fades against my will. Because I've never had that—that effortless, easy closeness and affection. It's always been on the other side of the looking glass. And there's a hollowness inside me that fears it always will be.

"Cora and I were just heading over to that new place in Winchester everyone's raving about for dinner. Would you like to join us?" Alfie asks.

I glance down at my shiny shoes. "Thank you, but no." I ignore the burning in my throat and tight squeeze around my heart.

"Going to a restaurant always causes too much commotion." I wave my hand. "You can't take me anywhere."

Alfie looks at me closely.

"Are you sure, Lenora? We'd love to have you."

"No, no. I'll be fine. Go on now—shoo."

Cora dips in a quick curtsy. "Good night, Your Majesty."

"Good night." I smile tightly and turn to walk away first.

The walk to the private quarters seems longer than usual, the halls emptier, the echo of footsteps louder. Winston opens the door and a maid greets me in the foyer. She says Cook will have dinner served shortly.

"Just a light meal, please," I tell her. "I'm not very hungry."

I head toward the empty parlor and switch on the television, just to have some noise. And I don't think about Edward again. I don't wonder where he is or what he's doing. I don't think about what it would be like if he were here—how we would have a drink before dinner and talk about the events of the day, maybe watch that silly *Honeymooners* show that's not funny at'all.

I move to the side table and poor myself a sherry. And I can feel Winston watching me. It's strange—usually I forget he's even in the room, but tonight, I notice.

"Are you all right, Queen Lenora?"

He speaks. That's unusual too.

"I'm fine."

After a moment, he speaks again. Gently persistent.

"It's my job to protect you from things that could hurt you. If something is, I'd like to know so I can deal with it."

I glance at the glass in my hand.

"Would you have a drink with me, Winston?"

I should be mortified to have thought the question, let alone asked it out loud. My granny Edwina is spinning like a top in her grave. But what's the bloody point of being

Queen if you can't make your own rules at least once in a while?

"It would be an honor."

I hand him a full glass and motion for him to sit on the sofa, while I take the chair by the fireplace.

"Tell me about yourself."

"Afraid there's not much to tell, Ma'am. I'm a man who enjoys his work."

I sip my sherry and the liquid warms my belly.

"What about your life? Your family?"

"I'm not married. I was an orphan before I joined the military."

"There must be someone? A sweetheart, perhaps?"

For the first time, he glances down and his eyes glitter with memories.

"There was a girl, when I was young. Her name was Melinda and her dad was a fisherman. I joined the military for her, to make something of myself . . . for us. While I was away in training, she went on the boat with her dad to help out. There was an accident at sea and she drowned."

I cover my mouth. "How tragic—I'm so sorry."

"It was a long time ago."

Those glittering eyes fall back on me and he says softly, "You remind me of her."

"Do I?"

He nods. "She was like a force of nature. Strong, steadfast . . . beautiful."

My eyes dart up at the compliment. Like some pathetic flower after a long drought—greedy for any drop of rain.

"You think I'm all those things?" I ask.

Winston exhales roughly.

"I think you are . . . magnificent."

He says it with a sacred awe, the way one whispers a saint's name in prayer.

I recall Thomas's words, from so long ago—when things were silly and simple.

I think Winston fancies you.

And I look at the man across from me, the man who would give his life for me—I don't know if I ever really looked at him before. He's darkly handsome, powerful, intelligent, dedicated. Desirable in every way a man should be . . .

But not to me.

My pulse doesn't throb when I look at him.

His eyes are the wrong color. Gray-blue . . . and I dream of dark emerald, like grass after a thunderstorm. His smile is straight and pleasing, not devilish and infuriating. The sound of his voice doesn't warm me or make my head go light. He doesn't say things that steal my breath away or make me want to laugh all at the same time.

Only one man does that. Only one ever has. And he's the one who left.

And I'm the one who let him go.

I set my empty glass on the table and rise.

"Thank you for the company and conversation, Winston. Let Cook know I won't be eating; I'm going directly to bed. We have a big day tomorrow. Good night."

He gazes down at me a moment, and then he nods.

"Sleep well, my Queen."

As I walk alone with my loneliness to my rooms, Alfie's words echo in my mind.

Love is bloody awful, Chicken.
Yes. Infatuation is no picnic either.

The following day, the glass-and-gold carriage rolls its way down the main thoroughfare of the city. It's a lovely-looking contraption—and awful to ride in. *Hot as a goat's ballsack*, my father used to say, though how he came by that information, I have no idea.

But it's tradition. Part of the summer festivities and celebrations the public looks forward to. The pavement is packed with people—cheering and laughing and holding up banners. Typically, the season culminates with a tremendous gala at the Palace—the Summer Jubilee Ball. This year, however, there will be no ball.

There will be a royal wedding instead.

Miriam and I sit beside each other in the carriage, waving through the windows to the crowd.

"Edward is still away on business?" she asks.

It's what we told the press as well, to preemptively explain his absence.

"Yes."

"He's been gone forever," she whines. "When is he coming back?"

"I'm not sure. A few more weeks, perhaps."

Then I change the subject. "I'm melting. If I go the way of the Wicked Witch of the West and disintegrate into a puddle, the throne's all yours, Miri."

These are the things we joke about in our family.

"No thank you very much," she replies in a singsong voice—her smile never wavering, like the professionals we are. "If they ever try to glue me to that throne, I'll abandon ship faster than you can say abdication. You and Edward better pop out some royal babies quickly after you're married."

The mention of Edward and babies makes my insides pulse with a mix of hesitant hope and cautious joy, and the near-constant ache of missing him.

But I smile and carry on. Because queens do many things, but I think we do that most often of all.

"How are we even related?" I tease my sister.

"It's a question I've asked myself more times than you ever want to know."

I start to laugh, but the sound is cut off by the sharp snap of breaking glass. And I squint at the window—staring through the perfectly round hole that's there now. That wasn't there before.

A pebble. *Must've been a pebble* is all I can think . . .

Until another shatter comes.

And another.

And the horses scream. And the glass explodes all around us, glittering shards falling down like sharpened raindrops. And the carriage churns and jostles like it's lost a wheel.

Then suddenly, Winston is here. In the carriage, pulling me and Miriam to the ground. He covers us—spreading himself on top of us, pressing us into the floor so hard I can't draw a breath.

He lifts his head and I look at his face. His lips are moving, telling me something, shouting—but it's as if the whole world has been plunged under water and I can't make out the words.

I strain so hard to hear . . . and then . . . everything goes black.

Edward

THIS WAS A MISTAKE.

I knew it on the first day, but I had to keep pushing, trying. I thought I could come out here to this gold mine and slip back into my old life for a time. I thought it would be easy, like flipping a light switch.

I thought wrong.

This doesn't fit anymore, none of it. I'm not the same man I was when I arrived back in Wessco . . . or when I carried a lovely, stubborn girl through the rain.

My priorities have changed. I have changed. Everything has.

I can't turn it off and I don't want to. Lenora haunts me. I lie awake at night in my tent thinking of the sound of her voice, the smell of her hair, the ever-changing shade of her liquid-silver eyes.

During the day, I wonder what she's doing. If she's all right. If those tools in Parliament are treating her well. I promised I would never let her fall . . . and then I left her there all alone.

She's the most alone person in the whole world.

The guilt eats at me, slices through me, right down to my bones.

But it's more than that. More than guilt or obligation. There's something else, something I don't know what to call yet—a constant push, an urgent pull from the center of my chest where my heart beats. A desperate straining desire to return home.

To return to her.

All these years I've been out here looking, searching for where I belonged and what I was supposed to do. For my purpose. And I've finally found it; I'm finally sure.

Lenora is my purpose. She is my reason.

And I have to get home to tell her.

In my tent, the three guards on my security detail watch as I stuff my belongings in my bag. They don't talk much and I think they probably hate my guts. For dragging them halfway around the world, into the jungle, sweating and miserable. Can't say I blame them.

Outside the tent, Ian Kincaid calls my name. I grab my hat, step through the flap and look around. He's at the docks, waving his arm at me. And it takes a moment to decipher what's in his hand.

When I do, my stomach plummets straight to hell.

Because it's a telegram.

An advisor from the palace—Smith something-or-other—
meets me at the airport in Indonesia with the royal plane,
an update and a proper suit. I don't sleep a wink during the
fifteen-hour flight. I spend the time torturing myself thinking that if I had been there, it never would've happened.
Fuck me.

I wash and shave, and when I slip my arms in the
sleeves of my suit . . . it doesn't feel like hell anymore. It
fits just right now.

I arrive back at the palace, and they tell me the Queen
is in the infirmary, so I run down the halls to get there.
When I push open the door and finally see Lenora—whole
and unharmed and herself—the worry and guilt that's had
me knotted up loosens its grip.

And I'm filled with blessed relief. Because she's here
and she's all right.

But then, as I continue to watch her across the infirmary . . . I start to feel something different entirely. Something twisting and ugly springs up.

Because she's in a chair, sitting very close to the bed,
chatting with that chud Winston. He's shirtless except for
a large bandage stuck to his chest and the sling cradling his
arm. They talk in soft, familiar tones—almost intimate—
then Lenora smiles at him. And it's a real smile. The kind
that dances in her eyes and lights up her whole face.

And I want to shoot the bastard. The same way they
shot the evil fuck who tried to hurt her—right where they
found him, on that same day, in an abandoned building
across from the parade route.

I walk into the room. "Well, isn't this nice?"

Lenora turns at the sound of my voice, and for a moment she looks happy to see me.

"Edward!" She stands. "When did you get back?"

Despite the fuse that's been lit in my head, my eyes drink her in deeply. They've missed her. "Just now."

"Duke Anthorp." The bodyguard greets me, dipping his head in a bow.

"Winston." I turn to face him. "Thank you for what you did. We are . . ." I glance at Lenora, then back again. ". . . forever in your debt."

And though resentment sizzles in my throat, the words are true.

I loop my arm around Lenora's shoulders, pulling her good and snug against me. "Come along, love. Say good-bye to your little friend."

She looks at me strangely, but then turns to the guard. "Good day, Winston."

And I guide Lenny out of the room. In the hall, I step back and look her up and down again—checking for injuries.

"Are you all right? Truly?"

"Yes, I'm fine." She nods, her face soft. "Miriam, however, will probably have the vapors for a month." Then, hesitantly, she asks, "How was your trip?"

"Unproductive."

"Oh. Does that mean you'll have to leave again?"

"Perhaps. We'll see." I shrug.

I don't know why I say that—I'm not going anywhere. But then I get to the real problem . . . and my transformation into a horse's arse is complete.

"What was that about?" My jaw goes hard as I lift it toward the infirmary door.

Lenora blinks, the prettiest picture of pure innocence.

"What was what about?"

"You and the guard. You two seem awfully . . . close. Even more than before I left. Is that why you told me it was all right to go? Just what the hell's been going on around here?"

"You can't be serious." She looks at the door and then back at me, and her eyes darken to the color of sharpened lead. "You leave, for weeks, and now you're here and . . . you're jealous of Winston?"

"I don't get jealous, sweets. But I'm not a fool either." I try another tack and point at the door. "You realize he's fucking your sister, don't you?"

Lenora gasps, eyes going wide.

"Oh, apparently, you didn't."

Michael and I saw them humping against a tree in the garden a few days before I left. Miriam is an independent girl and I didn't get the sense she was being taken advantage of, so I minded my own business. But Lenora is another damn story altogether—she is all my business.

"You can ask Michael if you don't believe me. I guess it makes sense—she is the spare. Or has he worked his way up through the ranks to you now? Is that how it goes?"

Her dainty hands clench into tight fists. "The only fool here is me. Because I was happy that you were home." She shakes her head. "It's a mistake I won't make again."

It's the hurt in her voice that breaks through the asinine. Heartbreak mixed with aching disappointment.

What am I doing? What the fuck am I doing?

"Lenny, wait—"

"Go to hell."

"Lenora . . ." I grab her arm, but I barely touch her before she cries out and her face pinches with pain. I let go, breathing hard, looking for how I harmed her.

"What's wrong with you?"

She lifts that stubborn chin. "Nothing."

"Don't lie to me."

She's favoring her right arm. As carefully as I can, I grip the sleeve of her cardigan sweater.

"Let go!"

And I pull it down her arm. Revealing a thick white bandage wrapped around her bicep. There's a crimson discoloration in the center where the blood seeped through.

It's like I've taken a sledgehammer to the chest, the kind that smashes your heart to pieces.

"Christ almighty. You were shot?"

She yanks her arm away.

"It's nothing. It just grazed me."

"Why wasn't I told immediately?"

She slips her arm back through the sleeve of her sweater.

"We thought it best to keep it out of the press."

"I'm not the press! I'm going to be your husband!"

She glares at me, all fiery defensiveness. And then she throws my own words back at me.

"But you're not—at least not yet."

Lenora takes a breath and straightens her skirt.

"Now if you'll excuse me, I have a country to run."

Head raised and back straight, like a moving stone statue of the perfect queen, she walks away.

Leaving me to watch her go.

My plan is to let Lenora settle down and then in the private quarters, to explain some things to her—hash it all out. And this time, try not to massively fuck it up.

I don't expect her to be done with her duties for some time; the sun is just setting and the sky is a soft, dove gray. So I walk out past the gardens to visit Thomas's grave.

But when I arrive, someone else has already beaten me there.

"If you were here, I'd hit you!" Lenora paces in front of the gravestone, shaking her fist. "And it wouldn't be any dainty-girl slap either. Oh no—it would be a punch right to the balls! Honestly, Thomas, what were you thinking? What have you done?"

She collapses onto the bench beside the grave, the indignation draining out of her.

"He's going to hate me," she whispers brokenly. "I'm going to ruin his life and he doesn't even know it yet. He's leaving behind a life he loved and I have nothing to offer him in return. Nothing he values. One day he's going to hate me for that and when he does, it will shatter me."

I step out of the shadows.

"I'm not going to hate you."

Lenora jumps up from the bench, wiping at her

cheeks. "You shouldn't listen to private conversations! It's rude."

"I know. I'm a very rude man." I take a step closer. "But I swear, I won't hate you."

I gesture toward the bench. "May I sit with you?"

She glances at the empty bench, then back at me, with an unsure nod. I sit down, leaning forward, resting my elbows on my knees. Cautiously, Lenny sits beside me.

"I was angry when Thomas died," I tell her softly. "At God and the world and the whole fucking universe. But mostly I was angry at myself. Because I should've been here."

I look at his headstone, and it's still raw, still wrong. My eyes burn and my throat is tight. "And I would've ripped my lungs out and given them to him to save him. But there was nothing I could do. Except promise him that I would care for you, protect you . . . marry you."

Lenora stares at her hands in her lap.

"I don't want to be an obligation to you. A promise you have to keep. The thought of it turns my stomach," she says.

I shake my head. "But you're not. It's why I was already on my way back to you when the telegram came. Why I couldn't stand to be away any longer. You are more to me now."

Her eyes are two round pools of silver in the fading light of the day.

"How can you be sure?"

"You have to trust me, even just a little. You have to try. I'm a man who knows his mind. I know that I want you—that I've wanted you from the first. And if that means accepting the life that comes with you . . . then it's worth it."

Her delicate brows draw together.

"Won't you miss it? Won't you miss the freedom, the adventure?"

I chuckle and shake my head, because she still doesn't understand. I put my hand over hers.

"Making a life with you will be my greatest adventure, Lenora."

Her breath hitches in her throat.

"Oh . . . oh my."

"I want us to start again," I tell her. "Start over, better. No parliaments or titles or crowns or marriage arrangements. Let's just be you and I—Edward and Lenora—two people who met in the forest. Can we do that?"

Her words are said in a tone I've never heard from her before. Unsure and vulnerable.

"I want to; I want that with you. I'm just not sure how we do that."

"Then I'll go first." I stand and hold my hand out to her. "Hello, I'm Edward Langdon Richard Dorian Rourke. I've been to every continent on the globe. I've touched the bottom of oceans and the tops of mountains, and in my expert opinion the very best place in the whole wide world . . . is right here."

Lenora stares at my hand, and ever so slowly she reaches out and places her small one in mine, playing along.

"It's nice to meet you, Edward."

I bow my head.

"The pleasure's all mine."

I take a seat on the bench and gesture for her to stand. "Now you."

"Oh, yes, right." She stands, fiddling with her hands, and her pink tongue darts out, licking her lips. The Queen is adorable when she's nervous.

"I'm Lenora Celeste Beatrice Arabella Pembrook. But you can call me Lenny . . . as long as no one is around to hear you say it. I'm a queen, so, you know, most days . . . I rule."

I want to clap for her. *Well done, sweet, funny girl.*

"We should probably say something nice about each other now—a compliment. That's what people do when they first meet, yeah?"

Lenora nods.

I look at her face and try to think of something she hasn't heard a thousand times before. Something as true as the day is long.

"You're the prettiest lass I've ever seen. The first time I saw you, I felt like I'd been the one thrown off a horse—you knocked me on my arse. You're fierce and funny and the choices you've had to make haven't been easy, but you've carried on. I admire that. I admire you."

A shy smile kisses her lips when she takes her turn.

Her eyes drift over my face, my cheeks, my nose, my mouth. "I'm not going to tell you that you're wickedly handsome, even if it's true. I think you already know that. You're brave and bold and more honorable than you let on. You fascinate me, even when you're just sitting there breathing. You always have. I want to know you, Edward. Every piece and part that makes you, I want to know."

It's the best compliment I've ever received. Full stop.

I stand and offer her my arm—like a gentleman.

"Take a walk with me in the garden?"

Lenora slips her arm through mine.

"That would be lovely."

The sky is darkest navy now. I guide her down the lantern-lit path, and the air is heavy with jasmine and rose.

"What's your favorite food?" I ask.

"Shepherd's pie. And you?"

"I'll eat anything." I shrug.

After a moment, Lenora asks, "What is your favorite time of year?"

"Summer. What about you?"

She grins sheepishly. "Winter."

We stroll silently a bit more, until I ask, "Favorite color?"

"Yellow." She tilts her head up to me. "You?"

"I'm partial to gray."

Lenny stops dead in her tracks. And pulls her arm from mine.

"Oh no, I take it back—this will never work. Definitely not."

I laugh.

"What did gray ever do to you?"

Her smile is small and secret—a pretty lock I can't wait to open.

"It's a long story."

I move closer, and brush back a hair that's come loose from her bun.

"I'd like to hear that story. Will you tell it to me?"

Our eyes meet, and it feels like the ground and the air and the stars shift all around us. Becoming something different. Something new.

"All right." Lenora nods.

And I nod as well.

"All right."

CHAPTER 13

Edward

AFTER OUR TALK AT THOMAS'S GRAVE, things change between Lenora and me. Slowly . . . and yet not slowly at all. The closeness, the intimacy that's been building, flows freer, easier—like the swelling bud of a flower whose time to bloom has finally come.

There's no stopping it—and why the hell would anyone want to?

One afternoon I go to her office, because I see now the direct approach is better with her. Laying things out, discussing them fully—Lenny gets uneasy when she's caught unawares.

And for what I have in mind, I want her very, very aware.

She looks up from behind her desk when I walk through her door without knocking.

"Hello."

I dip my head. "Hello, Lenny. Are you busy?"

"Not so much. Just reviewing some documents."

I glance at the clock on the wall and out toward the window.

"No meetings scheduled?"

"No."

"Excellent." I nod, then stick my head outside the door to tell the guard, "We're not to be disturbed."

I shut the door behind me. And then . . . I lock it.

Those gorgeous gray eyes flare so very wide, I feel it right in my cock.

Leisurely, like a cat stalking, I approach her desk, letting my gaze drift down over her butter-yellow chiffon top with its cute, prim collar.

"You're looking very pretty today, Lenora."

"Thank you. You look very pretty too."

She giggles when she realizes what she's said.

Sometimes I forget just how young Lenora is. How sheltered and unworldly. Inexperienced. But at moments like this—when the faintest blush stains her cheeks and the plump mouth that I dream about at night smiles so shyly—she reminds me.

"I've been thinking about something—almost constantly, actually—and it's something we need to discuss."

Her head tilts with curiosity. She stands.

"This sounds serious."

My aching balls couldn't agree more.

I sit on the cushioned chair, leaning back—watching her every move—while she moves to the sofa just across from me. Lenora sits prettily, legs crossed at the ankles, hands demurely resting in her lap like the gracious lady she was raised to be.

"What would you like to discuss, Edward?"

"Fucking."

And she flinches so hard she almost comes out of her seat. I smirk shamelessly while she unleashes her fiercest scowl.

"Must you call it that?"

"I really must, love."

"Why?"

"Because I like the word. I like the way it sounds—the specificity. The heat."

"Can't we refer to it as . . . the marriage act?" She seems proud of herself for having thought of it.

"God, no."

"Why not?"

"Because 'the marriage act' sounds like something your great-grandparents did a hundred years ago. And no one wants to think of old granddad and grandmum when they're talking about fucking."

Lenny covers her face with her hands.

I take mercy on her. "We'll come back to the names for things another time. We're getting off topic. For now, let's compromise. We'll call it . . . sex. Or making love."

She nods, agreeing. But her little hands are now clasped together so tightly, her knuckles are white.

"Lenora . . . are you afraid of making love?"

She looks down at her hands. "This is a very personal conversation, Edward."

I make my voice go gentle. Soothing. "I'm going to be your husband. We're going to belong to each other in every way. There's nothing to be embarrassed about. This is something I need to know for you, something I want to know."

Her hands relax and her shoulders loosen, just a bit.

"I'm not afraid of making love. It's just . . . unfamiliar. I don't really know how it's done properly."

"You don't know how it's done as in . . . you don't know *how it's done*?"

I make a visual depiction with my fingers—forming a circle with one hand and penetrating it with the finger on my other.

And I'm rewarded with an eye roll and a quick chuckle. "No, of course I know the specifics of it. Dr. Hatchet explained."

I pause. "Doctor . . . Hatchet?"

This is going to be a corker, I can tell.

"He was the personal physician to the King when I was twelve."

I nod cautiously. "And he's the one who told you about the birds and the bees?"

"Yes." She swallows. "He was very thorough. He had diagrams."

I nod again. "Of course. Diagrams are always helpful."

Lenora narrows her eyes, like she's trying to figure out if I'm mocking her. I keep my features utterly neutral, but it's not easy.

"And how old was Dr. Hatchet?" I ask.

"He was . . . well . . . more than a few years older than Father. He was totally deaf on his right side and suffered from cataracts . . . and he kept forgetting my name. He retired the month after."

Bloody hell.

"Didn't your mother tell you anything?"

I always thought that's how it worked with girls.

"After I spoke with Dr. Hatchet, Mother came to see me."

"And what did she say, then?"

"She patted my shoulder and said it's all much nicer than it sounds."

That's when the laugh escapes—can't help it.

"Don't laugh at me." Lenora frowns.

I hold up my hands. "I'm not laughing, I swear to God."

Her mouth puckers into a little pout. "You're literally laughing in front of me, Edward."

"I'm sorry." I rub a hand down my face. "Truly. You just . . . you caught me by surprise."

"Yes, that's me," she says dryly. "I'm just full of surprises."

After a moment, I'm able to stop laughing. I clap my hands, ready to get to work.

"All right, so I'm thinking we should start slow. Talk over all the things that come before making love, that lead up to it. And then we'll practice, so you're comfortable on the wedding night," I explain.

"Like lessons? I was always very good at lessons," she says in a way that's so fucking adorable, I may lose my mind.

"I bet you were, sweetheart. And these will be our . . ."

"Love lessons," Lenora finishes.

"Yes, I like that. Love lessons."

I half expect her to get a pad and pen from her desk to take notes. But she doesn't, and that's probably for the best if I'm not going to start laughing again.

"Right. So . . . sex usually begins with the eyes. Looking, gazing . . . wanting another person so much, your skin gets hot with the desire to touch them."

"I think we've got that part covered." Her voice goes airy. "I like looking at you, Edward."

My smile is slow and full. "I'm happy to hear it. You're my favorite person to look at too. After looking, you move to physical contact. Caressing a shoulder, holding hands."

"We've done that," she says huskily.

"Yes, and you liked the hand holding?"

"Very much."

I look into her eyes and swear from the bottom of my heart, "I'm going to make sure you like it all very much. I promise, sweet girl."

The faint blush comes again, but her smile is so tender and grateful, it steals the breath right out of my lungs.

"What comes after touching and hand holding?" she asks.

"Kissing."

Her eyes go straight to my mouth. She stares with an innocent hunger, a pure, unexplored desire. And it calls forth a hundred images in my filthy mind of all the ways I want to have her, take her, push her, pull her, ride her—all the ways I'll be able to very, very soon. The crotch of my trousers tightens and I'm hard as granite.

"Should we try it?" I ask.

I don't breathe as I wait for Lenora's answer. And

then she says the most beautiful word in any language.

"Yes."

Lenora

FOR A FEW LONG MOMENTS, Edward . . . looks at me. It makes my stomach swoop and my skin hot, just as he described. Like I've been in the sun too long. Flushed . . . but everywhere.

It feels very . . . naughty.

"Have you ever been kissed, Lenny?"

"Once. A Belgian prince kissed me during a ball. He just sort of grabbed me and flicked his tongue around in my mouth, like a lizard."

Edward curses.

"They tackled him and, you know . . ." I shrug. "Removed him from the country."

There's a glint in Edward's eyes that feels almost dangerous, but in a good way.

"Is that it?"

"Yes. That's it."

He leans forward and his voice is different. Darker. Almost hypnotic—a commanding, alluring voice.

"Come here, Lenora."

I blink at him, like a suddenly cornered owl. "Here?

Now? You want to kiss me *now*?"

"I do. Very much."

I glance toward the window. "But it's the middle of the day!"

Yes, yes—I sound moronic. I'm aware.

And so is Edward. He smirks devilishly. "All sorts of fun can happen in the middle of the day. Come closer and I'll show you."

My breath catches in my narrowed throat, and I don't know why I'm so damn nervous. I've been present during the negotiation of military treaties with heads of state that could've ended in war, without batting an eyelash.

And yet, somehow, this feels bigger. More important.

I rise to my feet. But I can't seem to make them move in his direction. At least not fast enough for Edward. Because he stands too and steps toward me with that large, loose, confident stride.

"Can I tell you a secret?" His voice brushes over me like the touch of a soft feather. Calming and smooth.

"All right."

His eyes drift over my face, before settling on my lips.

"I've been obsessed with your mouth since the first time I saw you." His hand cups my jaw and this thumb grazes my bottom lip. "How it would feel, what you would taste like. I've dreamed of your lips, lass."

He wraps his arm around my lower back, pulling me closer until we're pressed against each other—thigh to thigh, stomach to stomach, my breasts against the warm, solid wall of his chest.

Sensation pulses through me and it feels . . . wondrous.

Edward's palm slides along, spreading across my hip, holding me, fingers clenching. My nose brushes the hollow of his throat, and I breathe in the warm scent of his skin—sun and sand and summertime.

"Don't be afraid."

I look up into his eyes, my voice a breathless whisper.

"I'm not afraid."

My mind has finally caught up to what my body already knows. These strong arms . . . his arms . . . will always keep me safe.

Edward leans down and brushes his lips against mine, a gentle, sweet touch. And then again, firmer. And still again, grazing back and forth. His mouth is warm, his lips full. And my heart beats so fast I can feel it drumming against his chest.

I lift my chin, reaching toward him. And Edward kisses me again.

Thrilling joy and excitement, and burning, burning need all sing in chorus inside me. Edward's lips engulf my bottom one, sucking gently, and a streak of heat blazes to my lower stomach.

I think I gasp or maybe moan. I don't know if I'm breathing and I don't care. All that matters is the glorious feel of his mouth on mine.

"Do you want more?" Edward asks against my lips.

"Yes," I breathe out. "Teach me."

He looks down at me, his green eyes dark, almost black with hunger.

"Open your mouth for me. Give me your tongue, Lenora."

I'm nodding mindlessly, and his mouth swoops down and the press of his kiss comes back again. This time I open for him and his firm, hot tongue plunges between my lips, slowly stroking my own. And I feel brave and beautiful . . . and wanted. I stroke back, rubbing my tongue against his, mirroring his movements.

He groans deep and hard from his chest. And even with a crown on my head, I've never felt so powerful. That sound. I want to make him make that sound again. Longer and lower.

The flesh between my legs is throbbing now and my hips swivel against him, all on their own. The strong bands of Edward's arms wrap around my back, lifting me off my feet so my face is above his. And still our lips move on each other's and our mouths press and our tongues swirl and I never want it to end.

My hands wrap around his shoulders, his neck, his corded muscles contracting under my palms. I sink them into the golden silk of his hair and he groans again—making me feel more like a queen than I ever have before.

His chest expands against mine hard—both of us breathing heavily. Edward tears his lips from mine, and they rake across my chin, my jaw, to my neck. I feel the decadent wet lick of his tongue and the bite of his teeth on my skin.

Yes . . .

And I gasp senseless words, but Edward understands.

Please . . .

Then I'm falling as he sits back on the sofa, taking me

with him. His lips return to my mouth and his hand slides into my hair, cradling my skull, turning me how he wants me. I feel the touch of his palm on my face and I cover his with mine, wanting to touch him in every way I can. Wanting to burrow closer, feeling a pull in my chest from my heart to his.

My Edward . . .

A voice whispers in my head—it's the first time I've thought of this man I'm going to marry as mine.

Mine.

What a lucky girl I am.

Edward's lips slow, and then with one final kiss, they still. And our foreheads press against each other's and we look into each other's eyes, panting, breathing the same air.

"Did you like it?" he asks.

I smile and laugh giddily.

"I liked it so much."

I move forward and Edward pulls back, teasing me—making me chase his lips.

"How much?"

"So much . . . I want another lesson."

He chuckles, then pulls me close across his lap and we begin all over again.

And it's as if something inside me—some joyous part of me that I didn't even know was sleeping—has finally been awakened, with his kiss.

CHAPTER
14

Lenora

F OR THE LAST TWO WEEKS, Edward and I have been practicing our kissing. In my office, the gardens, the library . . . one time in the chapel, God save our souls. And judging by his reaction—the manly groans that my stroking tongue pulls from his throat, the way his fingers grasp at me desperately, the way he grows thick and hard and thrusts his arousal against me—I think I'm getting the hang of it. Sometimes, we combine the touching and the kissing, over our clothing, and it is . . . incredible. A whole new world of sensations and feeling.

Everything with Edward is incredible.

Tonight, there's a dinner party at the palace, a pre-wedding celebration. It's a small affair, only about three hundred guests. Alfie is there with his children, and Michael as well—he'll be serving as Edward's best man. But dinner parties are my least favorite sort of event—because of the rules, the protocol. No one is allowed to start their meal before the Queen takes her first bite, and when I place my fork down across my plate, no one is allowed to take a bite afterward. So basically, the entire evening is spent with every eye on me, and it's all traditions and rituals.

And during after-dinner cocktails—politics, of course. Even on a night meant to celebrate the upcoming royal nuptials, politics reigns supreme.

"I respectfully ask you to reconsider, Your Majesty. All of our neighboring nations have contributed troops."

Lord Strathmoore, a slick, greasy-looking marquis who never met a war he didn't like—or profit from—disagrees with my recent decision to reject joining an international military intervention in Malaya. Many of the lords disagreed with me, but none as vocally as Strathmoore.

I sip my liqueur and shake my head. "And if all the nations jumped off a bridge, would you ask Wessco's boys to hold their noses and jump as well? No. I don't believe it's our battle to fight."

Edward stands beside me, his arm almost brushing the sleeve of my burgundy satin dress. From the corner of my eye, I see his chin dip slightly and though we haven't discussed international issues in depth, I believe he agrees with me. And I value his opinion—not because we're going to be married, but because he's an intelligent, experienced and worldly man.

"We will be a laughingstock."

I shrug. "Man's greatest fear is being laughed at. Women don't share that worry—we're laughed at practically every day of our lives."

Edward lifts his glass to me. "Well said, Your Majesty."

Strathmoore shifts his gaze. "You fought in the war, Anthorp. What is your opinion on military intervention?

Edward's voice is firm and confident, but low with an almost reverent tone. "War is . . . surprising."

"Surprising?" Strathmoore repeats.

"A man goes into it thinking he knows what to expect. Guns and bombs, cannons and killing. But the actual brutality of it—watching the life fade from a young lad's eyes, seeing men lose their limbs and others lose their souls to barbarity—it's surprising. Something that has to be experienced to be truly understood."

"Have you become a pacifist, then?"

"Not at all. I have no objection to going to war for a just cause, a noble cause. But as the Queen said, risking the lives of boys you send to a fight that is not ours, just to show that you can, displays more fear and cowardice than strength."

Later, when Strathmoore has moved on to another conversation and Edward and I stand alone, I look at him. Letting my eyes stroke over the way his black tuxedo molds to his muscular form, and his thick, blond hair—now shorter than when we first met—still has a few strands falling forward over his forehead, hinting at his wild, roguish side.

"You're very dashing tonight, Edward."

Yesterday, Miriam told me all about flirting, and shared some pointers—so I'm giving it a go.

"And so well behaved. Following all the 'shoulds' and 'shouldn'ts.'"

His eyes alight on me.

"And does that turn you on, love?"

My heart does a little flip, but I give him a daring smile.

"It does."

He brings his glass to his lips, smirking.

"Noted."

Edward has been staying in Guthrie House—the previously empty residence of the Crown Prince or Princess—since he arrived at the palace. But after dinner, after I dismiss my maid for the evening and walk into my bedroom, Edward is there. Reclined on my paisley chaise longue, his arms folded behind his head, his long, powerful legs stretched out.

I really ought to be appalled that he's here without permission . . . but I'm really not at'all.

"That dinner was fucking painful." He pulls his tie loose and opens the top buttons of his shirt. "So many sticks up so many arses . . . the awkwardness and boredom is going to haunt me for days."

I cross my arms.

"Is that why you've snuck into my room? To complain about the bane of dinner etiquette?"

Smoothly, he rises from the longue and stalks over to me. "Actually, I've snuck into your room for another reason."

"Love lessons?" I suggest with a raised brow.

His eyes go to my lips. And I run my tongue along the bottom, because I've learned that it drives Edward mad. His throat ripples as he swallows hard.

"I have a very particular lesson in mind for tonight—but that's for later. For now, I was wondering if you wanted to see what a real good time is all about? I could show you. I want to show you."

Something about the way he says it makes me think I'm not going to like this one bit . . . and I'm going to love it all at the same time.

"What do you say, Lenny?"

I say his favorite word. "Yes."

"Why do I have to take my hair down, again?" I ask Edward from my vanity table.

"You'll see," he calls back from my dressing room.

I pull out the pins from my hair and shake out the bun. Dark waves cascade down my back. I leave my bangs swept to the right and tie back just the sides of my hair, leaving the rest long and full almost to my waist. It's styled neatly, but still down as Edward requested.

When he catches sight of me in the dressing room door, he freezes. And then he whistles. "Outstanding."

And pleasing electric tingles dance over every inch of my skin.

Edward goes back to strolling around the dressing room, sliding the hangers aside, looking for an appropriate outfit for whatever this "good time" entails. He pauses at a peach silk nightgown and fingers the lace trim.

"This is a surprise. I had you figured for a flannel pajamas type of girl. Or . . . burlap, to match your personality." He winks.

And I give Edward "the finger"—just like his brother taught me.

It amuses him immensely.

"Ah—that's the one." He holds up a pleated skirt and a royal blue short-sleeved blouse with buttons up the front and a draped-bow neckline. It's a casual ensemble, something I would wear around the palace if the day ever came that I had nothing to do. "Put these on."

"This is a terrible idea," I remind Edward.

"So you've said."

I grasp the tight web of ivy that covers the shadowed south corner of the wall that surrounds the palace property and climb.

"Ridiculous. And stupid."

"You've mentioned that as well," he says from below me, where he's positioned to catch me if I slip. "Almost there."

"I don't understand why we have to sneak out."

"Have you ever done it before?" Edward asks.

"No."

"That's why. Everyone should do everything once. Even you—especially you."

When we reach the top of the wall, I sit, waiting,

while Edward lifts himself over, landing easily on the pavement on the other side.

He lifts his arms up toward me. "Jump."

I cross my arms instead. "Why can't security come with us?"

"Because then everyone will know who you are—I want you to blend."

"I've never *blended* a day in my life."

"You will tonight. Jump, Lenora."

With a huff, I push off the wall . . . right into Edward's arms. He sets me down and scoops my pumps up from where he tossed them over earlier, slipping one on each foot.

"Although," he grins, "you look bloody fantastic in that skirt. Did I mention that? Almost changed all my plans when I saw you in it."

I look up and down the dim, deserted street. Not even the moon is out tonight and the air is cool on my bare arms.

"How do you feel?"

I've never been outside the palace walls without security. Not once.

"Naked."

Edward's mouth quirks. "That would be a whole different kind of good time." His hands slide up and down my arms, warming me. "You're not naked—I'll be your armor tonight."

He guides me to the open-topped teal Cadillac convertible waiting at the curb, but I stop short before I slide in.

Because suddenly the full ramifications of what we're

doing settle in. Panic's icy fingers grip my lungs and it's like I can't breathe and I'm breathing too much at the same time.

"Edward . . . I can't . . ."

"Lenny, look at me."

"So much could go wrong. No one will know where I am. What if there's an emergency? An international incident? What if—"

Warm, worshiping lips swallow my words. They move against mine with steady, sultry strokes, stoking a calm pleasure in the very center of me. Safe arms engulf me—capture me—holding me dear and close, and I'm surrounded by the scent of summer, the scent of Edward.

He looks into my eyes, brushing my cheek. "I've thought of all that. I've taken care of it. Trust me, Lenora."

It's difficult. More difficult than I imagined. Letting go, putting my faith in another person. It goes against all my instincts, everything I've been taught.

But for Edward, I'll try. For him, I will.

"All right."

He closes the car door, trots around the other side and slides in behind the wheel.

And we're off.

Edward

LENORA STANDS ON THE PAVEMENT, tilts her head and reads the sign above the door.

"The Horny Goat."

I stand beside her. "It was a whorehouse back in the day."

"You've brought me to a whorehouse?"

"'Back in the day' being the key words."

She frowns. "It's a terrible name for a whorehouse. Did they specialize in bestiality?"

I peer down at her. "I'm surprised you know that term."

She shrugs a pretty shoulder. "I read things."

And I laugh. "It may have been a terrible name for a whorehouse, but it's a fantastic name for a pub."

I take her hand and open the door and we walk into the best damn pub in all of Wessco—with sticky floors, crooked walls, a rickety roof and a one-of-a-kind character of an owner named Donald Macalister behind the bar.

"Donald and I served together in the war," I tell Lenora.

He spots me as we step up to the bar, grinning around the toothpick between his lips.

"There he is! Edward!" He ruffles my hair and engulfs me in a bear hug.

"It's good to see you, Donald, damn good." I smack his back.

I didn't long for many things while I was away, but

when I did, it was for moments like this. A laugh, a drink, taking the piss with an old friend who knows me inside and out. It's always the simplest moments we miss the most.

"How are you, mate?" He straightens up, gripping my shoulders. "As if I have to ask. It wasn't enough you were born with a silver spoon up your arse, now that pretty face has moved you into the palace? It's no wonder the Qu—"

And then he sees Lenora. And goes stock-still with shock.

Behind the bar, Donald's wife notices her too. "Jesus, Mary and Joseph."

Donald starts to bow.

"Nooo . . ." I warn, because a bow will draw attention. "Don't."

He holds still, the toothpick dropping out of his mouth.

Lenora looks to me, at a bit of a loss.

"Say hello, love. You're terrifying the man."

She waves at him with her fingers. "Hello, Donald. It's a pleasure to make your acquaintance. You have a very . . . colorful establishment here."

And the three-hundred-pound, six-foot-five man . . . just stares. I wave my hand in front of his face. He doesn't even blink. Lenny's bewitched him.

"All right then." I catch Donald's wife's eyes. "Two pints, please, Mary. And a lifetime of secrecy."

That snaps Donald out of the trance. He pours us two Guinnesses and slides them across the bar to me. Then he looks Lenny in the eyes.

"Come by anytime you like, Your . . . uh . . . Ma'am.

Enjoy a drink or a dance—what you do and say here will
never leave this room." He taps the bar. "You have the
word of Donald Macalister on that."

With my hand on her lower back, I guide Lenny to a
table in the back corner. She takes a sip from her mug and
a line of foam clings to her upper lip. I want to lick it off.
But she beats me to it, swiping it with her tongue.

"Still feeling naked?" I ask.

"No." She smiles, glancing around. "It's . . . nice. No
one's looking at me. I can't remember the last time no one
looked at me."

For a bit, we just enjoy our drinks. But the band is
good tonight. A foursome playing quick-tempo folk songs,
the kind of music that begs to be danced to.

"Fancy a dance, lass?" I ask.

And Christ, she lights up for me—comes alive right
before my eyes. So much joy inside her just waiting to let
loose.

"I would love to."

I take her hand and for the next hour, we swirl around
the dance floor. Spinning and turning until her hair is
damp at the nape of her neck and we work up a thirst for
another pint. We share a slice of Mary's sweet cake, eating
with our hands and Lenny sucks at the tip of her fingers,
driving me mad.

The band starts a new set with a slower tune and lyrics of love and loss. Amongst several other couples—who
don't pay us any mind—I guide my girl back to the dance
floor, take her in the circle of my arms and rock her close.
Holding her tight, resting my lips against her hair, our bodies pressed and aligned—a divine torture.

As the last notes of the song echo in the air, I tip Lenny's head up and slant my mouth over hers in a quick, hot kiss meant to brand—to mark and remember this moment.

Then the sad, slow song is swept away by the sharp quick slide of a fiddle. Murmurs of approval ripple through the dance floor and Lenny throws her head back and laughs—lusty and full and beautiful.

She clasps the hand of my bended arm and my other hand holds her waist . . . and our fast feet are off again, dancing the next hours away.

Happiness makes the Queen silly. Animated. Unreserved. She whistles the entire ride back to the palace and giggles as we scale back over the wall undetected. Back into her world—our world.

As we walk through the quiet palace hand in hand, the occasional servant gives Lenny odd looks. Most likely because of her clothes, the change in hairstyle—or it could be the glow on her cheeks and the breathtaking smile that hasn't left her lips.

When we get to her bedroom, she spins in a circle in the center of the room. "That was amazing!" Lenora's hair fans out behind her. "Wasn't it amazing?"

"Amazing," I murmur, not taking my eyes off her.

"I am curious about one thing," she says.

"What's that?"

"Earlier you said you'd thought of my concerns about an emergency, that you had taken care of it. What did you do?"

"Ah." I nod. "I gave your sister an envelope with our location inside and instructions for it to be opened in case of a catastrophe."

Lenny gapes at me. "You trusted Miriam with that?"

"Your sister isn't as clueless as she puts on. She's actually smart enough to make everyone believe she's clueless, so no one ever expects anything of her."

"Hmm . . . interesting theory."

"I'm an interesting man."

Something in the words or the way I say them catches Lenora's attention. She moves toward me in slow, deliberate steps—reaches up, feeling the stubble of my jaw, and then she kisses me. It's the first time she's taken control, initiated a kiss. I move my mouth with hers, letting her lead, willing to follow wherever she wants to go.

She rocks back to her heels, looking up at me, her voice soft and quick, as if she wants to get the words out before she changes her mind. "Can I tell you something, Edward?"

I nip at her chin. "Anything. There is no wrong between us, Lenora."

She nods and swallows a breath.

"All the dancing, and beer, has made me feel very . . . brave. And I've been imagining . . . thinking . . . I want to see you. All of you. Beneath your clothes. I want to look at the man I'm going to marry. Will you show him to me?"

There's so much to her, my chest clenches with it. So many secret sides and layers to strip away and discover. Parts I think she's just discovering about herself—parts we can spend our lives discovering together.

Without hesitation, I grip the back of my shirt and pull it over my head, dropping it purposely to the floor. I feel her eyes on me—as hot and heavy as a caress. Her gaze trails over the muscles of my arms, my shoulders, down the center of my chest. Her eyes drop lower, tracing every ridge of my stomach and down the path of hair that leads lower still.

My hands work the buckle of my trousers. And still she watches. I push them down—I'm not exactly the shy type—stepping out of them, and her pretty eyes flare wide as my hard, thick cock bobs against my stomach, reaching for her. Wanting her.

Lenora stares, all innocent curiosity that makes me throb. Her voice is breathy.

"Does it always look like that?"

"Around you? Always."

Her eyes skim down my legs all the way to my toes . . . then slowly drag back up again. Seeing everything, missing nothing.

"My experience is limited," she breathes out, "but I can't fathom God making another man as perfectly formed as you."

Pure, primal male pride pulses through my veins. And I want to have her—conquer her—claim her and keep her.

Holding my eyes, Lenora takes a step back and reaches for the buttons on her blouse.

"You don't have to." The words scrape up my throat. "I want you to . . . fuck, you have no idea how much I want you to . . . but only if you truly want to. There's no rush—we have all the time in the world."

Her eyes are clear with challenge, bold with bravery

. . . but the tips of her ears are glowing hot pink, and I know this isn't easy for her.

Still, she lifts her chin and opens her blouse, skimming it down her arms to the floor. She reaches behind her back, and in a moment, the satin brassiere falls away—and my breath catches at the sight of her pale, high, perfect breasts and dark pink nipples that were made to be sucked.

I don't move. I don't breathe. I say nothing that might disturb her or give her pause. Because now that it's begun, I'm desperate to drink in all of her.

The skirt goes next—she slides it past the swell of her hips, down her petite, shapely legs—leaving her only in delicate lace garters, opaque white stockings and satin knickers.

Without a sound, Lenora dips her head, unhooks her garters and rolls the stockings down each leg. Then she slips her knickers off too. And I eat her up, devour every inch of her, with my greedy eyes.

She stands before me, bare and breathtakingly beautiful. Like something from a dream, a fantasy—full breasts, a tiny, trim waist and a beckoning bush of pretty dark curls between her legs.

I pull in a breath of air and slowly circle her. I don't touch her—I don't dare—if I do, we'll be skipping a whole bunch of lessons tonight. Her hair flows in mahogany swirls down her back—brushing the top of the firm, perfect globes of her arse.

The things I could do to her. The things I will.

"You're exquisite." I press a single kiss to her temple. Then I close my eyes, breathe deep and regain my control.

I move around, standing in front of her—my voice

coming back to me, strong and firm.

"I had a lesson in mind for tonight. Words—the names of things."

Her brows furrow. "The names of things?"

I wrap my fist around my cock and stroke it meaningfully.

"The names of things."

Her cheeks go red, but she manages to roll her silver eyes. "I'm not an idiot, Edward. I know the names of things."

"Dr. Hatchet again?"

"Well . . . yes, mostly, but—"

"And what names did the good doctor teach you?"

"All the proper words, of course." Her eyes slide down and I grow even harder under her gaze. "Penis, vagina, areola—"

"No." I shake my head. "No. Those aren't the words I want to hear from your puffy, perfect lips."

She narrows her eyes. "Well, what do you want?"

"I want to hear you say *cock*."

Lenora's eyes flash to mine. And she frowns.

"Those are cheap words. Vulgar words."

"They're real words. Hot words. Sensual words real people use in the throes of passion and fucking and lust and love. If you can't bring yourself to say it, sweetheart, you've got no business getting anywhere near it."

Lenora lifts her chin and lets out a shuddery breath. And then she looks me right in the eyes—stunning in her stubbornness—and that beautiful bud of a mouth gives me exactly what I want.

"Cock."

And it's fucking sublime. So good I could come with three pumps of her pretty hand.

"Dick." I say it like an order.

"Dick." Mine twitches at the sound of his name in her lovely, lilting voice.

Her pupils are dilated and her nipples are two tight, rosy points begging for my mouth. I lick my lips and take it up a notch.

"Pussy."

A ghost of a smile tugs at the corner of her lips.

"Pussy."

Instinctively, my eyes drop to hers . . . and my mouth waters.

"Sweet, wet, pussy."

It's going to be—there's not a doubt in my mind.

"Sweet, wet, pussy."

I lean in closer, so our noses are just inches apart. And my voice is low and ragged now—filthy.

"Cunt."

"I hate you."

And I laugh. Because this, now, here . . . *her* . . . nothing has ever felt so good in my life.

"Say it, Lenny," I tell her softly, almost begging. I run my fingertip across her collarbone, feeling the thrum of her pounding heart. "Say it for me and I'll give you a kiss."

She inhales slowly, her breasts rising—her nipples just grazing the hairs on my chest. And Christ, she looks so delectable I want to pounce on her. I want to spread her out, hook one leg over my shoulder and thrust into her, hard and fast, right here on the goddamn floor. I want to pump into her for hours, until her voice is hoarse with pleasure and her pussy is so full, I drip out of her.

And then I want to take her all over again—in every way I know how. Fuck those pouty lips, come down her throat, have her from behind, on her knees, teach her to ride me until she scours my back with her fingernails, because it just feels so . . . damn . . . good.

But I won't do any of that. Not tonight. Because it has to be slow. It has to be right.

For her . . . it has to be perfect.

Her eyes shine with boldness now. With challenge. Because retreat is not in my Lenny's vocabulary. She rises up on her toes, bringing her mouth so close to mine, I can taste the sweetness on her breath. Her tone is sultry, teasing—accentuating every consonant.

"Cunt."

My eyes slide closed with bliss. "Hmmm . . . good girl."

I open my eyes and slowly sink to my knees in front of her.

She peers down at me, tantalizingly bewildered.

"What are you doing?"

I smirk up at her. "I promised you a kiss. I'm giving it to you."

I hold her by her hips, lean forward and envelop her pussy in a deep, open-mouthed kiss. My lips suck on her gently, and my tongue strokes slowly up and down between her folds.

"Ohh!"

She tastes sweeter than I'd even imagined. The scent of her curls here is floral too—fresh and clean—lilacs in the snow. The softest, prettiest pussy—I could stay here on my knees for her all night long.

"Edward . . ." She rises up on her toes, before settling down into my lapping, lashing mouth on a long, serrated moan. "I . . . ohhh . . ."

"Do you like it, sweets?" I ask against her hot, wet flesh.

"Yes . . ." Her breath puffs from her mouth. "Do you like it?"

I look up so she can see the truth in my eyes.

"I do . . . so much."

She bites at her bottom lip. "Are you sure?"

I kiss her thigh, her hip. "Let me show you how much I like it."

I guide her to the chaise longue, lay her down and spread her knees with my hands. I kiss up her pale, smooth thighs and across her tiny waist, groaning at the feel of her soft skin beneath my lips. I rest my chin on her pelvic bone and smile into her searching gray eyes.

"Can I tell you another secret, Lenny?"

"All right?"

"I've dreamed about these lips too."

Then I bow my head and worship my Queen.

Lenora

THIS IS NOT NORMAL. It's some deviant thing he learned while traveling. A sin—it's too good not be a sin. One of the big ones, I'm sure—deadly. And that makes sense, because my heart beats so hard and my breath is so short, I feel like I might die.

And I couldn't care less.

Just the sight of Edward's blond head between my legs makes me cry out with need. With passion. My moans fill the room in a voice that sounds nothing like me. My back bows and my hands stroke through Edward's hair and across his smooth, taut shoulder blades—needing to feel his skin.

"Jesus . . ." I draw in a moan at the hot, slick sensation of his wet moving mouth.

Edward looks up at me with the devil in his eyes.

"Edward."

Then he dips his head back down and takes his time —playing me like a fiddle, making long leisurely strums with his tongue and pressing humming open-mouthed kisses against my flesh. He grasps my knees, spreading my legs wider and drags his tongue up and down through my wet lips. And then he spears me with his tongue, pushes it inside in firm, thick thrusts. It's wicked and dirty and incredible.

I lift my chin and groan loudly at the ceiling. Because it's all so much . . . everywhere. Building, surging—yes— a brutal, beautiful onslaught.

And then his tongue is replaced by the firm press of his finger sliding in and out of me. My muscles clench hard around him without a thought, wanting to keep him there—keep him inside—because he feels so good inside.

"Fuck," Edward groans, the hot pant of his breath fondling my thigh. "I knew it. I knew you'd be tight just like this."

He kisses my tender skin, nipping with his teeth and scratching with his stubble. "Lenora, do you touch yourself, pleasure yourself? In the shower, the bath, the bed?"

And I don't even care anymore—there is no modesty or shyness, no secrets. It's as Edward said . . . there is no wrong.

"Yes."

He reaches for my hand, kissing the tips of my fingers, sucking them into his mouth, wetting them with his tongue. "Show me how you do it. The pace . . . the rhythm . . . show me, love."

Not following his command is not even a consideration. I slide my two fingers through my . . . pussy . . . to the juncture, spreading my lips and unashamedly rubbing my clitoris in firm, slow circles. And it's always felt good, but never like this. This is liquid, illustrious pleasure.

Edward growls my name and he's on me again. I feel the wet heat of his mouth on my fingers as he licks at me, feasts on me—like a famished man's first meal. Like he wants to consume me . . . and I would let him. My fingers move faster and my hips rise. And I thrust shamelessly up into Edward's mouth.

His hands slide under me, squeezing and kneading my arse, before lifting me up to his relentless lips. He pushes my slippery fingers aside with his chin, and his tongue—his glorious tongue—takes over, pressing flat against me, dragging back and forth over my clitoris in perfect sensual circles. Building and building, and yes . . .

My nails dig into the cushion of the chaise, grasping for something to hold. My head tilts and I scream as pure, piercing pleasure pounds through me. My vision goes white and it's like I'm flying, soaring, swirling. The feel of Edward's strong hands and sure mouth makes it go on, prolonging the deep sensual bliss.

Slowly, I sink back to myself, breathing in racing gasps. Edward peppers soft, gentle kisses on my pelvis and stomach, before gazing up at me. And I want to lose myself in his emerald eyes. I could. I could disappear forever into him and be insatiably happy.

I reach for him, touching his brow, his regal cheek.

And I beg. "Show me how to do that to you. To make you feel like I feel."

He flexes his jaw and his eyes go dark.

"You're sure?"

I nod. "I'm sure."

He rises, standing beside the chaise, the hard shaft of his . . . cock . . . jutting out, weeping fluid at the tip. Edward slides his fingers between my legs, gathering my wetness and bringing his hand to his erection—coating it, stroking. He takes my hand and wraps it around his . . . dick. It's warm against my palm, smooth as silk and rigid as steel.

He's too thick, too large for my fingers to circle all the way around, but by the pleasured hiss that whistles between his clenched teeth, that doesn't seem to matter.

He moves my hand beneath his, and we're pumping together in long, tight strokes.

"Harder." He groans. "Grip it harder."

When I squeeze tighter, he releases my hand—leaving me to my own devices. I bring my other hand between his legs, cupping his heavy testicles, palming the delicate skin there.

"Yes . . ." Edward grunts.

And his face . . . his face is beautiful . . . contorted in hungry, surging gratification. And I want more. More moans and grunts—I want to wring those sounds from his lungs. So without thinking, I lean forward and take the tip of him between my lips.

He shouts, smacking the cushion behind my head violently, curving his spine, leaning over me—his hips jabbing in shallow thrusts. And it's amazing. Edward's not even touching me and I can feel the sweet, delicious sensation between my legs throb to life. Building and building all over again.

He cups the back of my head, gently, pushing forward, feeding me more of him. I run my tongue along his length, tasting the manly tang of his skin, suckling hard to taste him more. And there's such power in it. I was weaned on power—to keep it, wield it—but this intimate power is something new and miraculous.

Humbling and heady at the same time.

This giant of man, who could break me with his bare hands, stands above me, but is utterly at my mercy.

Pleading in a way that makes me moan with him.

"That's it, sweet girl . . . take it . . . take it just like that."

And I do. I relish in the taking of him.

Edward pulls back, suddenly, out of my mouth—he strokes himself fast above me, then with a deep, long groan his thick, hot semen pulses from him—splashing on my chest, my breasts, my nipples.

When it's over, he grips my hair and yanks my face up, plunging his tongue between my lips with a raging, desperate force even while his chest heaves to recover his breath. After a moment, his tongue slows, gentles, and his fingers stroke my face tenderly. He goes down on his knees, kissing my forehead, my cheeks, before resting his forehead on my thigh.

"Christ almighty . . ."

I run my fingers through his hair. But then, something occurs to me and my hand stills.

"Hmph."

Edward rubs my knee soothingly. "What is it?"

I frown deeply.

"Dr. Hatchet definitely left some parts out."

And Edward laughs—a joyful, masculine rumble right from his chest.

"God, you fucking delight me, Lenora. Nothing on earth will ever delight me as much as you."

CHAPTER
15

Lenora

PREPARING FOR A ROYAL WEDDING is like preparing for war—everything must be coordinated, staged, executed to perfection. The palace may have a staff of hundreds, but just as there are orders that can only be given by a general, there are responsibilities that can only be performed by the bride and groom. Dignitaries to entertain, luncheons and brunches to attend, invitations that must be personalized, proclamations that must be planned, dress-fitting appointments that must be kept, and thousands of thank-you notes that must be signed by hand.

I despise thank-you notes. If I could, I would ban them from the damn country, just to save myself the trouble. One can dream . . .

The next two weeks go by in a blur of duty-filled days. Edward and I see each other, of course, but it feels like we share more longing glances across rooms than actual time together.

And then suddenly, D-Day is here.

Or more to the point . . . the night before D-Day. Both Edward and I are in the palace, but we might as well be in two separate countries. He's spending the evening with the male relatives and lords who have a role in the wedding. They're in the private library on one side of the palace, while I'm stuck with my bloody batty aunts, cousins and other female relations in the music room on the other side.

The men get cigars, liquor and probably stag films . . . while we ladies get tea and crumpets and a private performance from a renowned female opera singer.

But tradition is tradition. And this is who we are—so this is who we must be.

When the opera singer concludes her last song, the sky is black from the moon being snuffed out by heavy clouds. We all clap gently.

And now begins the mind-numbingly polite, pointless chatting portion of the evening.

"Where will you and Prince Edward be honeymooning, Your Majesty?" Matilda, my uncle Warwitch's wife, asks.

Edward received his new title last week—Prince of Wessco—in a ceremony he would've missed if he'd had his way. But he attended because it was expected.

He attended for me.

"Saint Augustine's. A small, privately owned island off the Dutch coast."

There's a sparking flash of white in the sky outside the large arched window. Lightning.

"And do you have all your unmentionables packed for your new husband to enjoy?" my cousin Calliope—the one who told a "fictional" story about a young queen's death by poisoned wedding cake earlier—asks me.

"The staff is taking care of the packing," is my non-answer reply—a trick I learned from my father.

Because the answer is yes. I wanted delicate and beautiful lingerie, but I also wanted things that were meant to be torn, shredded. Articles that would shatter Edward's self-control—that would make him feel wild, like he makes me feel.

When I needed advice on choosing such things, I was sure just whom to go to. And when I did, Miriam flung her arms around me and exclaimed, "I knew you were my sister!"

But I'm not going to tell any of these women that. Because they aren't my friends—most I barely know and those that I do, I don't like at'all.

A burst of thunder rattles the window, turning my head again.

And I realize there's somewhere else—somewhere infinitely better—I could be, right now.

I pop up from my chair. "I have to go."

From across the room, my sister desperately mouths the words, *Take me with you.* And then she winks at a waiter, clearing drinks from the table.

"Go where?" asks Lady Dorchester—the most notorious gossip in the Wessco aristocracy.

"I . . . ah—"

"Urgent government business." Cora Barrister comes to my rescue. "We just got the call. Very urgent. The Queen must go." She turns to me, a knowing look in her sparkling blue eyes. "You must go straight away, Your

Majesty."

"Yes." I take Cora's hand, squeezing. "Thank you, Cora."

The thunder crashes outside the window again.

"Until tomorrow, Ladies."

They each dip their head to me as I make for the door. In the outer hall, I kick off my shoes, pick them up . . . and I run. I run through the halls of the palace and I don't stop running until I get to the other side. To the library.

I don't knock—I don't have to. There's a guard outside, and I'm the bloody Queen, so he opens the door for me. The library is filled with deep chattering voices and thick ashy smoke. It's so thick, Edward spots me before I spot him.

"Lenora?"

That brings the attention of the men in the room straight to me. They all bow and immediately stop talking. Automatically, my back straightens and my face slides into neutral.

"Pardon the interruption. There is a matter I must speak with Prince Edward about."

Edward follows me out into the hall.

"Leave us," I tell the guard.

"What's the matter, Lenny?" He cups my jaw. "You're all flushed."

I glance at the door to the library. "Are you . . . enjoying yourself?"

"Not even a little. If I have to spend five more minutes talking to those pompous wankers, I'm going to climb up, take your great-uncle Ethelbert's historical gun off the wall and shoot them all."

I nod, chuckling. "There's something I want to show you. But we must hurry or we'll miss it."

Edward gestures for me to wait and steps back inside the door. "Gentlemen, there is urgent wedding business that needs my attention. But . . . the bar is stocked, the cigars are plentiful, so please carry on and enjoy yourselves. Good evening."

He comes back out into the hall, arms open. "I'm all yours."

I take his hand. "Come on, then."

And we both run. I lead him down the hall of portraits, where dozens of my ancestors watch over us, and then passed the Capella Suite—the room where I and all my siblings were born. Finally, we reach the narrow white door at the very end of the Eggshell Hallway—named after the wallpaper that gives the appearance of cracked eggshells.

"Where are we going, Lenny?" Edward asks.

"You'll see."

Behind the door is a winding staircase with narrow brick walls and no windows. And I lead Edward up and up and up, until finally . . . we're there. We exit through another door at the top and walk out onto the roof of the Palace of Wessco. It hasn't started raining yet but the breeze is cool and clouds are low. I spin in a giddy circle before him, the air crackling with electricity and static all around us.

Then, grasping Edward's hand, I point to the sky a bit farther out from where we stand. "Watch . . . there."

And as if I commanded it, the lightning flashes in a jagged, bright line of white against the pitch-black sky.

Another strike comes just a few seconds later—tinting the clouds in dark purple. And then another, and another in hues of orange and pink. Because the palace is so high, every strike of lightning is visible for miles around. It's a light show—nature's fireworks. A few seconds later, the thunder booms so loud I feel it in my bones.

Edward smiles at the sky. "It's beautiful. Amazing."

"I used to come up here when I was a little girl. When I was . . . well . . . when I was lonely. I would watch the lightning and feel the thunder tremble and I knew there were others, seeing and feeling the very same thing. And it made me feel—not alone."

He turns to me, his features tight and his eyes bright —burning with emotion.

"You were the first person I thought of when I saw the storm," I tell him over another boom of thunder. The vibration rattles beneath our feet. "The first person I want- ed to share it with . . . the only person. I wanted you to know that."

He takes my face in his hands and slants his mouth across mine. I can taste desire on his tongue—feel his need, his want for me, with every press of his lips. The bristles of Edward's stubble tickle my cheek as our mouths move and meld. The kiss is hot and hurried, and then with the next great burst of thunder . . . the kiss becomes very, very wet.

The rain shower pours down over us, slicking our clothes to our skin, drenching our hair, our bodies, our fused lips.

Edward presses his forehead to mine and the water runs in little rivulets down his cheek.

"Come to my room."

I nod, because I would go anywhere with Edward.

And it's such a big change from who I was just a few short months ago. And yet, following him feels like the rightest thing I've ever done.

We run through the pouring rain down to Guthrie House. In the foyer, we don't wait for the staff to bring us towels, but instead go right up to Edward's bedroom.

I try to wipe the water off my face and arms with my hands.

"You're always getting me wet."

Edward comes up behind me, with a towel in his hands, chuckling, "I do seem to have that effect on you."

He rubs the towel over my arms, my neck, patting my dripping hair. I feel his mouth right up against my ear, and I shiver at the promise in his voice.

"We need to get you out of these clothes."

I glance back at him over my shoulder. "It buttons down the back. Will you help me?"

He smirks, making my knees go wobbly. Slowly, he undoes the buttons of my mint-green dress, one by one. "It's my honor to serve my Queen."

His rich voice is so smooth and decadent, I can't even tell if he's joking.

When I step out of my dress, Edward shakes it and hangs it on the back of the chair to dry. He's much less careful with his own clothes—his shirt ends up in a slapping wet heap on the floor, before it's joined by his trousers.

And Edward is naked and I'm practically naked, but there is no shyness. No awkwardness or anxiousness.

I gaze at the impressive, hard erection between his legs . . . and I am not ashamed to want it. Crave it. Desperately. To want to touch his cock with my hands, my fingers, my mouth, my tongue—touch him everywhere and for a very long time. The thought creates a throbbing ache low in my stomach—because I yearn to feel his touch in return.

It's just like Edward said . . . we're going to belong to each other.

But I think we already do.

"There's something I want to show you," Edward says.

But he doesn't move, and neither do I. We look into each other's eyes, like we're reading each other's minds. Because the next thing I know, we're pressed right up against each other, arms wrapped around each other.

Edward bends his neck, kissing me furiously, greedily.

"Fuck, I've missed you."

I taste rainwater on his lips.

"I think about you every night," I confess between kisses.

"So do I," Edward says. "If I think about you any more, I'm going to jerk my dick right off."

I convulse in his arms, laughing wildly.

"It's not funny. I'm not joking," Edward insists, backing me up toward the bed—a dangerous, predatory glint in his eyes. "It's a very serious matter."

He lifts me under my arms, onto the bed. I'm on my knees, eye level with him, my arms on his shoulders, and slowly our laughter fades away.

Edward looks down between us and sighs as he traces the waist of my black silk knickers. "I like these."

His hand skims up my waist, slipping a finger under the strap of my bra. "But this . . ." He shakes his head mournfully and clicks his tongue. "This monstrosity has got to go."

He makes quick work of the clasp and slides the satin down my arms—tossing it over his shoulder. And then he stares at my breasts, like he's hypnotized. He cups one in his large hand—rubbing the nipple with his palm.

My head rolls on my neck. "What's this lesson called?" I moan.

He licks his lips. "This lesson is called, your tits are beautiful and if I don't get my mouth on them right now, I'm going to go mad."

And then he's kissing me, climbing on the bed with me, laying me back and sliding on top of me. And the weight of him—the feel of his taut, tan chest pressing down on me—is electric. Heavenly.

Edward kisses down my neck, then lower still over my collarbone. He holds my breast up for his mouth—his lips closing around my nipple with a groan. And then I can't hear anything except the sound of my own gasps and my own pounding heart.

"Oh . . . oh . . . yes . . . please . . ."

The feel of Edward's sucking mouth, his swirling wet tongue, robs me of all my senses. He licks his way over to my other breast—palming and pinching the first as he laves and flicks at my nipple.

I feel the hard ridge of his cock—hot and big—between my legs. Pressing against me. Sliding up and down against the tight cleft of my opening—separated only by a thin, shifting, strap of silk.

"Edward—?"

"We won't." He kisses my breasts, nibbles around the soft swells. "It's all right, Lenny. Not yet—I promise." His breath is warm and minty on my face as he lifts up onto his elbows and smooths my hair, looking down at me with so much affection in his eyes.

"Trust me."

I cover his hand with mine and twine my leg around his—pulling him closer.

"I do. I trust you."

And my body goes loose and lax with that trust. Edward shifts his hips, thrusting up—he doesn't penetrate me, but his erection slides up and down against my knickers, between my lower lips. I'm slippery and warm from the rubbing, gliding, wet friction. His hips retreat, then push back again, and the hard head of his cock glides back and forth right over my clitoris, igniting a spike of hot pleasure that tears through me. I tingle everywhere and burn for more.

"Oh . . . oh . . ."

Edward holds my gaze while his hips circle again and again. "Yes?"

"Yes," I gasp. "Oh, yes . . ."

"Do you want to stop?"

"No," I pant.

His hard cock hits that spot again, and my back arches and my muscles clench—to get closer. To get more.

"Don't stop, Edward." My voice is keening, shameless.

Edward drops his forehead to the pillow beside me, and as his hips pump wilder—harsher—his breath bites out in pants against my neck.

He palms my bottom, pulling me against him—giving me more, taking me farther, higher. "Move with me, love. Yes . . . just like that."

My arms clutch at him and my hips rotate—matching his thrusts. Edward turns his head, slanting his mouth over mine, sucking on my tongue. And the beautiful sensation is rising, filling me with feeling. Like I could burst with bliss.

And then I do. And Edward bursts with me. I feel his hot semen on my stomach, and his grunts in my ear.

"Fuck, fuck . . . fuck . . ."

The masculine carnal sounds of his release feed my own and I moan into his shoulder, pressing my teeth against his skin as the pulsing pleasure wracks through me —and I go tight and stiff beneath him. Both of us taking and giving and feeling the rapture of the moment together.

Later, after Edward has gotten a cloth from the washroom and cleaned us both up, and we lie in a heap of tangled limbs in his bed, he presses his lips to my temple.

"This isn't why I brought you to my room, I swear."

He thinks on his words, and then rephrases. "Well . . . it's not the *only* reason."

I smile. "Yes, you said you wanted to show me something."

He kisses my forehead, then slips from the bed. I sit up so I can watch him cross the room. I admire his tapered waist, the hard swell of his arse, and how the muscles in his back ripple as he moves.

There was a time I thought God had forsaken me. But looking at the bare perfection of this man, I realize . . . I must be God's most favorite person ever.

I pull the blanket over my shoulders and shift to sit on the side of the bed, my feet hanging off. Edward opens his top bureau drawer, takes something out and walks back to me, crouching down.

His hair falls forward into his eyes, and his grin makes him look young and boyish and so very handsome. "Give me your hand."

I hold my hand out to him and he slides the ring—his mother's ring—off my finger.

Then he walks over and throws it out the window.

"Edward!"

"Don't argue with me about this. That ring is cursed."

He comes back to me, and this time he doesn't crouch down.

He kneels.

Edward flips the box open and inside is a ring—a perfect pearl surrounded by small glittering diamonds on a gold band.

"Edward!" I gasp. "Is this your pearl?"

"No." He shakes his head. "It's your pearl now."

He takes the ring from the box, holding it between his fingers. His voice is rough and his eyes are tender. "Will you marry me, Lenora? Will you be my wife and let me be your husband? Not because your kingdom demands it, but because you want to?"

I've never been a crier, but it looks like that may be changing too. Because tears well in my eyes and blessed happiness clogs my throat.

"Yes, I will marry you, Edward, because I want to. And because I think my favorite title will soon be that I am Yours."

He slides the ring on my finger and lets out a shout of joy. I laugh as he lifts me up, wrapping my legs around his waist and slanting his mouth across mine in a deep, sweet kiss that goes on and on.

And it's perfect. A moment of perfect, pure happiness. The kind you remember and look back on and cherish your whole life.

But those moments of pure happiness are much like the cherry blossoms Thomas and I once admired in the garden. They're so beautiful when they come, but you have to enjoy them while you can . . . because they don't last forever.

CHAPTER 16

Edward

"ARE YOU NERVOUS?" Michael Fitzgibbons asks, in the vestibule behind the altar in St. George's Cathedral. In the last months he and I have become very close—good friends—and there was no one else I could imagine asking to stand beside me as my best man today.

I snort. "No."

"Most grooms are usually terrified the day of the wedding," he says. "And this is bigger than most weddings."

I peer out the door—celebrities and royals and businessmen of every stripe pack the pews. Cameramen are stationed in the chorus box to convey every moment to the thirsty public. Outside on the pavement you can't even move through the throngs of people waiting for a glimpse of her . . . of us . . . wanting to be a part of this day.

"I just want to get it over with. Have her be mine, officially."

Michael smiles impishly. "The Queen's a keeper, yeah?"

The anxious palace events secretary, the one in charge of this whole show, scurries into the room. "The Queen has arrived outside. Places, please, Prince Edward, Lord Michael."

I tap Michael on the back. "She certainly is that."

I stand at the altar, in my officer's military uniform, spine straight, arms folded behind my back, the perfect image of a storybook prince. The music begins—the mournful notes of a piano first, then bagpipes, then strings and horns . . . all building and swirling together into a surging rendition of the bridal march.

The congregation stands and double doors open, and there in the center . . . there she is.

Wrapped in snow-white satin and lace, snug around her waist, long in the back, elegant through the shoulders and down her arms . . . she shines like an angel fresh from heaven. There's a lace veil over her face, so I can't make out her features yet, but the tiara on her head—a new one of emerald and diamonds that was commissioned just for this day—winks and sparkles as she walks. Alone.

Because she's not being given away. She's giving herself.

As she glides down the aisle to me, I press my hand to the breast of my shirt pocket, feeling the hard ridge of my brother's glasses, and I send my whispered words out across the ether.

Thank you, Thomas.

Thank you for bringing us together. For seeing what my destiny could be before I did.

I was made for this . . . for her. To cherish her, protect her and challenge her, to guide her and follow her—to be the man she needs, so she can be the woman, the queen, she was always meant to be.

At last, she arrives by my side, facing me.

Slowly, I lift her veil, revealing the shimmer of her diamond eyes, the rose hue of her porcelain cheek, the delicate china of her tiny nose, and the soft swell of her pink lips. My voice is low, so only she can hear my whisper of rapturous awe.

"Dear God, Lenny . . . you take my breath away."

Her answering smile is worshipful and lovely.

I offer her my arm, and she threads her lace-covered limb through mine, and we turn toward the altar and step up together to the Archbishop. The cathedral is bursting with thousands of guests—the wedding is televised, so there are millions more watching—but when the time for vows comes, it's just she and I . . . Lenora and Edward. In this moment, together.

Surrounded by the glow of candlelight and the sweet scent of lilies, we look into each other's eyes and pledge our lives—ourselves—to one another.

"I, Edward Langdon Richard Dorian Rourke, take thee, Lenora . . ."

"I, Lenora Celeste Beatrice Arabella Pembrook, take thee, Edward . . ."

". . . to be my wife,"

". . . to be my husband,"

"to have . . ."

"and to hold . . ."

"from this day forward . . ."

"for better or worse . . ."

"for richer, for poorer . . ."

"in sickness and in health . . ."

"to honor and cherish . . ."

"to honor and cherish . . ."

"till death shall we part."

"till death shall we part."

We slide simple bands of gold onto each other's fingers, and it's as though the words, the pledge, the promise is being wrung from the depths of our souls.

"All that I am is yours . . ."

"All that I am is yours . . ."

"all that I have, I give to you . . ."

"all that I have, I give to you . . ."

"with my body, I honor you . . ."

"with my body, I honor you . . ."

"within the sacred laws of man . . ."

"and the love of the Father, Son and Holy Spirit."

"Amen."

"Amen."

The Archbishop clears his throat, and his voice echoes through the cathedral as he proclaims, "I now pronounce, henceforth, that they be man and wife. You may kiss your bride."

I may . . . and I really, really must. Can't wait another damn second.

I wrap my arm around her waist and pull her in close. I cup her cheek and bend my head and kiss my beautiful wife. Our lips move together with passion and tenderness, but more than that—with joy.

Then, to the sounds of the congregation's applause, we walk together back down the aisle. Security didn't want us riding in the open-topped carriage, because of the earlier attempt on Lenora's life, but she wouldn't hear of it. She insisted. The people will want to see us, celebrate with us, she said.

And when my stubborn girl makes up her mind, it's futile to resist.

So I take her hand and lead her down the stone steps of the cathedral, through a hail of falling white petals. I help her step up into the cherrywood carriage and climb in behind her. Together we ride through the streets toward the reception at the palace, waving to our people, who are overjoyed for us.

And this time . . . I don't mind the waving one bit.

Lenora

ALMOST THE ENTIRE FIRST HALF of my and Edward's wedding reception is spent taking photographs. Official photographs, private photos, portraits, exclusive photos for the press, shots with us together, shots with us alone, shots with the full wedding party and parts of the wedding party . . . photos with the page boys and flower girls. The marriage of a queen is a once-in-a-lifetime event, a historical occasion, so it's to be expected.

Photos are a royal's full-time job.

Finally, Edward and I are permitted to go to the party. We dance and drink wine and feed each other cake. And still the cameras capture each moment.

And then I'm whisked away from him—one final time—to get a few shots on the balcony, in my dress with the setting sun behind me. I step back into the magnificent ballroom and a voice comes from my right.

"You look very happy, Chicken."

I walk to him, where he leans against the large, round marble column.

"I am, Alfie. If all arranged marriages ended up like this, every royal should have one."

He chuckles and the wonderful, jolly man who has been such a kind constant in my life shines his sparkling blue gaze down on me.

"He would be so proud of you . . . for so many reasons."

My throat tightens and my eyes grow warm with emotion.

"You have already surpassed all he hoped for you."

I put my hand on his arm, his shoulder, squeezing.

"Thank you, dear Alfie."

I wander around the ballroom, nodding to guests and re-turning their well wishes—looking for my new husband.

My husband.

How in the world did that happen? Just the words in my head make my arms and legs go giddy and my stomach tumble with simmering desire.

Edward is much different at large functions than I am. My father would've said he's good at "working a room." He's confident, jovial—an entertaining host and easy con-versationalist. The type who's never had an awkward mo-ment.

Which is why I think nothing of it when I spot him chatting it up with an attractive, tall blond woman across the way. I've never seen her before, but as I get closer I see she seems to be just a bit older than me . . . except there's an air of worldliness about her. Of experience.

And then I hear their voices.

"We can sneak off right now—I'm quick but talented; you won't regret it."

"You're embarrassing yourself. And you're barking up a very wrong tree."

"Perhaps not for long. They say the Queen is as cold as—"

Edward's harsh voice chokes off her reply. "Not an-other fucking word."

A fire rages, right near my heart. Maybe it's because I've never known this kind of happiness, so I've never thought about what I would do to protect it. To keep it. Turns out, I would do a hell of a lot.

They notice me—she notices me, and bows.

"Your Majesty. It's—"

"Don't 'Your Majesty' me—who the hell do you think you are? Or more importantly, who the hell do you think I am?"

Her eyes dart around the room, filling with mortification.

"You think you can walk in here—into my palace, my wedding—and proposition my husband right under my nose? That I'm the type of woman who will let that go unanswered?"

I don't hiss, because I'm not a snake or a cat—my words are careful, calculated and completely committed, because I'm a queen.

I snatch her wrist in my grip. "Try to take what's mine again and I will burn everything you love to the ground. And then . . . I will burn *you* to the ground. Now go."

I turn away, dismissing her as she scurries off. And that's when I see that I may have been louder than I realized. Because they're all there—dignitaries, the Prime Minister, the Archbishop, the Advising Council—looking at me, and judging by their expressions, they all heard me.

I cross my arms and lift my nose.

"I'm not sorry. Not even a little."

Edward laughs . . . and it warms me right down to my toes. Then he takes me in his arms and kisses me—deep and lusty—bending me back into a full dip. And that gets the attention of the whole ballroom. There are gasps, several murmurs of approval and more than one camera flash.

It's just like a movie.

Or a fairy tale.

Toward the end of the reception, I change into an ivory traveling outfit with gold filigree with matching gloves and cap, and Edward swaps his uniform for a blue button-down shirt and navy jacket, without a tie. We say our goodbyes to the crowd at the palace gates and climb into a Rolls-Royce, in a burst of flashing camera bulbs. We arrive at the airport hangar where the royal private jet awaits to take us to our island honeymoon.

Once we're seated in the soft leather seats, it's as if my limbs are weighed down by a hundred pounds and my eyelids have completely thrown in the towel.

I yawn big and wide.

"It was a long day," Edward says, toying with the netting on my cap.

"It was," I agree, even though it's technically only eight in the evening. "A long, lovely day."

He kisses my forehead and gently pushes my head to his shoulder. "Sleep now. I have plans for you—for an even longer, lovelier night, and I want you well rested."

Everything warms—my cheeks, my stomach, my heart. And that's the last thought I have, before dreamless sleep swallows me whole.

"Wake up, Lenora," a melodic voice calls, pulling me to consciousness. Then it goes dirty with suggestion. "Open your eyes, Lenny, and I'll give you a kiss."

My eyes pop open straight away.

Smirking like the devil he is, Edward pecks my lips and wiggles his eyebrows. "I'll give you a proper kiss later. We've landed—the car's waiting."

"Oh. What time is it?"

"Just after one in the morning."

I stretch my arms, and check my hair and makeup in the mirror. Then I stand and bump into the long, fluffy coat Edward is holding open for me.

"Put this on," he says. He's wearing one too.

"What in the world?"

That's when the cabin door opens and a whirl of frigid air bursts through it. I blink as I look out the door—at the dark sky and giant white mounds of snow that surround us.

Maybe I'm still asleep.

"This . . . doesn't look like Saint Augustine's Island."

Edward nods. "There's been a change of plans."

"Where are we?"

"It's a surprise. You'll see."

And something in the way he says it makes my stomach flip with excitement. I slide into the coat and Edward gestures toward the plane door.

"After you, Your Majesty."

The car is heated when we climb in, with a thermos of rich hot chocolate waiting for us. We slip our coats off and drive for about an hour, on winding roads flanked by big, tall, snowy evergreen trees.

Edward pulls a black silk scarf from his pocket and holds it up.

"We're almost there. I want you to put this on."

I raise an eyebrow. "Kinky."

Edward told me all about "kinky" a few nights ago. Very intriguing.

His strong lips slide into a chuckle, then he wraps the scarf around my eyes, blocking out my vision completely. Moments later the car rolls to a stop. I feel the brisk wind on my legs when the door is opened, and Edward's large, warm hand envelops mine as he guides me out of the car.

"Don't let me fall," I tell him.

"Never," he says, against my ear, before sweeping me right off my feet, into his arms. I rest my hands around Edward's neck as he carries me.

It's only later that I realize that through all of Edward's surprises and changing of plans, the kinky silk scarves, and the carrying me around . . . I never hesitated. I never questioned or worried that he would allow me to be hurt or embarrassed.

I never doubted him for a moment.

The temperature changes again, and though I can't see, I hear a door close behind us and I know we're inside. I'm set on my feet and the coat is stripped away.

Edward unties the scarf and slides it from my eyes.

And my breath leaves me in a rush.

Because it's a bedroom, but the ceiling is curved, domed—it and the full wall in front of me are made entirely of clear glass.

We're on a hillside, covered by snow and dense forest. But above us, the sky is jet black . . . except for a river of the most magnificent colors. Swirls of greens and reds and deep purple—all dancing together. What did Edward call it in his letter, so long ago? *A living symphony of color.*

Aurora borealis.

"We're in Finland," Edward says from behind me. "This is called the North House. There are smaller, simpler cabins down the hill for rent, but you don't have to worry—I've bought them all out too. I'll make a campfire for you, outside if you like. It's just us here, now. Just you and I."

And it's all . . . so much. A flood of feeling washes through me, drowning me, and I put my hand over my mouth but I can't keep it in. And I burst into great, heaving tears.

Edward takes me in his arms, holding me as I shudder with sobs.

"Don't cry, Lenny."

And I try to explain, to make him understand.

"I never thought I would have this."

He tips my head back, wiping at my tears. "Aurora borealis?"

"You." I grip his shirt and look up into those beautiful eyes. "I never thought I would have you. I never even let myself hope for you, dream for you, and yet somehow here you are. You have changed my whole life, Edward. You've changed me, and I couldn't do this alone."

He smiles gently and strokes my face. "Yes, you could."

"But I wouldn't be me, not who I am now. I would be some other, emptier version of me." Another tear falls and another, and my voice breaks. "You are my joy and my heart . . . you are my home . . . and I would be lost without you."

He holds my face tight in his hands, and his words are low and forceful. "You will never be lost. I will be with you always. The vows were wrong. When death comes, he can have my body . . . but my soul will stay with you, I swear it."

And my heart is so very full, so full of all that he has given me and all that I feel for him.

Edward

*S*LOW, SLOW, SLOW . . .

It's a mantra in my mind, a reminder. A restraint.

Because, God damn, how I want her. Not even in my wildest, most selfish adolescent days did I want to take and take a woman like I want to take her.

Wild and hard, lazy and long.

I kiss her soft lips, and touch her face, and move us backwards toward the bed. And Lenny looks up at me, her eyes round and silver as the moon, and she reaches for my shirt, opening the buttons one at a time. She may be the innocent, inexperienced one, but when she pushes my shirt off and skims her hands across the burning skin of my chest . . . and follows those hands with her velvet kisses . . . I'm the one trembling.

I may not be a king, but here, now—she makes me feel like one.

More than a king—her hero, her husband, her mesmerized slave, her ravenous lover—it's all the same now. All wrapped up together.

Lenora's mouth trails down my stomach and her torturous wet tongue traces the ridges of my abdomen. My hands clench tight at my sides—yearning to grab and tug and pinch and cup.

But I let her have her way—let her explore and taste until her sweet heart is content.

She bites her lip and pauses at my navel, suddenly unsure.

But then my little Queen rises to the occasion . . . and sinks down on her lovely knees just for me.

And, fuck, my cock aches at the sight.

My trousers are opened and the belt slid out with the hiss of leather. Then quickly, like she just can't wait for it, Lenny pulls my trousers down my hips, freeing my hot, rock-hard flesh. I step out of the pool of fabric at my ankles and I feel her needy, keening breaths against my thighs.

She grips my dick in her delicate hands and slides her palm firmly up the shaft, just like I taught her. Lenora wets her lips, opens her mouth and takes me in the fantastically wet, scorching cavern of her mouth, where she worships me with tight suction.

My head rolls back on my neck and my eyes close

and I can't fucking watch her anymore, or I'll come on her tongue.

She moans around me—I hear it, I feel it.

And my control stretches to a tenuous, razor-thin thread.

I grip her arms and yank her up—harder than I should. I kiss her until she can't breathe, can't think—sucking on those velvet lips, grazing them with my teeth, dominating her with the thrust of my tongue.

And my heart pounds in my ears, *slow, slow, slow* . . .

I undo the pearl buttons of Lenora's suit jacket and slip it off. Her arms are lithe and long. Delicate. I raise them straight up over her head as I breathe deeply. I look into her simmering eyes and let her see the bare, raw desire in mine. How much I adore her—how blessed I am that she's mine.

I skim my palms down her bare arms. Then down her sides, stroking the pale flesh of her breasts with my thumbs along the way.

The skirt is gone next. I get on my knees and slide it down her legs, leaving Lenora only in a thin ivory satin slip. I kiss her stomach on my way up, the lilac-scented valley between her silken breasts. My large hands slide up her thighs, pushing the slip over her head—so she's bare to my eyes . . . to my heart.

Then, one by one, I pull the pins from her hair—removing her cap and unraveling her bun until her hair falls loose down around her in a wild, wavy dark curtain. It accentuates her features—her skin is paler, her cheekbones higher, her gray eyes brighter.

And it's all for me. I'm the only man who will ever

see her like this.

I give her a smile with all the tenderness I have, as I bring her in against me, our warm skin sliding. I lift her up so her breasts are right there for my lips' taking, wrapping my mouth around her nipple—flicking it hard and fast with my tongue and sucking and sucking on the hard points until her high-pitched voice calls my name for mercy.

Her hands comb through my hair, caressing my jaw, bringing my face up to hers. "Make love to me, Edward." She looks up at the ceiling, then back into my eyes. "Make love to me under this magical sky."

I spin around and lay Lenora down on the bed. Her pink mouth is parted and panting and her tousled hair framing her. And she opens for me like a flower—arms stretched, knees spread—uninhibited and unashamed and perfect and mine.

I climb over her, toss her legs over my shoulders, and then I feast. Licking and tasting between her legs, making her pussy wet and clenching, making her moan and gasp my name—my bride, my wife, my beautiful fucking girl.

"Edward . . . Edward . . ." she chants, pulling at the strands of my hair hard.

I kiss down her inner thigh, her calf, rising up on my knees, between her legs, and I drag the broad, bell-shaped head of my cock through her slick, slippery heat.

Up and down, past her opening again and again, pausing but not dipping in.

Lenny's hips rise up—craving, begging.

"Is this what you want?" I whisper.

She writhes beneath me, eyes drunk with pleasure and

lust and need.

"Yes . . ."

I open her up wider, drape her legs across my thighs. My palm slides up the slick center of her stomach, kneading her breasts, stroking her nipples, then back down. I rub her tight little clit with the pads of my fingers on one hand, and slip two fingers into her pussy with the other.

And I work her slowly, pumping into her as she gasps and groans.

Lenora lifts her chin, her face twisted with passion and craving for more.

"Please, please, please, please . . ."

I slip my fingers from her and grip my cock, sliding again to her slick, hot opening.

"Yes . . . yes . . . Edward . . ." she chants.

I press inside her, just the head.

Slow, slow, slow.

Her muscles resist, but her wetness eases the way. I want to curse with the sensation of her—the hot snugness that makes my vision go dark. But I won't. This moment is too precious for those words.

"Lenora, look at me," I rasp.

When her eyes rise to mine, I grasp her hips and thrust all the way in past her virginity, embedded fully in the depths of her wet, gripping heat.

She arches her back and cries out.

For a moment, I don't move . . . but when I do, it's down into her arms. I lie on top of her, hovering above her, pressed as deeply into her as I can be. I gaze into her beautiful eyes and brush back her damp hair and I feel the caress of her hands on my arms, my back.

"All right?" I ask.

"Yes," she nods. "Yes . . ."

And then I move. Hips circling in slow, shallow circles—kissing her, loving her with my mouth—building it back up, wanting to give her ecstasy . . . give her the whole world.

My lower pelvis rubs her clit with every swerve of my hips.

Again and again and again.

Lenora's chest rises and falls, harder, faster, and heat surges back into her eyes.

"That's it, love," I coax. "That's it . . ."

And Christ, the feel of her—more than I dreamed in my wettest fantasy. Every ridge and rope of her muscles inside is slick and tight and clamping.

I suck at the tender skin of her neck, breathing hard. And her moans fill my ears. Louder and harsher with every roll of my hips. Fantastic, carnal sounds that makes my balls tighten and my cock swell.

The sounds of lust and love and life.

"Edward! Edward, Edward . . ."

She grasps at my shoulders desperately and her heels press against my arse. And I kiss her mouth deep and long —licking the sounds from her lips, holding them inside, keeping them for myself.

I feel it when she comes. It's in the pulsing clench of her beautiful pussy, in the long, broken sob of her moan, in the squeeze of her arms that cradle me tenderly even as she finds her peak.

Electric heat races down my spine. My hips thrust wildly, roughly, and I groan helplessly against her shoulder as my cock jerks, filling her up, coming hard so deep inside her.

Afterward, I lift my head and look down into Lenora's eyes, kissing her gently and brushing her hair back. I don't ask if she's all right, because I know she is—I see it in her smile and the tender tear that streaks down her cheek. I pull her against me, into my arms, both of us boneless and spent and satiated.

CHAPTER 17

Lenora

S TANDING UP FROM MY CHAIR, I lean my hands on the table and address the Advising Council.

"So let me see if I have this right. Parliament wouldn't consider my legislation until I was a married woman. Because they wanted a queen who was a traditional wife and assurances that my husband would 'curb me.' And now that I'm married, and have been married for nearly four weeks, they refuse to consider the legislation because they're claiming I'm somehow being controlled by my husband's cock?"

My uncle's jaw drops.

Radcliffe could be on the verge of a heart attack.

And Tweedledum gasps in outrage. "Your Majesty!"

"Oh, man up, Tweedle!" I smack the table. "I need you. I need all of you. Because we have to send a message loud and clear that while Prince Edward's cock is certainly magnificent enough to do the job, the Queen is controlled by no one. Least of all by Parliament. So they'd best get off their arses and do their bloody jobs!"

My council stares at me in shock.

Except for Alfie and Edward. They're trying very hard not to laugh. And failing miserably.

Edward isn't an official member of the Advising Council, but since we returned from Finland he's been coming to the meetings, and later we discuss the issues in private. Sharing my thoughts with him and hearing his opinions is often very helpful.

Now is not one of those times.

"Prince Edward, Lord Ellington . . ." I scowl.

Edward's eyes dance at me with humor. Because for some reason, he just loves getting me all riled up.

"While I'm happy you find me so entertaining, do you have anything helpful to add to the discussion besides hilarity?"

Alfie shakes his head, his face bright red and busting with a grin.

Edward leans back in his chair, arms crossed and mouth quirked—regarding me with that handsome arrogance that makes me want to kiss him all the time.

"As a matter of fact, I do, Your Majesty."

"Please, enlighten us, then."

"You don't need to send a message. What you need . . . is a good shovel."

"A shovel?" I ask. "I don't follow."

"They're politicians," he explains. "Dig up enough of their dirt, and they'll do any damn thing you want."

Dirt. Hmm.

Slowly, I nod.

"That sounds very . . . efficient."

Edward

THE FOLLOWING WEEK, ten of the most influential leaders in Parliament meet in the large back office, at the Queen's request. She wears a candy-pink dress trimmed in black that hugs her perfectly and high black pumps with little bows and a heel so sharp she could stab someone through the heart with it. But it's the look in her eyes I enjoy the most. Anticipation, excitement, vengeance and victory.

She's like a sleek, small, silver gun—beautiful but lethal. It's an intoxicating combination.

"Good morning, my Lords." Lenora folds her hands in front of her and smiles sweetly. I lean against the wall . . . just watching her.

"Please observe the files in front of you. There is delicate information that has come to our attention, about each of you. We wanted to make you aware that we are aware of this information . . . and that we have documentation to prove it. For your own protection, of course."

They tear open the files. A few of them may actually shit themselves.

Lenora taps her lip, furrowing her brow worriedly.

"Although, the problem is . . . I do tend to speak without thinking when I'm upset." She looks each of them in the eye. "I am a woman after all. There's no telling what secrets I may tell—or to whom—when I am thoroughly put out. It could be the press, the authorities . . . your *wives*."

Slowly she walks in front of them, letting them stew for a bit.

"My suggestion to each of you is to not upset me. To vote on the upcoming legislation in a way that will please me. In short . . . do not piss me off. For your own protection, of course."

Then she's back to smiling again. And it's sort of terrifying.

"Also—"

"There's an *also*?" Stinky Winky objects.

My vicious girl grins. "There *is*, Lord Winkerton—do not interrupt me again. As I was saying . . . also, I have decided that the mandatory military service program will include all citizens of Wessco—men *and* women."

And the old men lose their minds—grumbling and shouting.

"That is an outrage!" Lord Plutorch bellows.

"It's an affront to womanhood!" Count Malmunch trembles with indignation.

"For Christ's sakes, it's what's best for the country," I counter.

Lenora takes not an ounce of their shit.

"I will not have half my subjects under the thumb of the other. Not while I am Queen. This law will open up skill sets and opportunities to women that men have always exclusively enjoyed. It's a step toward equality."

She stares them down.

"That's all for today. Vote well, my Lords. And remember these folders . . . I know I will."

She turns and takes my arm, and together we walk out the door.

I escort the Queen to her office. Quickly. Wanting to toss her over my shoulder and carry her off like a Neanderthal back to his cave.

I slam the office door behind us and lock it—and then we attack each other, all twisting, grasping limbs, kneading hands, worshiping mouths and gasping breaths.

I lift her onto the desk and step between her pretty spread legs.

"You were amazing," I say, and kiss her hard and long, thrusting into her mouth with my tongue.

Then I pull her pink dress over her head and toss it on the floor. Giving me an eyeful of her pristine tits, hidden only by a brassiere, and lace knickers and garters that I want to shred with my teeth.

"It felt amazing," she pants, kissing my chest, my chin—anywhere she can reach.

"I'm so proud of you." I dip my head, laving the globes of her breasts, sucking on her rosy nipples. "You didn't even blush when you said *cock* to the Advising Council. Twice."

Gripping her arms, I stand Lenny up and spin her

around. Kissing her neck, her back, bracing her hands flat on her desk—bending her over just right.

I tug my trousers down and tear her lace knickers . . . and I groan when I drag my cock through her slit and feel how slick and hot she already is for me.

"I'm going to have to come up with filthier words to make you blush now."

She giggles like a vixen, glancing over her shoulder —her silver eyes wide and curious.

"There are filthier words?"

Grinning, I hold her steady at her hip—and thrust into her tight, silken pussy that was made for me to fuck.

"Always," I rasp against her hair. "There's always filthier, love."

Two months later
Palace of Wessco

While the Americans in the States have their Thanksgiving, here in Wessco, we have the Autumn Pass in mid-October. It's part harvest festival, part patriotic celebration —to commemorate the feast after the final battle that earned Wessco her independence.

There are parties and fairs, the banks are closed and the palace gates are opened, and the monarch gives a rowdy speech from a platform in the front courtyard that's televised live.

Last night, Lenora practiced her speech for me . . . while my head was buried between her thighs and my tongue did its best work to distract her. She moaned, gasped and screamed it—but she knew the speech inside and out.

But now, the courtyard's packed with people and Lenny's up on the platform, looking ghastly pale. One good gust of the brisk breeze might blow her right the fuck over.

I grab Winston by the arm. "Something's wrong with her. I'm going to bring her inside—make sure the path is clear."

He nods and I move up the stairs to the Queen's side.

"And, we would like to . . ." She closes her eyes, and even her lashes seem ashen.

I lean over and speak into the microphone. "To thank each of you for coming out today, to enjoy the fall celebration! Happy Autumn Pass, everyone!"

There's a swell of applause and Lenny rests her head against my arm. I turn us toward the side entrance to the palace and she whispers weakly, "Please get me inside."

I keep my arm around her back, rubbing slow circles and guiding her toward the door. "Easy now, love. I've got you."

And I do have her—my hold is firm and strong. But that doesn't matter.

Because no sooner are we over the threshold than Lenora's knees give out and her eyes roll back. I catch her before she falls, but she's fainted away in my arms.

"Lenora!"

Fear is cold, and brutal. It stops your heart, freezes

your blood and tells you you'll never be warm again. It claws up from your stomach and lodges in your throat.

"Get the doctor, now! Lenora!"

I don't know how long I sit outside the infirmary while the doctor is with her, but it feels like fucking days. The others are here—advisors and secretaries and that moron Prime Minister, Bumblewood.

I don't talk to them—I don't talk at all. I sit and I pace . . . and I pray.

Because I think about Thomas and how fast he got sick, how quickly he went. And in my mind, I keep seeing him, in his bed with that sheet lying still over his face. Not moving, or breathing. Just gone.

I grind my palms into my eye sockets, trying to push the picture from my brain. But it holds tight.

Finally, the doctor emerges . . . and heads straight toward the Prime Minister.

My long strides get to him first, blocking his way.

"Tell him one word about my wife's condition before you tell me and I'll rip your tongue out and strangle you with it."

The doctor closes his mouth. And nods.

I guide him to the corner, away from the flock of vultures.

"What's wrong with her? Is she ill? Will she recover? What does she need?"

His smile is infuriatingly fucking calm.

"Her Majesty is dehydrated."

All right—water. Not so bad. Lenny needs to drink more water.

"And exhausted," the doctor says.

Damn, that's my fault. Of course she's exhausted. She's got an insatiable bastard of a husband who keeps her up all night, doing everything in bed *but* sleeping.

"And she's slightly anemic," the doctor adds.

Iron. She needs iron—red meat has iron.

"I've given her some supplements and orders to rest."

I nod and nod—while looking out the window, searching for the best spot to graze the cattle I plan to buy immediately.

"Queen Lenora is expecting, Prince Edward."

My brain stops short. And the whole world freezes in time. For a moment I don't move; I'm not sure I even breathe.

"Expecting? You mean a baby? She's having a baby?" I point to myself. "Our baby?"

The old man smiles broader, chuckling, and nods.

"Not today, but yes. Congratulations."

Holy hell. It shouldn't be a shock, not with the way I've been at her, but still it is. I laugh—stupidly giddy, and fucking cocksure proud.

"Thank you, Doctor."

I grab his hand and smack his back, even though I've never liked the tosser. But I like him now because he's given me the best news I've ever heard in my whole life.

I like everyone right now. But I like Lenny most of all.

So I run in to see her as fast as I can. And I scoop her

up from the bed—set her in my lap—and kiss the daylights out of my pregnant wife.

CHAPTER 18

Lenora

I THOUGHT I UNDERSTOOD maternal instinct—
that base, primal urge to protect your future, your legacy. It's what I felt for the public the first day I wore
the crown. I wanted to care for them, provide for them,
watch them grow strong and become all I knew they could
be.

I still feel that way. But those emotions are just a
shadow of what I feel for this child growing within me.
The first months were . . . sick and draining. Edward
would rub my back as I vomited into a bag in the backseat
of the car, and then I had to rinse my mouth and negotiate
with some foreign leader. It was perfect misery.

But now, in my fourth month, the sickness is gone
and when I press my hand to the firm bump of my abdomen . . . it's miraculous. I have food cravings—an insatiable hunger that drags me into the kitchen at midnight, to
Edward's great amusement—in search of Cook's home-

made custard cream biscuits and Marmite spread, straight from the jar.

But there are other cravings as well. My desire to make Wessco prosperous and peaceful thrums through me with a whole new intensity. Because I'm not just doing it for my people; I'm doing it for this child and any that will come after. They will inherit from me whatever we make of this country—and I'm determined to pass on only the best.

Although we've announced the news to the public, I don't look terribly pregnant. At my advisor's insistence, the palace has hired stylists to dress me—who know just how to hide the growing bulge with the right pattern, jacket, belt. So that I don't appear awkward or vulnerable. Or weak.

Today it's a navy and white gingham shirtwaist dress and matching cardigan sweater, for my meeting with the Advising Council.

"Who wants to go into the casino business?" I ask them.

And, except for Alfie, by the looks on their faces, the answer is none of them. Bloody downers.

I stand, clapping my hands. "I have it on good authority that illicit gambling halls are all the rage amongst the aristocracy. You must have heard whispers about them."

Edward is my good authority—and he heard about it from his friend Donald Macalister. Apparently, the lords and ladies of Wessco get all dressed up in their finest gowns and jewels and masquerade ball masks to hide their identities—and attend parties where they drink Champagne and gamble thousands and thousands of dollars away at the tables.

Edward snuck out of the palace and attended one of the events himself, just a few evenings ago. He wouldn't let me come along that time—too dangerous, he'd said.

Because gambling is illegal.

But I'm going to change that.

"The next legislation I want to present to Parliament is to legalize gambling."

And there Tweedledum goes with the sign of the cross.

"Just think of it, my Lords. We could become the next hottest tourist destination."

"Like Monaco?" my uncle says.

"Exactly! And there will be licensing fees, regulatory fees, service jobs, tax revenue . . . the possibilities are endless."

Sheffield, Radcliffe and the Tweedles seem to start to warm to the idea. But Lord Norfolk is as cold as ice.

"Absolutely not. It's a sin. It's immoral."

"There are many activities that are considered immoral; we don't outlaw them all," I counter.

"You will be contributing to the degradation of our country," he argues.

"Rubbish!" I shoot back, rubbing my stomach absentmindedly. "It's going on anyway—right under our noses. By regulating it, we will prevent exploitation, and the government will get their piece of the pie."

He points his finger at me. "I do not support this!"

Edward stands, his voice hard and heavy as a sledgehammer.

"The Queen doesn't need your support, Norfolk. She

will have your obedience. If you can't give it, you'll step aside and we'll find a man who can."

"We, Prince Edward?" Norfolk taunts. "Do you now speak for the Queen?"

I don't hesitate, I don't balk . . . it's the easiest thing in the world to say. Because it's true. "He does speak for me. We are of one mind in all things. His word is as good as mine."

Edward's eyes dart to me—surprised.

Because this is . . . a big deal. It's meaningful. Power-ful. It matters. Edward knows it, and the council knows it, as well as I do. By giving Edward the power to speak for me, I'm surrendering a piece of myself to him. Sharing my authority as freely as I share my thoughts and my body with him.

But it's not difficult, letting go of these reins. Because Edward will never let me fall.

A few days later, we sit on the sofa in my office—together, but both of us are working. I turn to him, and tell him what's been on my mind.

"I want to make a new position on the advising coun-cil, for you. I want you to be my First Advisor. How do you feel about that?"

His eyes narrow, as he considers it. "Why do you want to do it?"

"Because it's true. You're the first person I go to for advice, whose opinion I trust the most . . . if the title fits, you should wear it."

A frown pulls at his lips.

"What is it?" I ask.

"They're going to say I hold sway over you."

"You do."

"Yes, but . . . you are the Queen. And I'm perfectly content to be the husband of the Queen. I don't want to be the reason you are diminished in anyone's eyes."

And this is why I'm the luckiest woman in the world. Why I want him to have the position, the title . . . because I want everyone to give him the respect he deserves, the respect he's earned . . . by being all he is.

I take Edward's hand. "We won't let that happen. We'll show them that we share this life, and I am a stronger Queen because of that. Because of you, because of us. And . . . if they still think what they will, I don't give a damn. As long as it can't hurt us, Edward, I don't care."

He mulls this over. And then he smirks.

"Are you sure it's not just because of my magnificent cock? I am outstanding at sticking it in you."

Laughter bubbles up my throat, but I hold it in. And look him right in the face. "Hmm . . . yes, you're right. It probably is just that, after all."

Edward tickles me—mercilessly. And I attack him back; he's ticklish under his arms. We roll around and our papers fall off the sofa and eventually we fall off the sofa too. And Edward settles me on top of him, so my knees straddle his waist and we end the day making sweet, laughing love right there on my office floor.

Seven months along in my pregnancy, it's safe to say that I've stopped walking. After all, no rational person can describe what I'm doing as walking.

It's a waddle. Just like a penguin. A queen penguin.

Edward thinks it's adorable. Crazy man. He asks me to walk around our room at night—the way some men ask their wives to do a "striptease"—just so he can watch me, with warmth in his eyes and that arousing smirk on his lips.

I'm waddling down the palace hall right now, with my darling husband walking beside me, on our way to Parliament. So I can sign the law that passed last week in both Houses, which legalizes gambling in Wessco.

Until the Archbishop of Dingleberry intercepts us.

"Good afternoon, Queen Lenora, Prince Edward." He bows his head.

"Archbishop." Edward nods for us both.

"Your Majesty, I've been wanting to speak with you about Princess Miriam. The Holy Father is very concerned about her behavior. He was hoping you could speak with her, bring her to heel."

Miri is in love. Again. With a butcher . . . or is it a baker?

Whatever went on between her and Winston all those months ago was brief and meaningless—as is her pattern, apparently. This is the fourth . . . no, fifth time she's been in love—I almost forgot about the young duke from Spain who still sends her flowers every single day.

My sister is in love with the idea of love. The rush and swirl of it.

But it's not real. Her feelings for these men dissipate like mist in the morning.

It's not the same emotion that throbs through me when I look at my Edward. If he lost his looks or his charm or his dirty, teasing voice, my devotion for him wouldn't waver. I'd still want to be near him, with him, caring for him, all the time. And I know deep inside, where knowledge is automatic and instinctual, that he feels the same for me.

But Miriam's adventures of the heart are harmless. They hurt no one. And the people adore her antics—they follow her love life like some dramatic real-life afternoon soap opera. All they need is someone to get amnesia and the comparison will be spot-on.

And maybe, if she keeps at it . . . one day she'll find a genuine love. I do truly wish that for her.

"Princess Miriam is a grown woman now," I tell the Archbishop. "She makes her own choices, and frankly, I have more important matters to address."

Edward and I try to walk away, but his voice stops us. Again.

"She is behaving like a wayward, wanton woman. The Pope is considering excommunicating her."

That stops me. And slowly, I turn toward him, lowering my voice.

"I see." I tap my fingers together. "Princess Miriam is independent and compassionate; those are good qualities for a princess to have. I don't always agree with her choices or views—but to be frank, I couldn't bloody stand *your* views through the years, and yet you're still here."

My words become clipped and cold and very, very final.

"So, if the Pope moves to excommunicate my sister or publicly shame her in any way, be sure to tell him I'm perfectly willing to follow old cousin Henry's example and start our own damn church."

The Archbishop gasps, and if the man had pearls he'd be clutching them.

"And I'll make Miriam the head of it."

Edward's mouth twists into a grin. "The Wessco Church for Wayward Wanton Women. It's got a ring to it."

"Indeed." I nod.

I address the Archbishop. "If the Holy Father wants to lose an entire country of Catholics, that's his prerogative, but from one head of state to another, I wouldn't recommend it. Be sure he understands. Now are we quite finished, Archbishop?"

I love the look of chastisement on a powerful man's face in the morning.

"Yes, Your Majesty."

"Very good."

My husband offers me his arm, and his approving chuckle, and together we walk . . . and waddle . . . away.

Edward

I T'S AFTER TEN IN THE evening when I return to the palace, after a dinner in honor of the visiting Canadian Prime Minister. I attended alone, as I've attended every function for the last month—the final month of Lenny's pregnancy. She's felt too ungainly and uneasy to get all decked out in her formal-wear and go out to major events. It's miserable work without her, but it's my job as the Prince of Wessco . . . and my job as the husband of Lenora.

I walk in the door of our bedroom, tugging at my tie —eager to get out of these clothes and have my wife give me a good, long welcome home.

"Evening, love," I tell her. "How was your night?"

"Uneventful." She sits at her vanity, brushing her hair. "Don't get undressed. I'd prefer for you to sleep in your own room tonight."

I stop unbuttoning my shirt and stare at her. Because never mind the ridiculous statement—her voice, the set of her mouth, the way she won't even glance at me . . . it's all wrong.

"This *is* my room."

"No, it's not. Your rooms are across the sitting area; you've just never used them until now."

I walk toward her, looking at her face closer. "Fucking you from two rooms over would be difficult—even for me."

She flinches.

"What's wrong with you, Lenny?" She was fine—better than fine—when I left. Happy. "What happened?"

She stands, rubbing the massive swell of her stomach over her powder blue nightgown. "I'm uncomfortable and not sleeping well and I just want to be left alone. Can't you do that for me?"

Her eyes are flat. As lifeless as her voice.

"I can't, actually."

"You mean, you won't."

"Correct, sweetheart—I absolutely won't. Not until you tell me what the hell is going on in that head of yours to bring this on."

I dip my chin, trying to catch her eyes. "What is it?"

Her eyes slide closed and her breath catches. But then her features harden, go blank . . . and out it comes.

"Winston came by to warn me . . . to show me some photos that will be published in the papers later this week."

"What sort of photos?"

"Photos of you."

She moves to the writing desk, picking up a stack of half a dozen black-and-white pictures. She holds them out, away from her body . . . like they're toxic.

I flip through them—one by one. And a cold ball of rage gathers in my stomach, growing thicker, larger, with each image.

They're grainy photos of me in a dim corner of a restaurant, holding the hand of a young blond woman. From the long angle, it appears we're gazing into each other's eyes. I toss them on the desk, where they scatter and flutter to the floor.

And I regard my wife. "Would you like an explanation?"

"I think I deserve one," she bites out.

"Her name is Daniella. She's the fiancée of Colin Penderson, the man I'm working with to locate facilities for the boys' club I'm creating in Thomas's honor." I point at the photograph. "The three of us met for a working dinner. I was shaking her hand—that's why I'm touching her. And if you look here," I jab my finger at the corner of one photo, "you'll see the buttons on Colin's coat, because he's not in the frame, but he's standing right there."

Lenny's expression barely changes at all. "That's a very . . . thorough story, Edward. A perfectly logical explanation."

"And you don't believe a word of it."

She shrugs. "I didn't say that."

"What exactly are you saying, Lenora? Do you think I'm fucking her—is that it?"

Those sharp silver eyes cut me right down to the bone.

"It's not like you would be the first. Every king of Wesco has had mistresses, and every prince his whores. There were even whispers about my father, though I don't believe they ever reached Mother's ears."

"I don't give a shit about princes or kings. If there's something you want to know, stop dancing around it and ask."

She raises her chin and straightens her spine. "Were you with her?"

"Was I *with her*?" I repeat, scathingly. Mockingly. "What a reserved way of phrasing it. So dignified, so sanitary. Is that where we are again? Back to the polite, proper words for things?"

I slam my fist on the desk and the lamp falls off, smashing on the floor.

"I'll take anything from you, Lenny. I'll take your frustration, your anger, your suspicion—hell, I'll even take your bloody hatred—but what I will not accept, *ever*, is your indifference. So don't put that goddamn mask on with me."

I walk around the desk, looking down on her, face-to-face. "Now let's try this again. Ask me what you want to know. The words are right there on your lips—you can taste them, can't you? Fucking ask."

And Lenora doesn't disappoint.

"Did you lie to me? Are you lying to me now?" She steps closer, her voice rising with each word. "Did you meet her? Did you kiss her? Did she touch you?" She shoves me with her hands. "Did you fuck her?" And beats at my chest with her fists. "Did you? Did you?"

I grab her wrists, trapping them between us. "No. *Never.*" The word growls out of me, between gnashing teeth. "You think I'd do that to you? That I'd obliterate my vows, betray our child . . . hurt you that way? Is that who you think I am?"

Her gaze slides toward the floor, but I grip her chin, forcing her eyes to mine.

"Look at me. If that's the kind of man you think I am, then what the fuck have we been doing all these months?"

And she searches my face, her eyes shimmering like two broken diamonds. Her mouth opens and closes, then eventually, the soft, strangled words come out.

"I don't think you're that kind of man."

I let her go, stepping back.

She looks down at the photos and one by one, tears fall down her cheeks. "But she's very beautiful. And I'm—"

"*You* are beautiful." I take her face in both my hands, gently now, cupping her cheeks and swiping her tears away with my thumbs. "Christ, you are all I see. Don't you know that? Even when you're not with me . . . you're all I can see."

Her face crumbles, collapses into a sob. And I pull her into my arms, pressing her against my chest.

"I do, I do know that," she cries. "I'm sorry."

"Shhh . . ." I pet her hair, rocking her.

Her hands twist in my shirt. "I'm sorry, Edward. I just . . . I don't know what's happening. I'm so tired and there's just so much . . .

"I know, I know."

So much responsibility, so much to do, so much weight, so much worry. Never ending and always.

"And I feel like I'm losing my mind. I—"

I tilt her head and cover her mouth with mine. Her lips are pillow soft and puffy from crying.

"It's all right. It's all right, now." I soothe her.

And I kiss her again and again until she settles. My lips trail over her face, swallowing her tears and drinking her pain. I stroke her tongue with mine, cup her breasts, kneading the sensitive mounds, stroking her nipples, coaxing moans from deep inside her.

I take her to the bed and strip her slowly. I drag my mouth, my hands, over every inch of her tender flesh, until she writhes, and nothing exists in the world except what I'm doing to her. Between kisses and moans, I promise and whisper that she is my beautiful girl, my lovely lass, my sweet, my only . . . my everything.

Because she is.

We lie on our sides, chest to back, and I make love to her with gentle, smooth thrusts from behind. Lenora reaches back for me, her hand on my hip, my thigh—pushing me forward, urging me deeper, to give her more.

And I do. Christ, I do.

I slide my arms beneath her and across her breasts, holding her shoulders, rocking up into her, until the pleasure ripples through us and we come at the same time—her, with a perfect, keening cry and me, with a hoarse, ragged groan.

I watch Lenora as she sleeps, with my hand on her stomach, feeling the moving life inside her—the life we made together. Her sweet lips part and her breath shudders in a hiccup, reminding me of the pain that pulled her under earlier. I throw the covers back, slip on my trousers and a half-buttoned shirt and tuck Lenny in snugly. Then I walk through the halls, down to the guard's quarters.

When I step inside, the men scurry up from the couches and chairs to stand and bow. My eyes go only to one man.

"I need a word," I tell Winston softly.

He follows me out across the hall to an empty room.

"Shut the door," I tell him, and he does. Then I stand in front of him, fists clenched at my sides, feet spread.

"For now, in this moment, I am not a prince and you are not a guard. We are just men—speaking as men—is that understood?"

His face and tone are impassive. "Yes, I understand."

"Good."

And then I pummel the bastard. Unleashing my rage and frustration, raining hard fists down on him like rocks.

"Motherfucking son of a bitch!"

He doesn't just take it. He blocks and jabs, we kick and crash, knock over a table and punch a massive, cracked, dent in the wall. In the end we're both bleeding, but I get leverage—and press him against the wall with my forearm to his windpipe.

I lean into his face so there is no mistaking me.

"Fill her head with that shit again and I'll kill you. Make her cry again . . . I'll fucking kill you slow." I press against his throat harder, my voice louder. "You will never have her. She belongs to me—she is mine. When I am dead and buried she will still be fucking mine."

I let the words sink in, and then I shove him back as I release him.

He gulps in air, hand to his throat, wheezing, "It's not about that."

I scoff, turning away.

"You wanted her to see those photos out in public?" he yells. "In front of a reporter? You wanted a journalist to catch her unaware and show them to her—now—when she's days from delivering? Is that your idea of how I should protect her?"

He shakes his head.

"No, no, I'll do my job properly. Protect her as she needs to be protected—truly—her and all who belong to her. I won't stop. You want to kill me for that one day, you're welcome to try."

I swipe at the blood on my lip with the back of my hand and point at him. "This happens again—you bring it to us, together. Not when she's alone—never again when she's alone. Do you hear me?"

He thinks on that, then he looks me in the eyes and nods. "Yes. All right, I agree."

A few days later, after the bile in my gut has had time to settle and the words don't taste quite so bitter, I lie in bed with Lenora. We're naked—just as I like her—with her head on my shoulder, her heavy breasts against my chest and her swollen stomach between us pushing into my side, my hand trailing up and down the curve of her spine.

"I want Winston to be made head of palace security. I want him in charge of everything. Covert programs, securing the palace grounds, trips abroad—he's to have all the resources he needs."

Lenora stares up at me. "You hate Winston."

My arm pulls her closer. "I hate him because he's in love with you."

She's quiet for a bit, tracing my stomach with her fingertip.

Then she sighs. "Edward—"

"It doesn't matter. He's the best at his job. He's completely devoted to you and to the Crown. He'll protect you at all costs and he'll be there to make sure you're safe when I can't." I rest my hand on her warm, tight stomach. "Both of you."

Her gaze glides over my face. "Is it difficult for you? To not be the one who protects us all the time?"

"I'm a man—of course it's difficult for me." I brush my hand through her long, dark hair, twining a strand around my finger. "I want to be everything for you, always. But that's not who we are. What kind of man would I be—what kind of husband, or father, or prince—if I let my pride put you at risk?"

"Not the man you are," she says softly.

"No, not the man I am."

Lenny picks up my hand and with the lips I still dream about, she places kisses at the tip of every finger and then in the very center of my palm.

"You are everything for me, Edward. Always. Never doubt that."

CHAPTER 19

Lenora

B Y THIS POINT, three days past my due date, all of me is uncomfortable, all the time—what with the small child literally sitting on my internal organs. So when the pain comes, slow and subtle twinges at first— a push of pressure—I don't recognize it for what it is.

But it keeps coming, more consistently, more rhythmically, and stronger each time—becoming sharp, squeezing, cramps . . . like my uterus is an orange being juiced.

Edward and I are walking through the garden, enjoying the breeze on a sunny summer day, when the strongest pain yet presses hard all around my middle.

"Oh!"

I bend at the waist, gripping Edward's arm. He cradles me through it, his hand on my back, holding me up, not letting me fall.

When it passes and I straighten up, I'm soaked from the waist down—the hem of my plaid dress, my legs, my shoes.

"Well . . . I guess that's it, then." Edward raises his eyebrows at the clear fluid still trickling down. "It's time."

Anticipation boils in my stomach, and I squeeze his hand.

"It's time."

When we arrive outside the Capella Suite, everything's in motion—people coming and going—excitement thick in the air. Oscar Pennygrove walks through the doors to the suite and Edward's jaw goes rigid.

"Why does Pennygrove get to go in and I don't?"

"Because this is how it's done. The way it's always been done."

Royals are born in palaces and castles. That's the way it works. Especially royals who are heirs to the throne. I'll have a doctor and nurses and top-notch medical treatment, but I won't have Edward. The men stay outside.

Love them or leave them, these are our traditions—a part of who we are, who my child will be.

And I may challenge Parliament and the Palace, and I will argue with my Advising Council—but what I won't do is toy with traditions that affect how my child may be viewed by the public or the Crown. That's a boat I will not rock.

This baby will be the leader of our country, an heir to my throne, and this birth will be by the book. The royal book.

"How it's always been done is bloody fucking stupid," Edward grumbles, nudging the rug with the toe of his boot.

"I know, but still . . ."

I finger his jaw, soothing the handsome, unhappy beast, bringing his eyes to mine.

"The next time I see you, I'll have a present for you— a new prince or princess."

His lips tug up in that handsome, boyish smile.

"Yes."

The head nurse, a husky dour-faced woman—because they always seem to be that way, don't they—gestures to the double doors of the suite. "Come along now, Your Majesty. We've taken care of everything."

A momentary jolt of fear hits me like a lightning bolt and I think Edward sees it. But the hall is full of people— assistants and guards and medical personnel—so he can't hold me the way I know he wants to. The way I want him to.

Instead he places a firm, lingering kiss to my forehead and points to the leather bench in the hall. "I'll be waiting, right there."

"No, no—you'll be bored. Go play squash or polo or . . . join a card game with Michael."

He looks into my eyes. "I'll be right there."

I give him a smile and squeeze his hand one last time. And then I let go.

Edward

I DON'T WORRY AT ALL for the first four hours. Not at eight hours or even twelve. I know enough about childbirth to understand that some births—especially first births—can take time. The servants bring food and drinks for me. Miriam and Alfie and Michael and Cora check in often, hoping for news. The Prime Minister stops by, some members of Parliament, as well as Sheffield and the Tweedle brothers—looking for updates.

At sixteen hours, I get uneasy.

At twenty, I'm concerned.

At, twenty-four, I start to worry. But the nurses come in and out of those double doors—nodding their heads and smiling that the Queen is fine, the baby is fine, all is well and things are moving right along.

Then twenty-eight hours have crawled by.

And thirty-two.

Thirty-six. And the nurses stop coming out altogether.

Thirty-eight hours after my Lenny went into that room, one finally emerges. And I unleash the sickening fear that's eating away at me like acid.

"What the fuck is happening in there?"

Her expression is tight, tart. "It's a hard labor, Prince Edward."

"What does that mean?"

"The doctor is doing all he can."

My hands fist and I want to tear the walls down.

"But what does that mean?"

And then the whole world stops—as a piercing, painful scream comes through those closed double doors. The kind that reaches inside you and twists your stomach . . . digs into your gut and claws at your soul.

"Edward!"

My feet fly toward the doors.

"Your Highness, you're not supposed to—"

And burst through them.

"Holy Christ."

It doesn't look like a room in a palace—it's all stark white and metal now. The walls are covered by sterile sheets; the nurses and the doctor are draped in white, their faces obscured behind masks and caps. There's a harsh bright light, a heart monitor, machines, a steel cabinet and trays of sharp, stainless-steel instruments. Pennygrove stands in the corner, covered in white—waiting, watching, and silent as stone.

Lenora lies flat on a table in the center, her legs raised and locked into stirrups at the ankles. There's a white sheet below and over her, and a curtain across her waist, hiding her view of the doctor and the lower half of her own body. The air is stifling—suffocating with the copper scent of blood and the heavy crush of fear.

"Edward," Lenora sobs, reaching for me.

And I go to her, grabbing her hand, crouching down close. I touch her face and smooth her hair. "I'm here, I'm here, I'm right here. I'm right here with you."

Her lip is crusted with dried blood, where she's bitten it through. And that small, insignificant wound wrecks me. Her face is a mess of pain and tears—her eyes filled with them, her cheeks flowing, her breaths coming and going in shuddered, stuttering gasps.

"They want . . . they want to put me asleep . . . and I didn't want to be alone."

My vision burns, blurs because she's hurting so much. And she's so afraid.

"You're not alone, Lenora. I'm right here, right here with you." I can't stop touching her. I want to shield her with my body, crawl onto that table and hold her until she's calm. I want to pick her up and leave this place—take her far away where none of this can touch her or hurt her ever again.

"It'll all be much easier once you're asleep, Your Majesty. More pleasant." The doctor's formless voice comes from behind the curtain.

"The baby, Edward." Lenora squeezes my hand tight. "Promise me you'll love him."

I stroke her face. "Of course I will. I promise. I already do."

"And you must tell him." Her voice breaks. "You have to tell him every day. It's very important. He'll be so sad inside if he doesn't know."

A lump of gravel clogs my throat, strangling me. "I will, I swear—I'll tell him every day." I kiss her hand, her knuckles. "We'll tell him together."

She closes her eyes then, breathing deep, slowly expanding her lungs. Wetness clings to her lashes like swollen raindrops, but when she opens them again, she's calmed.

Resigned.

The kind of resignation people have when they don't know what's around the corner, but they've already accepted whatever it may be.

She presses her hand to my face. "I love you, my Edward. I've loved you all this time. I was afraid . . . but I'm not afraid anymore."

I've tried to show Lenora all she means to me—I've worked at it, because actions always mean more than words. And I've given her words—sweet words, candid words, fervent words . . . but I've never given her those words. I didn't know they mattered so much to her.

"Lenora, I—"

But the nurse has already placed the mask on her face and Lenny is so drained, she goes right under in the blink of an eye.

"She's out, Doctor," the nurse says.

His voice changes to snapping, clipped commands. Urgent orders.

"Suction."

"Clamp."

"Forceps."

I don't let go of her hand. And I don't stop looking at her. Her coloring is terrible . . . her lips the color of chalk. I watch her breathe because there's a horrific, stabbing worry that if I look away, she might stop.

I hear the drone of their voices, the humming quick chatter of the nurses and doctor. And a slap of wet skin smacks the air.

And then . . . a baby's cry. It's loud and lusty and absolutely fucking furious.

"Wessco has a new prince," the doctor says.

Wetness streaks from my eyes, down my face, and I don't even care enough to wipe it away. I move in close to her, whispering, "It's a boy, Lenny. It's a boy. We have a son."

She doesn't answer. She doesn't move.

And the realization seeps in that something is wrong in this room. Off in the air. A new, healthy prince has just been born, but there is no sense of joy. The nurse's eyes above their masks are darting and alert. There is tension, apprehension . . . but no celebration.

Slowly, I stand and look over the curtain down below Lenora's waist.

And the bones in my chest contract and collapse and crumble to dust.

I've been to war. I've watched men die because they lost too much blood, and what Lenora is losing now . . . is too, too much. It soaks the table beneath her and puddles on the floor. The doctor is hunched between her legs, working with quick movements, and the nurse snaps instruments into his gloved palm—but nothing he does slows it down.

"Is she hemorrhaging?"

"You need to leave this room," the doctor answers, without raising his eyes.

A nurse takes my arm. "Come with me, Your Highness. You can hold the Prince in the next room."

I jerk my arm away, willing strength and authority into my voice.

"What's happening?"

"Go with your son, Prince Edward."

"I'm not going anywhere until you tell me what's happening to her!"

"The Queen is losing too much blood," the doctor

snaps, still focused on his work. "Her uterus is not contracting; there may be a rupture. If the bleeding can't be stopped, I have to operate and I cannot do that with you in here—so get out!"

"Please, Your Highness . . ." a nurse soothes. "Let him help her. Come on now. This way."

And I don't fight. I let them lead me from the room. Because I'm not there anyway. I'm somewhere else.

I'm in the woods around Anthorp Castle, watching a beautiful girl on a horse trying to catch the wind.

I'm in the foyer, a laugh in my throat, watching her raise her brow and cross her arms . . . completely enthralled already.

I'm holding her hand on a blanket.

I'm kissing her in her office.

I'm not afraid.

I'm kneeling for her in her bedroom.

I'm watching the lightning flash in her eyes on a rooftop.

I'm giving her a ring, waiting at the altar . . . loving her beneath a magical sky.

"Edward? What's happened?"

Alfie Barrister's worried voice calls me back. I look around the dark paneled walls of the hall outside the Capella Suite, where I'm sitting on a bench beside Michael. Miriam is here too, standing next to Alfie.

"Edward?" Michael coaxes.

"There were . . . complications," I say. "The doctor's sorting it out."

I stare down at my hands, not seeing them. I see only the mistakes, the regrets, playing out like a soundless reel of film.

"I was cruel to her when Thomas died. I . . . the things I said . . . that she didn't care. Why did I say that?"

"Edward . . ."

My voice is a distant shadow. "And I left. I left her for weeks."

"Edward."

"All that time, all those days, I'll never get them back now. I'll never . . ."

"Edward!" Miriam squeezes my hands, snapping me out of it, bringing my eyes to hers. "She's strong. Our girl is strong. You have to hold on to that."

A nurse approaches, standing just behind Miriam, speaking to me. "Would you like to hold the baby, Your Highness?"

"No, not yet. I'll . . . I'll hold him when his mother holds him."

"I'll sit with the baby." Miriam stands. "Lenora wouldn't want him to be alone."

She follows the nurse to the next room over, but the door is open and I can hear as she talks to my son.

"Hello there, little Prince. I'm your Auntie Miriam. We're going to have lots of fun—I'm going to teach you all the things you're not supposed to know." The sound of wetness rises in her throat as her voice clogs and cracks. "Your mummy has been counting the days to meet you. She's just . . . she's just been held up a bit longer. So . . . you and I will sit here together and wait for her."

And that's what we do. Each of us. For the next few hours, we wait.

She looks like a fairytale princess under a spell. Like Snow White after she bit the apple and fell into a deep sleep—with her dark hair, pale skin, thick lashes, silver nightgown and lips that have regained a hint of their rosy hue.

The doctor was able to stop the bleeding in time. Lenora needed three transfusions to make up for the blood she lost, but they didn't have to operate. They moved her to an adjoining room for recovery—a more fitting room—with velvet drapes and antique furniture and a four-poster bed with satin sheets and mounds of pillows. And now she sleeps, from the anesthesia, from the blood loss, from the trauma of the birth.

I sit at her bedside—her thoroughly enamored prince. I wait and watch and will her to wake up. My stubborn girl takes her time, of course.

But eventually, she sighs deeply and opens her bright eyes, blinking up at the ceiling. Her head turns toward me and before she makes a sound, I kiss her hand and give her the words.

"I love you, Lenora. I have loved you all this time and I will love you for all the time after this. And you will know it, every day. Every day."

Her lips spread into a dazzling smile. And her voice is soft and solemn. "I love you, Edward. And I promise to tell you every day. Every day."

And then her hand moves to her stomach and she looks down. "The baby?"

"He's a boy." I grin, my whole body finally sinking

into the elation of it.

"A boy?" She laughs with the joy of it. "We have a little boy?"

I nod. "Do you want me to have them bring him to you?"

"Oh, yes, please."

I ring for the nurse and prop Lenny up with a dozen pillows behind her. And they bring him in, wrapped in a blue downy blanket, and place him in her arms.

And she gazes down at him with so much delight, so much pure, devoted love, it's hard to breathe. Lenora pats the bed beside her and I slide on next to her, wrapping my arm around her back, tucking her close.

And together, we look at our boy—his precious nose and perfect tiny mouth and delicate eyebrows and his little cheek that's too soft to be believed.

"He has your hands," she says.

"He has your chin," I notice.

Lenora's eyes are shiny and wet. "Look at him, Edward. He's so beautiful."

And he is—I've been all over the world and he's the most beautiful thing I've ever seen.

She tips her face up to me. "So . . . what will you name your son?"

"You want me to name him?"

"Yes. He will get his title from me, he will be a Pembrook, but the rest . . . should come from you."

I look down at him, and then to Lenora, and my heart goes tight with all the devotion it holds for them. "I've been thinking . . . I would very much like to call him Thomas."

Lenny's eyes fill with tears, and I touch her cheek.

"But I don't want to make you sad."

She shakes her head, and the tears trickle even as she smiles.

"No, I'm not sad, I swear. It's perfect. Our Thomas . . . it's completely perfect."

CHAPTER
20

Lenora

Three weeks later

THERE'S A CLOCK ON THE nursery wall decorated with carved images of Humpty Dumpty, and the cat and mouse from Hickory Dickory Dock, and the cow that jumps over the moon. The tick-tock of it is like a soothing metronome . . . but I don't hear it. Not really.

Because when I'm nursing my baby, and gently rocking with him in the rocking chair, everything else just fades away. My advisors cautioned against breastfeeding Thomas myself. *"You'll have no time,"* they said. *"Too burdensome,"* they warned. *"Unseemly,"* they criticized. *"You're a Queen not a dairy cow."*

But one of the perks of being Queen is every once in a while, you get to make your own damn rules—and this was one I was making and keeping.

I run my finger over the dark satin strands of Thomas's hair, mesmerized. I relish in the feel of holding him skin to skin, and in the thump of his little heartbeat beneath my palm when I place my hand on his chest. His suckling slows and his eyes drag closed.

I can look at him for hours, basking in the wonder of his every sigh and breath.

I thought I understood how this would feel, I thought I knew, but motherhood is like how Edward once described war—surprising. Something that has to be experienced to be truly understood. The depth of my love for Thomas astounds me. It makes me feel invincible and . . . terrified.

Because there is nothing—*nothing*—I would not do for this boy.

Holding him is like holding my whole heart in my hand, but even more precious. And yet at the same time, there's a peace in it. A calm, perfect assurance that I am exactly where I'm supposed to be, doing precisely what I was always meant to do.

There are three certainties in my life, three things I know to the very bottom of my soul: I was born to be a Queen, I was born to be Edward's wife, and now, I was born to be Thomas's mum.

And for the rest of my days, if I never know anything more, those will be enough.

"It's time to go, love."

I look up at the sound of Edward's voice and see the soft tenderness that's always in his eyes when he watches us.

I slip my nipple from Thomas's sleeping mouth, pat

myself dry with a cloth and tuck my breast into my bra.

"Already? I lost track of the time."

"You always do." Edward smiles, lifting Thomas from my arms, so I can button up the top of my pleated periwinkle coat dress.

And then I do some watching of my own. Because seeing Edward hold our boy, watching him press a soft kiss to his little forehead—it pulls at a deep, primal part of me—and there's nothing on earth that could ever be sexier.

He lays Thomas in his ivory bassinet, winds the mobile and the soft, twinkling sounds begin to play. Then Edward turns to me, adjusting my wide collar and white spinner hat before handing me my short gloves.

And he leans down and kisses me with his firm, warm lips. I brush my nose against his, breathing in the scent of sunshine and summer and love.

"You look perfect." He tells me.

I straighten his burgundy striped tie, and reach up to brush the broad shoulders of his sharp, dark gray suit.

"You look perfect too." I tell him back.

Edward offers me his arm and we pass the nurse on our way out of the nursery.

"We'll return in about two hours," Edward says.

She dips her head. "Yes, Your Highness, Your Majesty."

We walk down the curved staircase through the grand marble foyer, outside to the waiting car that takes us to the ceremony for the yearly adjournment of Parliament. The MP's follow their own work calendar with a one-month holiday between the final and first official session.

One of the Monarch's duties is to begin and end the Parliamentary year with a blessing and a wine toast. Possibly several toasts if things go well.

It's how we roll.

And so, with Edward just behind my right shoulder, I stand beneath that familiar mural-painted ceiling as the Houses of Parliament and the Lords of the Advising Council stand and face me. All the friends and foes I've made over the course of my reign so far—allies and enemies that I'm sure will swap places and then switch back again as time goes on—because that's how royalty and politics and government work.

I hold my glass in my hand. "It has been a year of change and challenges and incredible, unexpected blessings." I tell them, my voice ringing with clarity and confidence.

I glance quickly back at my Edward, meeting his eyes, then face front again.

"Wessco has a new Prince and a new heir and together we stand on solid, secure ground as we turn our eyes toward the future."

I look at the faces of these ancient men, so set in their stubborn ways. My Parliament.

A mixture of pride and exhilaration surges in my chest as I recognize their expressions. The same countenances they wore when they looked at my father year after year. Some of them gaze at me with support and friendship, some with resentment or annoyance, but all of them —*all of them*—with respect.

For me. At last. Their Queen.

"We will do amazing things, my Lords . . . I can feel

it in my bones. I look forward to working with you next year and all the years that will come after."

I raise my wineglass. "For the good and glory of Wessco."

A wave of arms raise their glasses in return.

"For the good and glory of Wessco."

And we all drink.

My husband steps up beside me then and his glittering dark green gaze touches on me a moment before he turns toward our audience and lifts his glass.

And his rich voice resonates around the room. "Long live the Queen."

"Long live the Queen!" The Lords of the realm repeat and we drink some more.

Edward may have said, "Long live the Queen," but what I hear between his words, in his tone and in the way he looks at me is . . . *I love you.*

He gives me a wicked wink. And I clink my glass to his.

"Cheers."

One month later

One afternoon, Edward and I are at the dining table in the private quarters of the palace, enjoying an early lunch together.

"Miriam sent a letter," I tell him, holding up an envelope with my sister's familiar, bubbly writing.

Edward wipes his mouth with his napkin. "How is she enjoying Greece?"

Miriam got married. Again. Last month to a Greek Prince, fourth from the throne. I have no idea if it will last and frankly I don't think she does either. But she seemed happy, so for now, that's enough.

I show him a photograph of Miriam and her husband on a lovely sandy beach, with white-tipped waves crashing behind them. "So far, so good."

And that's when a dark-haired lad strolls right into our dining room. It's an unusual thing to happen, but he looks harmless enough—young, perhaps about thirteen—with a newsboy cap on his head and his hands in his pockets . . . and an unhappy frown on his face. He gazes at the paintings on the walls and the intricate plaster on the ceiling with one good eye and one wandering lazy one.

"And who might you be?" Edward asks.

"I'm Fergus, Prince Edward." He bows to us both. "Queen Lenora. It's an honor to meet you."

I raise a brow at the disagreeable-looking boy.

"Hello, Fergus. How did you end up in our dining room?"

"My dad's Jonathon, the upstairs butler. He made me come with him to start training me up. Hoping I'll earn a place in the household when little Prince Thomas has a place of his own."

"How old are you, my boy?" I ask.

"I'm ten, but I'll be eleven in the summer."

"Only ten? But that scowl makes you look older.

Don't you think you're a little young to be so cranky?"

The lad shrugs. "I'm not cranky . . . that's just my resting face, Your Majesty. Only one God gave me—can't do nothing about it."

"How's the butler training going so far?" Edward asks.

The staff of the palace consider it the highest honor to serve the royal family.

Fergus shrugs again. "Could be worse."

Despite the disgruntled disposition, there's something very genuine about his attitude. Honest and real. That's still a rare commodity around here.

Fergus's father, however, doesn't seem to appreciate those attributes.

"Fergus!" Jonathon hisses as he steps through the door from the kitchen. "I told you to stay in the kitchen, you idiot-boy!" He turns to us and in a much more measured tone, says, "My deepest apologies, Your Majesty and Your Highness, that he's disturbed your meal."

Edward holds up his hand. "He's fine. Let him stay."

Jonathon dips his head, then takes his place standing along the wall. And Edward asks the young Grumpy Gus, "How would you treat my son if you were a member of his staff?"

"Well . . . I'd make sure he had everything he needed —that's a good servant's job. But I'd want to treat him like a regular bloke as much as I could. The way I figure it, he'll have the whole world clamoring to kiss his arse— pardon my French, Queen Lenora. It might be good for a little prince to be treated like one of us normals, once in a while . . . even if it's just inside his own house."

My husband smiles at me. "I like him."

And I nod back, in agreement.

"Tell you what, lad," Edward says. "You mind your dad and complete your training, and when you come of age, I'll make you Butler of Guthrie House." He taps the table. "That's a promise. What do you think of that?"

Fergus takes a few moments to think it over. Then he nods, spits in his palm and holds it out.

"I accept your offer, Prince Edward."

Edward spits in his own hand, then he and Fergus—the future cranky Butler to the Crown Prince of Wessco—shake on it.

Three months later

The sun is just setting when I walk into the front parlor and look at the canvas Michael's painting. "Oh, that's coming along very nicely. Well done, Michael."

"I look like a horse's arse," Edward grumbles from the other side of the canvas. He poses for the portrait in a leather chair, wearing a perfectly fitted gray pinstripe vest and trousers with a dark blue tie and the cuffs of his white shirt rolled up just a bit. He's leaning back, his strong arms crossed with a smirk on his lips. Well . . . a smirk when his lips aren't too busy complaining.

He hated the idea from the very start. I had to bribe him with all sorts of dirty, shocking promises to get him to agree . . . although I suspect he would've agreed anyway.

The dirty, shocking promises just made it all more fun.

"Stop pouting! You look devastatingly handsome," I shoot back.

"I have a new filthy word for you Lenora—*taint*. That's exactly what I feel like."

I roll my eyes and shake my head. "This portrait is going to hang right behind my desk in my office, so I can look at my magnificent husband whenever I like."

"That reminds me." Michael puts his paintbrush down. "The portrait you requested is ready, Edward."

He walks over to us as Michael slips something out of his pocket. It's an oval locket made of gold—about the size of a half dollar. My husband opens it and inside is a tiny painting. Of me. My hair is down, framing my face in dark waves, as I gaze back over my shoulder with sparkling eyes. I look jubilant.

I look . . . beautiful.

Edward whistles. "Outstanding." He smacks Michael's arm. "It's perfect, mate. Thank you."

"How did you do this?" I ask Michael, but Edward answers.

"It was a candid shot, before they did your hair up on our wedding day—one of the hundreds and hundreds of photographs that were taken."

"I remember." I smile.

"The Palace was going to discard it, but I saved it and passed it to Michael so he could paint this for me."

Warm, wanted, tender tingles spark across my body —from the crown of my head to the tips of my toes and everywhere in between. It's how it feels when Edward swoops me off my feet . . . and in a way, that's just what he's doing now. But with words instead of his arms.

"What are you going to do with it?"

He reaches over and kisses me, quick but soft. "The same thing I do with all things that are most precious to me." He taps his front shirt pocket. "Keep it close."

And a year later, Edward would add a lock of Thomas's dark hair to the locket.

Edward

THAT NIGHT, Thomas lies in the center of our bed, swinging his arms and kicking his little legs. I can't stop the smile that comes to my lips as I watch him. Or the rush of possessive tenderness that drums in my chest as I look at Lenora sitting on the bed with him.

She smiles down at our sweet boy, delighted by his every move. "Sometimes I can't believe he's ours."

Her hair is down, long; we're both ready for bed. Lenora has given Thomas his final feeding and the night nurse will come to collect him soon, to put him down for the night. But these calm, quiet hours before then, that's part of our time with him.

Our time all together.

"I think I understand my father more now," Lenny says, picking Thomas up and cradling him in her delicate arms. "Why he was how he was with me."

I sit next to her on the bed, massaging the back of her neck gently.

"How do you mean?"

"He was older when I was born. He knew he only had ten, maybe twenty years with me—to teach me all the things I would need to know. I think that's why he treated me more like a protégé than a daughter." She runs the tip of her finger down Thomas's round cheek. "If I knew my time with him would be so short, I might be hard on him too. Because I would want him to be strong, like steel, so no one could ever hurt him. So they couldn't bend him or break him. This life, Edward—it's so easy to be broken by it."

Thomas's little mouth stretches into a yawn. Lenny kisses his cheek, then leans her head on my shoulder, gazing at him, her voice wistful.

"But we're young. We'll have years and years and years with Thomas. We'll be strong for him and protect him. And he will go to school and have friends. And he will run and play and laugh . . ."

"And he will swing," I finish for her.

When she looks at me, I stroke her cheek with my thumb. "I'll have swings hung in every corner of the gardens so you and our boy can swing anytime you like."

She smiles softly. "I think my swinging days are past, Edward."

"Not if I have anything to say about it." I press a kiss

to her pretty lips and wrap my arm around her. "They're only just beginning, Lenny."

EPILOGUE

Edward

Two years later

WE SIT ON A YELLOW checkered blanket, a full picnic basket and a bottle of chilled Champagne, courtesy of Cook, waiting nearby. I'm in my swim trunks and Lenora's in an outstanding red polka-dot swimsuit number that teases glimpses of all the best parts. Security is here, but far enough away that it doesn't feel like they're really here.

It feels like it's just us.

Our family.

Thomas runs along the shoreline, chasing the waves, with Nanny never far behind. The air is warm, but the water is brisk—though he doesn't care. Our little Prince plays hard, swings high, laughs loud and swims like a fish.

I hear Nanny squawk out a gasp and turn just in time to see Thomas wizzing into the ocean. I chuckle, and Lenora does too.

"He is utterly and completely a boy," she says, with adoring amusement.

Then she closes her eyes, tilts her face up to the sun and breathes deeply, a contented smile on her lips. She looks peaceful. Happy. Thoroughly loved, and it's a fantastic look on her. My chest tightens with my own soul-deep happiness—and pride—because I like to think I had something to do with that.

"Penny for your thoughts?"

Lenny turns her smile toward me and it's blinding. Then she gazes up the ridge toward Anthorp Castle, out to the forest, then back down across the beach and rocks and crashing waves.

"This is my favorite place in the whole wide world."

She says it with a sigh, almost reverently.

I rest down on my elbow next to her. Close enough to feel the heat on her sun-warmed skin and smell the lilacs in her hair.

"This old place? Why?"

"Close your eyes."

When I don't immediately comply, she puts her hands over my eyes—and I nip at her thumb with my teeth.

"Go on," she laughs throatily.

And right up there with Thomas's laughter . . . it's my very favorite sound.

"Close your eyes."

When I do, she tells me, "Now listen."

I do as I'm told for a few seconds, then I peek one eye open, meeting her soft gaze.

"I don't hear anything."

"Exactly. Nothing but waves and birds and the swaying trees. No people or duties, no cameras or press. Nothing for miles . . . but space. I can think here, I can breathe here, I can be myself here."

She lifts her hand and presses it tenderly to my jaw. "The me who wants to do nothing more than to be with you and Thomas every moment, of every day, for always."

I take her hand and kiss her palm.

"I love that you. But, then again, I love all the you's. Don't think I'll ever be able to pick a favorite."

"*All* the me's?"

I kiss her nose.

"Every one."

Lenora is doubtful.

"What about the me that's stubborn?"

"Adorable."

"Bossy?"

"Ravishingly sexy."

"And the me when I'm angry?"

"Even sexier. Makes me want to put that chastising mouth of yours to better use and find the nearest sofa or wall to work off all that passionate fury."

She laughs again—and I pull her closer, so we're both on our sides facing each other, just inches apart. My voice is rough and warm, like the sand beneath us.

"And when you're happy . . . fucking hell . . . I can't take my eyes off you."

She tilts her head, gazing up at me.

"I love all your you's too, Edward. My adventurer, my protector, my wonderful, wicked handsome prince."

"Good to hear it."

My hand travels over her outer thigh, across her hip, sliding up to the skin of her rib cage. My thumb strokes back and forth, slowly, just below her breast. And I'm about to kiss her—when a wet, two-year-old sand monster pounces onto the blanket between us.

"Mummy, Daddy—look!"

He holds up a small coral shell in his chubby hand—and Lenora and I react like he's struck gold.

"Good find, lad!"

"That's wonderful, darling!"

Thomas's thick, long-lashed gray-green eyes bounce between us.

"Swim? Come swim!"

I nod and scoop him up with one hand and pull Lenny up from the blanket with the other. And the three of us splash and swim and find a treasure trove of seashells until the sun goes down.

Late that night, a shifting in the bed wakes me. I open my eyes to see my Lenora slipping out from beneath the covers and drifting over to the window. For a moment I just look at her—her hair flows loose down her back in dark, shiny spirals. She's bathed in a halo of silver moonlight—it shimmers on her nightgown and kisses her pale, perfect skin with an iridescent glow. She's ethereal—a heavenly creature and a sin-tempting spirit all in one—and she takes my breath away.

I get out of bed and press up behind her at the window, wrapping my arms around her waist and pressing a soft kiss to her shoulder.

"Are you all right, love?"

She leans back against my bare chest.

"I had a dream."

"Mmm . . . was it the kind where we're naked?"

The vibration of her laughter passes between us.

"No, not that kind of dream."

"Pity." I rest my lips against her temple. "Tell me about it anyway."

Lenora's voice goes airy, faraway, like she's still dreaming.

"I was in a garden having tea, and all around me there was laughter and love and happiness. I could feel it in the air, like the warmth of the sun. And there were children . . . so many of them. There was a sweet girl with beautiful dark blue eyes and they called her Anna, for Mother. And there was a handsome little boy named Langdon and another named Edward . . . and he had your hair."

"Those are good names for good lads."

"And there was another girl—a tiny thing, but she was plucky. She copied every move I made." Lenora chuckles. "Even the way I held my teacup."

She shakes her head slightly, her voice soft. "And it felt, not exactly like they were ours, but still . . . like they belonged to us. To you and me, Edward."

Lenora turns in my arms, her eyes round and silver in the moonlight as she looks up at me.

"Do you think that's silly?"

I brush the back of my hand across her cheek, just to feel its softness.

"No, I don't think it's silly, sweet girl. I think it's a beautiful dream. A beautiful destiny. I think that laughter and happiness and all those lovely little tykes will be our dynasty. They will be the joys we leave behind."

I bend my head and press my lips to her silken neck, speaking the words against her skin.

"Mine and yours, forever and always."

Her hands skim up my arms, to my shoulders, then around my neck.

"Mine and yours, forever and always," she whispers, pressing her body against mine, leaning into my touch.

My wife, my love, my Queen . . . my life. I kiss her deeply—our tongues dance and our moans mingle. And then I sweep her up into my arms.

"Let's get started on them, straight away."

Lenny throws her head back and laughs as I carry her toward the bed.

"What a marvelous idea . . ."

She peppers my jaw with kisses, working her way to my mouth. Then she presses her lips to mine with all the sweetness and passion and tenderness she has to give.

Life can be an unpredictable, cruel beast—but I know down to the marrow of my bones that whatever comes our way, whatever happinesses or heartbreaks are in store for us, we'll face them together. Hand in hand, heart to heart, side by side, Lenora and Edward.

And when our bodies are dust in the ground and our souls are joined in whatever life comes after this one, the legend of our story and the echo of our love will live on forever.

The End

Turn the page to enjoy,

Royally Raised,

a bonus short story set 20 years

after the events of *Royally Matched*.

ROYALLY RAISED

New York Times Bestselling Author

EMMA CHASE

Henry

"I T'S UNCANNY."

"It's bizarre."

"It's fascinating. Look at her."

My brother, Nicholas, gestures towards my daughter, Jane, at the far end of the glittering, gold ballroom. At nineteen-years-old, Jane takes after my wife, Sarah, in beauty and build—dark cascading hair, a lovely face, long, lithe limbs, sparkling brown eyes with speckles of my green. She smiles and mingles with the press, as she glides towards the podium to answer questions about the newly established scholarship fund in honor of my grandparents, Queen Lenora and Prince Edward.

But her personality and demeanor are distinctly un-like Sarah. Or me.

"She's poised, self-assured, commanding even." Nicholas says as she takes to the podium—chin high, back straight, the very embodiment of royalty in action. "She's nothing like we were at her age."

"I know." I reply, bewildered. "Every responsibility I give her, every duty—she absorbs like a sponge. She thrives off of it."

"Mmm." Nicholas grunts. "All your years of reck-lessness, all Sarah's sweetness, and somehow you two managed to give birth to . . ."

"Granny." I finish for him.

"Yeah."

It's the damnedest thing.

"She'll make one hell of a queen, though." Nicholas offers.

"She will." I nod, with pride. But then I frown. "It sucks that I'll be too dead to see it."

My brother grins. "You could retire when she's a bit older. Step down. Live out your golden years away from the headaches of the capital and politics in one of the country estates with your wife."

For the first part his life, my older brother was all about tradition and following the rules, and living up to every royal expectation. And then he fell in love—and that love changed everything.

I shake my head. "There'd be too many comparisons. Too much second guessing of her choices and what I would've done. I won't do that to her. When Jane takes the throne it will be hers and hers alone."

As Jane begins to take questions, we turn our silent attention back to her. Until my sister-in-law slips into the room and up to my brother's side wearing a shimmery, knee-length red dress and strappy heels, her hair a mass of wild black curls. Even in her late forties, Olivia couldn't be described as anything less than a full-on knockout.

"Hey, guys." She whispers.

Nicholas's arm slips around her lower back, tucking her against his side.

"You're looking especially lovely, Olive." I say.

She gives me a glowing smile. "Thank you, Henry. It's date night. Date weekend, actually. We're going to Cannes and I can't wait." Her dark blue eyes go soft as she gazes up at my brother. "Are you ready?"

They lived the first five years of their marriage in the states—New York—with occasional visits to Wessco. That changed when Olivia became pregnant with twins, and the whole world seemed to go mad with royal baby fever. For her safety, they came home to the security of the palace walls—but then, after Langdon and Lillyanna were born, Nicholas and Olivia chose to stay and raise their children here. A few years later, they welcomed a third child—Thoedore—to their family.

The day I was crowned King, I asked my brother to become my First Advisor. Lucky for me, he agreed and although they have their own estate, they live most of the year at their apartments here in the Palace.

Nicholas grins wickedly. "Two glorious days alone with my stunning wife? Of course I'm ready, my bags are already in the car."

Olivia giggles, like a school girl in love.

Then she glances towards my daughter. "Janey looks great up there." And she snorts. "God, she reminds me of your Grandmother."

That seems to be the theme of the day.

Nicholas glances at his watch. "We should get moving." He nods, smacking my arm. "Henry."

"Have a good weekend, you two."

After they make a quiet exit, I fold my arms across my chest, lean back against the wall and watch Jane do what she does so well.

Until a reporter begins a question with, "Lady Jane —"

And my first-born cuts him off—right at the balls.

"Princess."

"I'm sorry?" the reporter asks.

Jane sighs, quick and impatient. "I am the Crown Princess of Wessco, the heir apparent—which means when you address me it will be as Princess Jane or Your Royal Highness. Perhaps, one day when you can get that right, I may stoop to answering your question."

Oh boy

She turns her head away to the rest of the crowd. "Next."

The same reporter lifts his hand tentatively. "Princess Jane—"

"Uh-uh," Jane raises her finger, like a sharp-voiced school teacher scolding a naughty pupil. "No interrupting. Shush." She dismisses him again. "Next."

A dozen memories from my adolescence come rushing back, and I shiver.

It's downright fucking spooky.

Later, I sit behind the desk in the Royal Office, the painting of my proud, elegant grandmother in her crown and robes hanging on the wall behind me. There's a comfort in its presence, like she's still here with me, having my back as she always did, in her own way. Grandmother and Grandfather raised me and Nicholas after our parents died, and the full appreciation of them—of their support and guidance—didn't really hit me until they were both gone.

And I missed them so much—I still do.

There's a knock on the door.

"Come in."

My oldest daughter pops her head in. "You wanted to see me, Dad?"

I set the document I was reviewing aside. "Yes, sweets. Sit down."

Her black designer slacks make a swishing sound as she glides into the office. She takes the chair across from me, folding her legs, her face serene and smiling.

"I wanted to talk to you about the press conference earlier."

"It was fantastic, wasn't it?" Jane's eyes glance to the painting. "I think Great-Granny would be pleased that another worthy cause has been created in her and Great-Grandfather's honor."

I smile tightly. "Yes, she would be. For the most part, you did very well, Jane—I'm proud of you."

Her pretty head tilts. "For the most part?"

"Well . . . there was that one interaction, with the journalist who misaddressed you. I wanted to discuss that with you."

"What about it?"

"You could've just let it pass."

She shrugs. "But I was right. He was wrong. Now he knows for next time."

This is going to be harder than I thought.

"While that's technically true, your response to him came off as rather . . . ," I swirl my hand, searching for the right word. ". . . entitled sounding."

Her brow furrows. "But I am . . . entitled. That's the point, isn't it? I'm entitled to the position, by birth. That's what is means to be the heir. Why shouldn't I act like it?"

"Just because you can do or say something, doesn't mean you should. You are the Crown Princess—your attitude reflects on all of us. You must behave," I choke out the next word, ". . . *properly.*"

Then I glance at the ceiling and brace for the lightning bolt that's sure to come down from the sky and strike me right in the arse. Because . . . the irony.

When it doesn't come, I continue.

"You should be humble, Jane. Show gratitude."

My daughter scoffs. "Why does a journalist deserve *my* gratitude?"

"He deserves your respect. They all do—they're our subjects, our citizens."

She rolls her eyes. *Cheeky*—and not in a cute way.

"I used to think I didn't need the press either, and I was wrong. When your day comes, this will go much easier for you if the press and the people are on your side."

And now she huffs. And folds her arms unhappily.

When our children were young, Sarah and I decided against spankings, it wasn't how we wanted to raise them. Now I'm thinking we were wrong in Jane's case—she's got too much of my petulant stubbornness. We probably should've beaten her, at least a little.

"You're making a big deal out of nothing, Dad."

I point at her. "The fact that you think so is exactly what concerns me."

"The people will have no other side to be on, but mine. When I'm Queen, they'll like it or as far as I'm concerned, they can piss the hell off."

Wow. Holy shit—*wow.*

I gape at her.

This is how Obi-Wan must've felt when Anakin turned to the fucking Dark Side.

"They could protest against you. Fight to overthrow you."

She waves her hand. "Revolutions are never successful anymore."

My voice rises. With frustration and also worry. For my darling daughter who thinks she knows everything.

"Successful or not, why would you want to govern a populace who is openly revolting against you? Why would you think that you even could?"

She shrugs again. "I'll have the military with me. They'll follow my orders—and I'll be smart enough to stop any rebellion before it starts."

What a beautiful little monster she sounds like.

"And that, dear girl, is called a dictatorship. Those never end well. For anyone."

My hand rubs over my face and I take a deep breath.

"The fact that you are the people's only choice is the very reason you should view this position as an honor. A service. A sacred duty, Jane."

Her features soften, sliding from stubbornness to thoughtfulness. And I think maybe—just maybe—I'm getting through.

"There is a trust between government and its people. An agreement. We govern them in conjunction with Parliament because they allow us to. And that is dependent on the monarchy putting the people's well-being above all else—above ourselves. The good of the country must always come first. The day you forget that, is the day you don't deserve to wear the crown—entitlement be damned."

Sometimes, I can make myself sound like Granny too.

Jane slips her phone out of her pocket and begins typing rapidly.

"What are you doing?"

"I'm writing this down. It's excellent advice."

The tension in my shoulders begins to ebb. Until . . .

"I want to make sure my biographer includes it."

Oh for fuck's sake.

"Jane . . ."

"No—I understand. You're right. I'll do better. I'll take this all to heart, Dad." She gives me a lovely, charming smile. "I'm very lucky you're so wise."

Now *I* roll my eyes. "Don't patronize me. I was patronizing the best of them, before you were anywhere close to being born."

She nods sweetly. "Of course, you were. There—got it." She puts her phone away. "Was there anything else? Sasha, Mellie and I are going to Monaco for the weekend. I don't want to be late meeting them."

"No." I sigh. "I suppose that's it for now. Do you want me to tell security to accompany you in plain clothes?"

Her little brow furrows. "Why?"

"Moving about in public will be easier if it's not obvious that you are who you are."

Jane looks genuinely confused. "But I like being me. Why would I want to pretend to be anyone else?"

I pinch the bridge of my nose. "Take a look in the history books—royals who enjoyed being who they were too much are not remembered kindly. And there's a reason for that."

Slowly she nods, playing at agreeing with me.

I invented that too.

"I'm so glad we had this chat, Dad."

Then she gets up, comes around the desk and hugs me, kissing my cheek. "I love you."

I hug her back, wishing she could be a little girl again —when it was all so much easier.

"I love you too, Janey. Be good, be safe."

"I will." She stands up and pats my shoulder. "We'll chat again soon."

And I want to slam my forehead into my desk.

Instead, after the apple of my eye breezes from the room and closes the door behind her, I spin in my chair to gaze at Granny's painting. One eyebrow seems raised higher than before, her smirk more self-satisfied.

"You're enjoying this, aren't you?" I ask.

And I can almost hear her answer.

Not so easy, is it, my boy?

"Go ahead—you and Grandfather have a good old laugh." I raise my tea-cup, toasting her. "Chuckle away."

The next time I look up from the work at my desk, it's dark outside—almost nine o'clock. Most days I make a point of eating dinner with Sarah and our children who aren't away at boarding school. But when I can't, Sarah holds off eating, so we can dine together.

I close up shop, wish my personal secretary, old Christopher, a pleasant evening as I walk by his desk and go find my wife. At this time of night, I don't have to search hard—there's only one place she'll be.

I hear their voices before I reach the nursery door, and the corners of my mouth automatically tug up into the best kind of smile.

". . . and then James climbed back into the sticky, giant peach ready to visit more amazing places and see the most extraordinary things!"

The snap of a closing book echoes, before a tiny voice objects.

"Wait! You can't stop there—I have to know what happens."

"That's the end of the chapter, Gilly." Sarah says in her soft tone. "You'll find out what happens next tomorrow."

Gilbert, our youngest, will be six in two weeks. If Jane was our honeymoon baby—well . . . slightly pre-honeymoon, if I'm being honest—Gil was our surprise. Sarah was forty-three when she gave birth to him, though the doctor said she had the uterus of a twenty-one-year old. Jane, who was fourteen then and Edward, our second oldest at a year younger than her, were mortified by the news that another sibling was on the way. They called us freaks of nature, the ingrates. While their little sisters, quiet Margaret and happy Isabel, who were ten and eight at the time, didn't know what all the fuss was about.

And yes, I was as proud as a studly peacock that I'd knocked my wife beautifully up so close to middle-age. It turned out, the last pregnancy was the easiest of the bunch for Sarah—she had no morning sickness, more energy instead of less, *insatiable* sex-drive . . . I was ecstatic about that part too.

I peak around the door just in time to see my son fling himself back onto the white carpet dramatically, arms splayed, his blond hair wavy and wild.

"Tomorrow will take so long! I can't wait!"

That sounds familiar.

Gilbert takes more after me than any of the others—energetic, rambunctious—a handful. But he's a joy. They all are.

When they're not giving us migraines.

"Please, Mummy. One more chapter . . . pleeeeeese."

When Sarah sighs, I know she's about to give in. And I'm not the only one who senses it.

"Prince Gilbert, don't pester your poor mother. Or beg, or whine. It is beneath you." Nanny Alice steps in from the adjoining room, her face stern and her brogue thick. "You have an early lesson in the morning." She claps her hands together, quick and sharp. "Into bed, now."

Gilbert's whole face scrunches into a frown.

"Nan-ny! She was going to say yes!" He waves his hand, his thumb and pointer finger pinched together. "She was this close and you ruined it."

Nanny Alice's lips pucker sourly. "Your Mummy has a soft spot for you—and that's why they keep me around—because I don't like you at'all."

Gilbert giggles like it's the silliest thing he's ever heard. Nanny Alice adores him and he knows it, but thankfully for us, she doesn't let the runt of the litter get away with anything.

As Gil climbs up onto his bed, I step into the room.

"Your Majesty." Nanny curtsies quickly.

I nod. "Thank you, Alice."

She dims the lights before slipping outside the door while we say goodnight. I slide my hand along Sarah's back and we step up beside the bed.

Blinking up at us, Gilbert yawns. "Can we plant a peach tree?"

I hear the smile in Sarah's voice. "Yes, we can. I know just the spot."

"Daddy, can we play rugby tomorrow? I've been practicing and I want to show you."

I brush my fingers through his crazy hair. Our little heathen.

"I'll have Nanny Alice bring you to my office after your morning lesson and we'll go out to the courtyard to play for a bit then."

He yawns again, longer this time.

"I really like the giant peach story. Do you think I could write a story like that?"

Sarah leans down over our boy, her voice hushed. "You can do anything you want, anything you dream, as long as you are good and honest and work hard at it." She peppers his forehead and cheeks with kisses, brushing her nose against his. "Goodnight my little love."

And then it's my turn.

"Sleep well, sweet boy. We love you."

He rolls away from us, onto his side, crushing his pillow into a heap beneath his head.

And with my arm around Sarah's shoulders, I guide her out the door, down the long endless hallway to our rooms.

It's a mild evening so we dine out on the balcony, beneath the black sky spotted with twinkling stars, at a table set with china for two. This time with Sarah alone—it's the best part of my day, any day—full stop.

Candlelight dances across her face making pink and soft orange shadows, and I'm struck not just by how utterly beautiful she still is, but how unchanged—constant. How she's been able to retain the same quiet strength and hopeful innocence she's always had despite the backstabbing, unsavory political world she lives in.

After we eat, I fill her in on my conversation with Jane, rubbing my temples as I recount it.

"She talked circles around me, I swear. It's almost emasculating."

Sarah chuckles and gives me "the look"—the one I love. A small smile, a gentle shake of her head.

"She talks circles around you because you let her. Because deep down you're delighted by how clever she is—how stubborn and strong and quick-witted she can be. Like your grandmother. You adore that about her."

I snort at being called out. Then I stare at the rumpled napkin on the table.

"She's spoiled, Sarah." I confess in a whisper. "Not to the point of rotten, but . . ."

My wife nods and straightens her back.

"Jane was born blessed—beautiful, intelligent. She's been raised in luxury and privilege by a family who loves her completely. She's never known hardship or tragedy.

She's been treated with deference by everyone around her —and she has more power than any nineteen-year-old ever should. I'd be shocked if she wasn't a bit spoiled."

"But we're not just raising a daughter! We're raising a queen. And it just all hit me today, that I don't think we're doing a very good job of it," I say miserably. "I didn't realize how . . . difficult . . . it is. A tightrope. And I have a whole new level of respect for Granny and Grandfather because God knows Nicholas and I did not make it easy for them."

Sarah toys with the rim of her wine glass thoughtfully. "I don't think it's the sort of task that's supposed to be easy. We've always tried to protect them from the harsher realities of life. Jane knows logically that she is more fortunate that almost anyone else in the world. But there's a difference between knowing that, and seeing it with her own eyes. Truly understanding the suffering others experience in the world and even her own country. Maybe, we've sheltered her too much. Sam and Elizabeth send their children on charitable missions every summer. They've done work in all sorts of places . . . perhaps it's time we do the same for Jane."

I shake my head. "Our children are different. They're targets—we all are—we learned that the hard way, years ago."

"I haven't forgotten."

"I don't like putting them out there, in danger. Needlessly."

Sarah tilts her head, regarding me. "But you're just fine with putting yourself there."

"It's not the same."

"But, now, it is the same. One day Jane will be you—she will sit where you sit, be faced with the same trials and choices you face. It would be cruel and dangerous not to prepare her for that. We're lucky that she still lives here with us—that she's just in her first year in Uni. But the time is quickly coming when she will be out of our reach, Henry. Her opinions will be set and we won't be able to influence her. If we have any hope of shaking her views, I'm afraid it has to be now . . . or never."

I rub the back of my neck and stare at my wife for a few moments.

"You're right." I chuckle, shaking my head. "Of course, you're right. You were always the brave one."

She smiles gently. Remembering. "Not always."

Sarah reaches across the table for my hand, and I give it to her without hesitation. "But you kept your promise. You kept me safe, so I could be brave. And I have no doubt that you will do the same for our daughter." She squeezes my hand. "I have *no* doubts about you, Henry."

Not for the first time, I gaze at Sarah's lovely face, at the absolute, unconditional trust in her dark eyes . . . and I know deep inside that I would be fucking *lost* without her. I would be nothing. Less than nothing.

Leaning forward, I bring her small hand to my lips. Then I cradle it in both of mine. "I'll call Sam in the morning."

Sarah

"**B**UT WHY DID WE have so many?"

Henry's voice reaches me from the bath where he's just finished his shower—a lighter extension of the conversation we began at dinner. I sit at the vanity table, my glasses off, rubbing moisturizer into my cheeks, tapping it below my eyes, wearing a rose and ivory silk nightgown.

My husband steps into the bedroom with a cloud of steam wafting behind him, rubbing a towel across his broad shoulders and damp head, wearing nothing. There's no concern that the staff will enter our rooms unannounced. That was nipped in the bud during the first weeks of our marriage—when Henry's valet walked in on one of our . . . friskier . . . moments.

Henry thought the whole thing was hilarious—but I couldn't look the poor man in the face for a month. So, my husband gave the staff strict instructions not to come into our rooms without knocking, at any time of day, unless the palace was burning to the ground.

There are Queen's quarters on the other side of the sitting room, but we've never used them. As if Henry would ever let me sleep anywhere but beside him. As if I'd ever want to. Sometimes, I still can't believe that it's real —that this is a life I get to have. The most miraculous happily ever after.

"I mean, why did we think having five would some-how be a good idea? I don't remember having that conversation. Do you?"

I glance over my shoulder, my eyes dragging up from his toes to his wild-green eyes. Henry was crowned at forty—a young King by any standard. He'll turn fifty this summer, and the grandest parties are already planned to celebrate the occasion. But besides the sexy dusting of light gray that joins the blond hairs on his chest, he's still taught and rippled in all the places a man should be.

I am a lucky, lucky girl.

"I don't think conversing had anything to do with it." My voice drops to a sultry level as I look him over. "It was more . . . you . . . always corrupting me with your wicked ways."

He catches my appraisal and his eyes darken. He tosses the towel aside and stalks over to me, a filthy smile taking possession of his mouth.

"That's not how I recall it." Henry leans down, behind my chair, tugging the strap of my nightgown off my shoulder and kissing the now bared spot. Then he punctuates each word with another hot peck, climbing towards my neck. "I think you have always been too damn delectable for your own good, love."

He drags his nose, up over my ear, giving me goosebumps with his breath, to my temple. "Mmm, you smell amazing."

Then his simmering eyes meet mine in the mirror. "Christ, look at you."

I groan and cover my face. "Uh, please don't." I drop my hands and turn towards him in the chair. "Do you know those crinkles I get around my eyes when I laugh? I realized the other day, they're there all the time now. I'm so old."

He makes a thoroughly disgusted sound and pulls me up from the chair. "That is some top-notch rubbish right there." With his arms around me, he leans back, looking down at me.

"You are every bit as beautiful as the day I first saw you in that pub." He chuckles. "When you stuck your book in my face and told me to smell it."

I laugh, pressing my face against his chest. "You make it sound dirty."

"I like to think it was dirty. The best kind of foreplay. It certainly reeled me in."

Henry runs his hands through my hair, leaning back again, looking down at me adoringly. "But you know what —I was wrong. You're not as beautiful as that day. You're even more exquisite now."

He kisses the tip of my nose.

"More beautiful than when I was twenty-five?" I ask doubtfully.

"Oh, definitely." Henry sighs, and brushes my hair back. "You're a woman now." His knuckle strokes my jaw. "An incredible mother, an activist . . ."

I glance away, blushing, but Henry chases me with his gaze.

". . . a beloved Queen."

My eyes drift back up to his and his loving fingers caress my face.

His voice is low, rough with gentle sincerity. "Watching you become who you are has been the greatest privilege of my whole life, Sarah."

The sweetest tenderness swells in my throat.

"You're a king." I tease. "I'm pretty sure that's supposed to be the greatest privilege."

"No." Henry shakes his head, kissing the inside of my wrist, where his name is etched beneath my skin. "No. Even more than that."

And the emotion, the deep all-encompassing love that I feel for this man—my wonderful, precious husband—my darling, amazing King, expands in my soul and brings tears to my eyes.

I melt against him with a sigh. "Oh, Henry."

He bends his head and takes my mouth in a kiss hot with passion and need. I feel his arms encircle my hips, lifting me up and closer. My hands skim over his shoulders and my hair falls around us, encasing us in a magical world that's just he and I, and nothing else can reach us. And we taste each other deeply, kiss with the joy of the very first time and desperate urgency of the last.

Long moments later, I slide my lips across his perfectly stubbled jaw, nuzzling his ear.

And I whisper, "This is how Gilbert got here. I told you it was your fault."

Henry laughs into my neck, devilish and unrepentant as ever. And then he carries me to bed.

The End . . . for now

FOR EXCLUSIVE TEASERS, GIVEAWAYS,
AND TO BE THE FIRST TO HEAR
THE LATEST BOOK NEWS,
SIGN UP FOR EMMA'S **NEWSLETTER**:

http://authoremmachase.com/newsletter/

Turn the page for a free sample of
GETTING SCHOOLED,
a new hot and hilarious romance from Emma Chase!

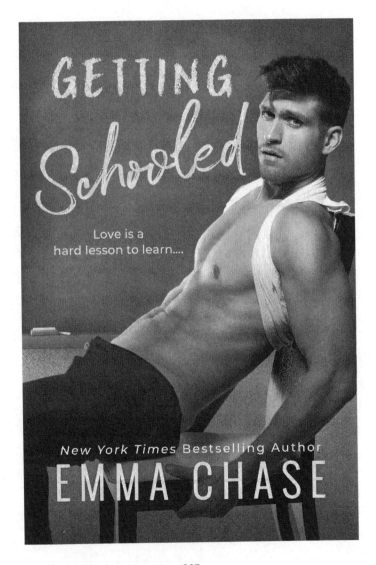

GETTING

Schooled

Love is a
hard lesson to learn....

New York Times Bestselling Author

EMMA CHASE

efore I head home, I put Snoopy in the Jeep and walk down to my classroom, where I'll be teaching US History in a few more days. I have a good roster—especially third period—a nice mix of smart, well-behaved kids and smart, mouthy ones to keep things from being too boring. They're Juniors which is a good age—they know the routine, know their way around, but still care enough about their grades not to tell me and my assignments to go screw myself. That tends to happen Senior year.

I put a stack of rubber band wrapped index cards in the top drawer of the desk. It's for the first-day assignment I always give, where I play "We Didn't Start the Fire," by Billy Joel, and hang the lyrics around the classroom. Then, they each pick two index cards and have to give an oral report, the next day, on the two people or events they chose. It makes history more relevant for them—interesting—which is big for a generation of kids who are basically immediate gratification junkies.

Child psychologists will tell you the human brain isn't fully developed until age twenty-five, but—not to go all touchy-feely on you—I think the soul stops growing at the end of high school, and who you are when you graduate, is who you'll always be. I've seen it in action, if you're a dick at eighteen—you'll probably be a dick for life.

That's another reason I like this job . . . because there's still hope for these kids. No matter where they come from, who their parents are, who their dipshit friends are, we get them in this building for seven hours a day. So, if we do what we're supposed to, set the example, listen, teach the right things, and yeah—figuratively knock them upside the head once in a while—we can help shape their souls. Change them—make them better human beings than they would've been without us.

That's my theory, anyway.

I sit down in the desk chair and lean back, balancing on the hind legs like my mother always told me not to. I fold my hands behind my head, put my feet on the desk, and sigh with contentment. Because life is sweet.

It's going to be a great year.

They're not all great—some years suck donkey balls —my best players graduate and it's a rebuilding year, which means a lot of 'L's' on the board, or sometimes you just get a crappy crop of students. But this year's going to be awesome—I can feel it.

And then, something catches my eye outside the window in the parking lot. Some*one*.

And my balance goes to shit.

I swing my arms like a baby bird, hang in the air for half a second . . . and then topple back in a heap. Not my smoothest move.

But right now, it doesn't matter.

I pull myself up to my feet, step over the chair towards the window, all the while peering at the blond in the navy blue pencil skirt walking across the parking lot.

And the ass that, even from this distance—I would know anywhere.

Callaway Carpenter. Holy shit.

She looks amazing, even more beautiful than the last time I saw her . . . than the first time I saw her. You never forget your first. Isn't that what they say? Callie was my first and for a long time, I thought she'd be my only.

The first time I laid my eyes on her, it felt like getting sacked by a three-hundred pound defensive lineman with an axe to grind. She looked like an angel. Golden hair framing petite, delicate features—a heart-shaped face, a dainty jaw, a cute nose and these big, round, blinking green eyes I wanted to drown in.

Wait . . . back up . . . that's not actually true. That's a lie.

I was fifteen when I met Callie, and fifteen year old boys are notorious perverts, so the first thing I noticed about her wasn't her face. It was her tits—they were full and round and absolutely perfect.

The second thing I noticed was her mouth—shiny and pink with a bee-stung bottom lip. In a blink, a hundred fantasies had gone through my head of what she could do with that mouth . . . what I could show her how to do.

Then I saw her angel face. That's how it happened.

And just like that—I was gone.

We were "the" couple in high school—Brenda and Eddie from that Billy Joel song. The star quarterback and the theater queen.

She was the love of my life, before I had any fucking idea what love was . . . and then, still, even after I did.

We broke up when she went away to college and I stayed here in Jersey—couldn't survive the distance. It was a quiet ending, when I went out to visit her in California, no drama or hysterics. Just some hard truths, tears, one last night together in her dorm room bed, and a morning of goodbye.

She never really came home again after that. At least, not long enough for us to run into each other. I haven't seen her in years—in a lifetime.

But she's here now.

At *my* school.

And you can bet Callie's sweet ass I'm going to find out why.

To keep reading, purchase a copy
from your favorite online retailer today!

About the Author

New York Times and *USA Today* bestselling author, Emma Chase, writes contemporary romance filled with heat, heart and laugh-out-loud humor. Her stories are known for their clever banter, sexy, swoon-worthy moments, and hilariously authentic male POV's.

Emma lives in New Jersey with her amazing husband, two awesome children, and two adorable but badly behaved dogs. She has a long-standing love/hate relationship with caffeine.

Follow me online:

Twitter: http://bit.ly/2reW1Dq
Facebook: http://bit.ly/2rgHAi3
Instagram: http://bit.ly/2jnzfpt
Website: http://bit.ly/2reCeUs

Follow me on Bookbub to get new release alerts
& find out when a title goes on sale!

BookBub: http://bit.ly/2IEDh8r

Also by Emma Chase

Getting Schooled

THE ROYALLY SERIES
Royally Screwed
Royally Matched
Royally Endowed
Royally Raised

Royally Series Collection

THE LEGAL BRIEFS SERIES
Overruled
Sustained
Appealed
Sidebarred

THE TANGLED SERIES
Tangled

Twisted

Tamed

Tied
Holy Frigging Matrimony
It's a Wonderful Tangled Christmas Carol

Made in the USA
San Bernardino, CA
03 November 2018